Praise for *The*

'I galloped through this excellent read; I was in suspense the whole time.'
Charlaine Harris, best-selling author of the True Blood novels

'I liked the book a lot, I devoured it in one sitting! *The Testing* has its own unique twist.'
HungerGamesTrilogy.net

'Charbonneau works action, romance, intrigue and a plausible dystopian premise into a near-flawless narrative.'
Publishers Weekly

'Reminiscent of *The Hunger Games* and *The Maze Runner*, readers will love this thrilling debut from Joelle Charbonneau... *The Testing* is the book of the season.'
Goodreads.com

'*The Testing* is definitely a dystopia that can stand out from the crowd and hold its head high. The writing was phenomenal and the ideas were so intricate and smart... I can't recommend this one highly enough!'
Total Teen Fiction blog

For Casey and Michael

A TEMPLAR BOOK

First published in 2014 by Houghton Mifflin Harcourt
First published in the UK in 2014 by Templar Publishing,
an imprint of The Templar Company Limited,
Deepdene Lodge, Deepdene Avenue, Dorking,
Surrey, RH5 4AT, UK
www.templarco.co.uk

Copyright © 2014 by Joelle Charbonneau
Cover design by James Fraser
First UK edition

All rights reserved

ISBN 978-1-84877-168-0

Printed and bound in CPI Group (UK) Ltd, Croydon, CR0 4YY

INDEPENDENT STUDY

THE TESTING 2

JOELLE CHARBONNEAU

templar

CHAPTER 1

EXAMINATION DAY

I slide the cool material of my shirt over the five long, jagged scars on my arm and examine myself in the reflector. Blue, long-sleeved tunic. Grey pants. Silver bracelet with a single star. The star and the smudges of fatigue under my eyes mark me as an entry-level University student. My fellow classmates show similar signs of having studied late into the night for today. After six months of taking the same preliminary classes, all twenty of us will be tested and sorted into the fields of study that will serve as the focus for the rest of our lives.

My chest tightens. I used to enjoy taking tests. I liked proving that I had learned. That I had worked hard. That I was smart. But now I am not sure what is real or what the consequences of a wrong answer will be. While my classmates are concerned about the test affecting the years ahead, I worry I will not survive the day.

Normally, I pull my hair back into a thick, dark knot in order to keep it out of my way. Today, I decide to leave it down. Perhaps the long waves will hide the evidence of months of restless nights. If not, maybe the cold compresses my mother taught me to apply to my eyes will help.

A wave of longing crashes over me at the thought of my mother. While contact between University students and their families is not expressly forbidden, neither is it encouraged. Most students I know have not heard a word from their loved ones back home. I have been fortunate. A Tosu official has been willing to pass along small bits of communication from my parents and four older brothers. They are well. My father and my oldest brother, Zeen, are creating a new fertiliser to help plants grow faster. My second oldest brother, Hamin, is engaged. He and his soon-to-be wife will be married next spring. His decision to marry has prompted our mother to look for wives for Zeen and my twin brothers, Hart and Win. So far, her efforts have been in vain.

Aside from my family, one other person has managed to get news to me. My best friend, Daileen, assures me she's studying hard and is currently first in her class. Her teacher has hinted Daileen might be chosen for The Testing this year. She is keeping her fingers crossed that she will join me in Tosu City. I am hoping she will fail. I want her to stay in a place where the answers to questions make sense. Where I know she will be safe.

A knock at the door makes me jump. "Hey, Cia. Are you ready? We don't want to be late." Stacia's right. Those who arrive late will not be allowed to take the exam. What that means for the future is unclear, but none of us wants to find out.

"I'll be ready in a minute," I yell as I kneel next to the foot of the bed and slide my hand between the bed frame and the mattress. My fingers search until they find the lump that makes me sigh with relief. My brother Zeen's Transit Communicator is still safe, as are the secrets it holds.

Months ago, I discovered the symbol I carved into the device to help lead me to the recorder and the confidences stored inside. When I finished listening to words I had no recollection of speaking, I cut open the mattress and hid the Communicator inside. Week after week, month after month, I tried to pretend that what the device revealed isn't real. After all, haven't I seen evidence every day that my fellow students are good people? That the professors and administrators working to prepare us for our futures want us to succeed? Some of them are standoffish. Others arrogant. None of the students or educators is perfect, but who is? No matter their flaws, I don't want to believe any are capable of the whispered, sometimes hard-to-make-out words inside the recorder.

"Cia." Stacia's voice pulls me from my thoughts. "We have to get going."

"Right. Sorry." I slip into my coat, hoist my University bag onto my shoulder and turn my back on my questions about the past. Those will have to wait. For now, I need to concentrate on my future.

Stacia frowns as I step into the hall. Her dark blonde hair is pulled back into a sleek ponytail, making her angular features look sharper than usual. "What took you so long? We're going to be the last ones to arrive."

"Which will make everyone nervous," I quip. "They'll wonder why we didn't feel the need to get there early and compare notes with everyone else."

Stacia's eyes narrow as she nods. "You're right. I love psyching out the competition."

I hate it. My parents taught me to value fair play over all else.

Stacia doesn't notice my discomfort as we trek past healthy trees, thriving grass and numerous academic structures. Not that she would say anything if she did. Stacia isn't one for girl talk or idle chatter. At first her silences challenged me to bring her out of her shell, as I used to do for my best friend from Five Lakes. Now, with so many questions on my mind, I am grateful for the quiet company.

I wave at a couple of older students as they walk by. As always, they ignore us. After today, the upperclassmen assigned to the same field of study will act as our guides. Until then, they pretend we don't exist. Most of my classmates have taken to ignoring them back, but I can't. My upbringing is too strong not to be polite.

"Ha. I should have known he'd be waiting for us." Stacia rolls her eyes and then laughs. "I'd bet my family's compensation money that he hovered around you during The Testing, too. Too bad I'll never know if I'd win that bet."

My heart skips as I spot Tomas Endress standing near the front door of the four-storey red-and-white-brick Early Studies building. His dark hair blows in the late-winter breeze. A University bag is slung carelessly over his shoulder. His grey eyes and dimpled smile are focused squarely on me as he waves and comes bounding down the steps. Tomas and I have known each other all our lives, but in the last couple months we've grown closer than I dreamed possible back home. When Tomas is with me, I feel smarter. More confident. And terrified that everything I think I know and admire about him is a lie.

Stacia rolls her eyes as Tomas kisses my cheek and entwines his fingers with mine. "I was starting to get worried about you. The test starts in ten minutes."

"Cia and I didn't feel the need to get here early and cram like everyone else. We're totally prepared. Right, Cia?" Stacia tosses her blonde ponytail and shoots me one of her rare smiles.

"Right," I say with more conviction than I feel. Yes, I have studied hard for this test, but the whispered words on the Transit Communicator make me doubt I could ever fully prepare for what is to come.

Not for the first time, I wish my father were here to talk to me. Almost three decades ago, he attended the University. Growing up, I asked hundreds of questions about his time here. Rarely did he answer them. Back then, I assumed his silence was to keep my brothers and me from feeling pressure to follow in his footsteps. Now I'm forced to wonder if something more sinister lay behind his secrecy.

There is only one way to find out.

The three of us climb the steps. When we reach the front door, Tomas stops and asks for a moment alone with me. Stacia sighs, warns me not to be late and stalks inside. When she's out of sight, Tomas brushes a hair off my forehead and peers into my eyes. "Did you sleep at all last night?"

"Some." Although with sleep comes the nightmares that hover just out of reach when I wake. "Don't worry. Being your study partner means I can answer questions no matter how tired I am."

While other students used their free time to relax or explore the United Commonwealth capital, Tosu City, Tomas and I spent all our spare moments with our books under a tree or in the library when the cold weather drove us inside. Most of our classmates assumed Tomas and I pretended to study in order to be alone. They don't understand my fear of what might happen if I do not pass this exam.

Tomas gives my hand a squeeze. "Things will get easier once we've been given our designated areas of study. You're a shoo-in for Mechanical Engineering."

"Let's hope you're right." I smile. "While I'd love to work with you, the idea of being assigned Biological Engineering scares the hell out of me." My father and brothers are geniuses at coaxing plants to thrive in the war-scarred earth. Revitalising the earth is an important job. One I admire. I might even be happy to consider it, if I didn't kill every plant I touched.

"Come on." Tomas brushes a light kiss on my lips and tugs me towards the steps. "Let's show them how smart students from Five Lakes are."

The hallway of the Early Studies building is dim. Only the sunshine that creeps in from the glass panes in the front door lights our way. Tosu City has strict laws governing electricity usage. While the production and storage of electricity are more robust than in Five Lakes, conservation is encouraged. During the daytime, the University only directs electricity to labs or classrooms that require extra light for the day's lesson. At night, however, the University has a much higher allotment of power than the rest of the city.

The second-floor examination room is well illuminated in honour of today's test. The lights make it easy to see the tension etched in my classmates' faces as they sit behind black desks, poring over their notes, hoping to cram one last fact that could make the difference between the futures they want and whatever else our professors might decide.

One final student arrives. I take a seat at an empty desk in the back. Tomas slides into the desk to the right of mine. I put my bag on the floor and glance around the room. Twenty of us. Thirteen boys. Seven girls. The future leaders of the United Commonwealth.

I am about to wish Tomas luck when Professor Lee arrives. For the past several months, Professor Lee has served as our history instructor. While most of the University teachers wear sober expressions, Professor Lee has kind eyes and a warm smile, which is why he's my favourite. Today, instead of the faded brown jacket he favours, our instructor is wearing a ceremonial purple United Commonwealth jumpsuit. The room goes silent as Professor Lee walks up and down the rows of desks. On each desk he drops a booklet of paper and a yellow pencil. I run my hand over the image in the corner of the booklet's cover. A lightning bolt. My symbol. Given to me in The Testing.

Professor Lee asks us not to open the booklet until further instruction is given. The booklet is thick. Back at Five Lakes, paper is harder to come by, so we use it sparingly and make sure to recycle every page when we are done. Here in Tosu City, learning takes priority over rationing.

My fingers toy with the pencil, rolling it back and forth across the black desk surface. Out of the corner of my eye, I catch Tomas watching me with a concerned expression. Suddenly, I'm in a different room. Eight students. A different male official dressed in ceremonial male purple. Eight black desks. Bright white walls instead of grey. Six boys. Only two girls in the room, one of whom is me. Tomas gives me the same worried look as I finger a pencil. The booklet in front of me is marked with the same lightning bolt, only this time, it is surrounded by an eight-pointed star. My symbol surrounded by the symbol of my group for The Testing.

The room in my memory disappears as Professor Lee's deep voice announces, "Congratulations on completing the basic studies required for all University students. Today's test, combined with evaluations from your professors, will determine which field of study your skills are best suited for. Tomorrow, a list will be posted with your test results, as well as which field of study you have been directed into: Education, Biological Engineering, Mechanical Engineering, Medicine or Government. All five fields of study are necessary to continue the revitalisation of our land, our technology and our citizens. While each of you has a preferred choice, we ask you to trust us to slot you into the career path that best suits the needs of the country. Do not attempt to guess which questions on the examination affect direction into a specific field of study. Any students with questionable test results will be given a failing grade and Redirected from the University student roster."

Professor Lee scans the room to make sure the impact of his words is felt. I can hear my heart hammer in the silence.

Finally, he continues. "Answer each question to the best of your ability. Do not give answers beyond the scope of the question. We are interested in learning not only how much you know but how well you comprehend the question being asked. Answers that go beyond the confines of the question will negatively affect your test results."

I swallow hard and wonder what the negative effect might be. A lowered score or something more?

"You will have eight hours to complete this examination. If you need a break for food, water or to relieve yourself, please raise your hand. A University official will escort you to the break room. If at any time you exit this room, you are not to leave the building or speak to anyone other than your escort. Either action will result in a failing grade and Redirection from the University. When you have completed the examination, raise the test booklet. I will collect the booklet and escort you to the door. What you do after that is up to you." He gives us a knowing smile before pushing a button on the wall behind him.

A small screen descends from the ceiling. Red numbers are displayed on the screen. Professor Lee pushes another button and says, "The eight-hour testing period starts now."

The numbers begin running backward, telling us how much time we have remaining to complete the examination. Paper rustles as test booklets are opened. Pencils are picked up. The examination to determine the direction of the rest of our lives has begun.

The first question makes me smile. *What is the Means Value Theorem? Please provide the formal statement and a proof in your explanation.*

Calculus. Something I'm good at. I answer the question quickly, give the formal equation for the theorem and provide a proof as to how it works. Briefly I wonder if I should also explain how the theorem applies to vector-valued functions or how it is used for integration. But then I remember Professor Lee's instructions. We are only supposed to provide the information requested. Nothing more. Nothing less. For a moment I wonder why, but then I decide it is because leaders must choose their words with care. In order to prevent conflicts, they must be certain their exact meaning is understood by the people who follow them. With that kind of responsibility facing those of us who make it to graduation, it is not surprising University officials wish to test that ability.

I reread the question, decide my answer is complete and within the scope and then move on to the next. My pencil flies across the page as I explain the Four Stages of War various governments inflicted upon one another and on the earth. I describe the next Three Stages, in which the earth fought back against the chemicals and other destructive forces unleashed upon it. Earthquakes, windstorms, floods, hurricanes and tornadoes swept across the globe, destroying in a matter of years what took humans centuries to create. The damage that for the past one hundred years the United Commonwealth has worked hard to repair.

My writing fills the pages. Chemistry. Geography. Physics. History. Music. Art. Reading comprehension. Biology. Each question brings a new subject. A different skill set. Most I can answer. My breath catches as I leave one blank. I am not certain what the question is asking for or what the answer might be. I hope I will have time to revisit it when I complete the rest. If not... My mind starts to drift to the words spoken on the Transit Communicator recording. The fate suffered by candidates of The Testing who dared answer a question wrong.

No. I pull my thoughts back. Worrying about the past won't help. I can only deal with the present.

According to the clock, I have just shy of four hours to finish my test. I roll out my shoulders and realise how stiff I am. Between tension and inactivity, my muscles are beginning to protest. My empty stomach is adding its complaints. While fear of failure urges me to press on, I can hear my mother's voice saying a brain and body need fuel to function at peak performance. I don't want to run out of time, but running out of energy and focus would be even worse.

I glance around the room. Every desk is occupied. No one else has taken a break. Will leaving the room to refuel be considered a sign of weakness by University officials? I scan the room for signs of cameras and find none. But just because I can't spot them doesn't mean they aren't there.

My stomach growls again. My throat is dry, and my eyes feel grainy. Regardless of how my actions might be perceived, I need a break. If I don't take a moment to recharge, the rest of my answers will suffer for it.

Swallowing hard, I close my booklet, place my pencil next to the papers and raise my hand. Professor Lee doesn't notice me right away, but some of the other students do.

Several give me smug looks, as though proud their stamina is greater than mine. Others, like Stacia, shake their heads. For a moment, I consider putting down my hand, but Tomas's encouraging nod makes me raise it higher in the air.

Professor Lee spots me, smiles and signals permission to leave my desk. My joints are stiff as I walk to the front of the class. A female official in ceremonial red is waiting for me outside the classroom door. She escorts me down the stairs to a room on the first floor where a table with food and water awaits. I fill a plate with chicken, slices of a sharp-smelling cheese and salad made of fruits, greens and nuts – all foods my parents encouraged my brothers and me to eat before important exams – and dig in.

I barely register the taste as I chew and swallow. This is not food to be savoured. It is fuel to get me through the next four hours. I finish my meal quickly and then use the bathroom and splash water on my face. Less than fifteen minutes has elapsed when I slide into my desk feeling far more alert than when I left. Picking up my pencil, I open the booklet and once again begin to write.

Questions on genetic code, historical figures, important breakthroughs in medicine and solar power collection are asked. My fingers cramp. The pages fill. I get to the last question and blink. *Please tell us your preferred focus of study and why you feel you are best suited to be selected for that career path.* This is my chance to convince the University administrators of my passion and ability to help develop our country's technology.

Taking a deep breath, I begin to write. All my hopes pour onto the page. My desire to help upgrade the communications system from our country's limited use of pulse radios to a sophisticated network that would be available to every citizen.

My excitement about new energy sources that would better power our lights and other devices. My absolute belief that I can make a difference in the technological future of the United Commonwealth.

Time slips away as I write and rewrite my answer, worried that one wrong word will change the focus of my career. One by one, my fellow students raise their booklets over their heads, wait for them to be collected and leave the room, until there are only five of us left. I am satisfied with my final answer and look up at the clock. Three minutes remain.

My mouth goes dry as I remember. I skipped four questions with the intent of going back later. Only, I spent so much time constructing my final answer there isn't enough time. My heart races as I flip back, hoping to answer just one of them. But I don't. The clock expires as I finish reading the first unanswered question again. Pencils down.

The examination is over. And I have not finished.

None of the questions I failed to answer are maths- or science-related – the subjects I believe are most important to Mechanical Engineering. I try to take solace in that as I hand my booklet to Professor Lee. But my failure to complete the exam makes it hard for me to hold my head up as I walk out of the room. All I can do now is hope for the best.

Tomas is waiting for me on the steps outside. The smile on his face disappears as he looks into my eyes. "How did it go?"

"I left four questions unanswered. If I hadn't taken a break for food, I would have finished."

Tomas shakes his head. "Taking a break was smart. I wouldn't have taken one if you hadn't. I was losing focus. You reminded me that it's important to step away and clear the mind. When I came back from my break, I reread my last answer and found two errors. I owe you for that."

The gentle kiss he gives me is more than payment enough.

When Tomas steps back, he flashes a dimpled grin. "I also owe you for the entertainment. The looks on everyone's faces when you walked out of the room were priceless. They didn't know whether to be impressed or intimidated by your confidence."

I blink. Confidence was the last thing I'd been feeling when I left the examination room. But Tomas's words make me stop and think. How would I have felt if someone else had raised her hand first? Had gone out for a snack while time ticked away on the clock? I would have assumed the student had no concern about finishing the test on time. In fact, the student's departure would have made me assume she would not only finish the exam but have time to spare. Tomas's words are a good reminder. Thinking something is true doesn't make it so. Perception is almost as important as reality.

The light starts to fade as Tomas and I walk hand in hand to the University's dining facility. Older students tend to avoid the dining hall, since every designated field of study has its own residence and kitchen. Most days, the only people using this hall are a handful of low-ranking University administrators, one or two professors and me and my fellow Early Studies students. The food provided is usually simple: sandwiches, fruit, rolls, raw vegetables. Nothing that requires great amounts of preparation or effort to keep warm. Despite the major milestone we have just completed, the food remains the same. No celebration for us. Not yet. Not until scores have been determined and fields of study assigned.

During the last six months as University students, we've

taken a number of tests. After each, the dining hall was filled with chatter comparing answers, lamenting mistakes and celebrating correct responses. Today there is none of that. Most of my fellow students keep their eyes on their plates as they eat. Some don't eat at all. They just push the food around, trying to look normal. Everyone feels fatigue from the test and anxiety over the results.

I pick at the bread and fruit. Worry makes it impossible to eat much more than a few mouthfuls. Tomas has no problem cleaning his plate. I guess I don't have to ask how he did on the exam.

Pushing away the remains of my meal, I ask, "Do you think they'll give us the results first thing in the morning or make us wait until later in the day?"

Before Tomas can speculate, a tenor voice says, "It'll happen first thing."

Tomas stiffens as our fellow Early Studies student Will grins and slides his lanky body into the empty seat next to me. Inside I flinch. Outwardly, I smile. "You sound pretty confident."

"That's because I am." His eyes gleam. "I overheard a couple of administrators talking. Pulling an all-nighter to make sure examination results are ready first thing in the morning wasn't on their top-ten list of favourite things to do." His smile widens. "They were seriously annoyed.

They don't mind making us lose sleep, but they don't like doing it themselves. So how did you guys do today?"

Tomas shrugs and looks down at his plate. For some reason Tomas won't explain, he doesn't like Will. Not that Tomas is ever rude. He's not. But the way he gives minimal responses speaks volumes, as does the look in his eyes. There is a wariness. A distrust.

"How about you, Cia?" Will asks. "I'm guessing you aced this like you do everything else. Right?"

I wish. "There were too many questions to ace them all."

"I know I flunked the questions on art history. I thought they wanted leaders who could help revitalise the country. How is knowing about a sculpture of a naked guy going to help? A naked girl..." He grins again. "Now, that's a different story."

I can't help but laugh and half listen as Will jokes about the various test questions and speculates on whether he'll be assigned his desired field of study – Education.

Will has a quick wit that I enjoy. He also has a great love for his family, especially his twin brother, Gill, who came to Tosu City for The Testing but did not pass through to the University. Not long after we began as University students, Will showed me a picture of him and his brother. Two identical faces with amused grins. Tall, thin bodies and ashen skin that speaks of a lack of healthy food in their home colony. Other than the length of their hair – Will's to his shoulders, and his brother's cropped short – the two were carbon copies right down to the love and happiness shining out of their deep green eyes.

It's the longing and love I see in his eyes that draw me to Will even as the accusations on the Transit Communicator warn me to stay away. I find it hard to believe someone who tried to kill both Tomas and me lurks under the friendly smile. But my recorded voice tells me that this is exactly who Will is. Which is why I keep close to him. I am determined to find out if that voice is right. About Will. About Tomas. About everything.

CHAPTER 2

We sit in the same classroom we were tested in yesterday. Waiting. Twenty students selected from the eighteen United Commonwealth colonies. Ready to learn how we will help rebuild our country.

I glance around the room. Most of my fellow students I've come to know. Will, who wants to teach. Stacia, who hopes to study government and law. Vic, a large red-headed boy from Stacia's colony, whose ambition lies with healing broken bones. A willowy brunette with waist-length hair, Kit, who flirts relentlessly with Tomas even as she tries to edge him out of the top spot for Biological Engineering. A boy called Brick claims he's happy to study whatever the United Commonwealth finds he is best suited for. Over half the students in this room are interested in being a part of the government in order to shape our country's laws. The one thing we have in common is our realisation that we control nothing.

I hold my breath as Professor Lee walks to the front of the class holding a clipboard. My heart hammers and

I try not to squirm as he says, "In my hand are the test results for your examination. Your name will appear in alphabetical order on this sheet. Next to your name will be an indicator as to whether you have passed and been assigned a field of study or have failed and are therefore Redirected to a field outside the University's scope. All students who did not receive a passing grade will meet a United Commonwealth official outside their residence at noon. That official will escort you to a location where you will discuss the next step in your career."

My pulse quickens. Is this part of the script every year, or has someone in our class failed this test?

There isn't time to ask as Professor Lee continues. "For those who passed, your designated field of study will be listed after your name. Tomorrow, you will be met by your course of study's academic adviser. You will be assigned to a student guide, who will help you move into your designated field of study's residence hall. You will have a week to settle into your space and get to know the people sharing your career path before your studies begin. I look forward to seeing many of you in my classes."

Professor Lee turns, hangs the clipboard on the wall behind him and walks to the exit. When he reaches the door, he looks back. "I congratulate you all on your achievements thus far. I know you will do great things in the future."

After one last smile, he walks out.

I'm not surprised that Stacia is the first one out of her seat. Chairs are pushed back, several of them overturned, as my classmates rush to the front to see what fate has in store. Someone gives a whoop of excitement. Anticipation laced with fear tingles up my spine. Slowly, I rise and walk towards the list.

At five foot two, I am the shortest girl in the class. Since I was the last to leave my desk, I find myself in the back of the group. Though I stand on tiptoe and crane my neck, the list remains hidden from view. But I can see the other students' faces clearly. Will getting slapped on the back by a short, dark-skinned boy named Rawson. Kit giving Tomas a big hug and keeping her arms around him even as he tries to pull away. Stacia stalking to the door. The tears glittering in her eyes send cold fear up my spine. Did she not get the area of study she wanted, or did the unthinkable happen?

Weaving in between bodies and finally pushing a grinning Will out of the way, I come face-to-face with the list. It is organised in alphabetical order by last name. I shift my eyes to the bottom, look for my name and find it.

VALE, Malencia – Pass – Government

I close my eyes, take three deep breaths and open them again. The words haven't changed. For some reason I can't comprehend, I have been assigned to the field of study I least want to pursue.

There must be a mistake. I fight the urge to run after Professor Lee and beg for an explanation. Did I not choose the correct words in my final answer? My skill lies in mathematics and in manipulating metal and wires, not in doublespeak and carefully constructed phrases. Why would the University administrators assign me to the area where I am most certain to fail?

Tears lodge in my throat but go no further. I will not let them fall. Not here. No one will see my disappointment. Not the administration. Not my fellow students. I refuse to let anyone know how hard I am fighting to keep my breath even and my hands unclenched. They will only see joy that I passed.

Curving my lips into a smile, I read the rest of the results and look for the names of my friends. I find Tomas first and grin for real. Biological Engineering. Pride and happiness shimmer through me. I look for him in the crowd and find him standing two feet away. I throw my arms around him and squeeze tight. The professors have made the correct choice. He will not disappoint.

Holding Tomas's hand, I find Stacia's and Will's names

back to back. Medicine for Stacia. Government for Will. Like me, neither received their preferred course of study, which explains Stacia's unhappiness. But they have both passed. Which is not true for all of my classmates. My personal disappointment fades. Beside Obidiah Martinez's name is one word: *Redirected*. I cannot help but wonder what consequences that word will bring.

It's the first question I ask Tomas after we leave the classroom and go to a spot outside where we are least likely to be disturbed. I can tell Tomas would rather talk about how I feel about my own test results. Once I assure him I'm fine, he says, "I'm guessing he'll get assigned to a tech team here in the city or sent to one of the colonies to help with construction. Don't you think?"

I'm not sure what I think. Obidiah isn't a friend. In fact, I don't think he could claim that standing with anyone here. A few have tried to engage him in conversation, including me. A week after arriving on campus, I saw him sitting by a tree, looking off into the distance. While his powerful build, fierce expression and exotic-looking braided hair would normally intimidate me into keeping my distance, the sadness I saw in his eyes had me walking towards him. The moment I said his name, his expression changed. Sadness was replaced by anger. He demanded I leave. I did. The experience was enough to keep me from repeating the overture. Now I wish I had.

"Are you sure you're okay?" Tomas asks as we walk back to my residence. He stops and looks down into my eyes. I feel the shield I've built against my emotions start to crack, and I bite my lip. Tomas touches my cheek and says, "If it's any consolation, I think they made the right choice."

The words punch the air from my lungs. "You don't think I'm good enough for Mechanical Engineering."

Tomas's hand touches my shoulder. I try to shake him off, but he holds fast. "I think there's no one I'd trust with the direction of our country more. Government isn't always just, and it isn't always fair. But it should be. I trust you to try and make ours both."

His words and kiss chase the doubts into the shadows, but they return when he leaves to pack for tomorrow's move. Tomas has faith in me, but I am not certain I can return his trust. Not in myself. Not in him. Not in anything.

Standing in my Early Studies quarters, I try to decide what to pack first. Since The Testing, I've acquired very little. Barely enough to warrant taking one of the additional bags they provided for the move to our new quarters. Just a few extra clothes, a couple of books and a small vase of dried flowers. The flowers were a birthday gift from home, although everyone thinks they came from Michal, the Tosu City official who escorted me to The Testing. Not even

Tomas knows the truth, since I don't want to risk trouble for the official or my family.

Today, the vase makes me think of my father. As I hold it, tears begin to fall. What would he think of the field I've been assigned? Would he be as confused as me? University administrators directed him into genetically manipulating plants. The evidence that their judgement was correct is cradled in my hands. My father is a genius at making growing things thrive. The passion he feels for his work is one of the qualities I most admire about him. I always assumed he'd made the choice to help revitalise the earth. I hadn't realised the decision had been made for him, and I have to wonder – if he had been the one doing the choosing, what would his choice have been? Was he, like Tomas, directed into the field of his passion, or was he like me?

Wiping away my tears, I dig into the mattress and pull the Transit Communicator from its hiding place. Bile rises in my throat. The stories recorded on the Communicator speak of a testing process run by the United Commonwealth government that is far from fair and just. Can I be an active part of a system that encourages Testing candidates to kill and be killed? Does the end result – my father's amazing work with plants and the hundreds of breakthroughs created by University graduates – justify the means? These are questions I cannot begin to answer until I learn whether the words I recorded are real or imagined.

Since all successful Testing candidates have their memories of The Testing removed, it is impossible for me to determine what really occurred during that time. But if I am clever, I can find a way.

I glance at the clock on my night stand – 11:04 a.m. According to Professor Lee's instructions, Obidiah will meet a University official outside this building at noon to embark on his new career path. While learning Obidiah's fate will not tell me if the recorder's stories are true, it will give me an idea of what the University believes is an appropriate punishment for failure. If it is anything like the stories on the recorder, I will have the answer I'm seeking.

I wrap the Transit Communicator in a towel and shove it in between the folds of clothes I have already packed. Then, grabbing a book, I lock my door and head downstairs. Will, Vic and a couple of my other classmates are tossing a ball in the open space next to my residence. Will waves me over, but I shake my head, raise the book I'm holding and keep moving.

Since Will and the other colony students are on the left side of the residence, I walk towards the two-storey grey stone structure to the right – the Earth Science building. Tomas and I have often used the bench near the entrance to study, so no one looks twice at me as I sit on the cold metal and pretend to read. From this vantage point, I have a clear view of the walkway that leads from the Early Study residence.

Soon I spot Obidiah's distinctive braids as he exits and stands on the walkway waiting for his escort. A large black bag weighs down his right shoulder. Carefully cradled in his arms is a battered guitar. I didn't know Obidiah played. I doubt any of us did. More surprising still is the wide grin that stretches across his face as he peers into the distance. Perhaps he is trying to put on a façade for those nearby, but I don't think so. For the first time since I met Obidiah, he looks happy. I try to imagine what I would feel after learning I was leaving the University.

Dejection. Failure. Heartbreak.

Obidiah appears to be experiencing none of these emotions. I think back to that moment months ago when he looked so alone. And I wonder. Did he really fail the test? Or was he so unhappy here that he sabotaged his score in the hopes he would find his way back home?

I see two University officials approach. One in ceremonial red. The other in purple. Obidiah nods at whatever they say and falls in step behind them as they lead him down the walkway to the north.

Making sure not to lose sight of them, I close the book

in my hand, stand and slowly walk on a parallel course. Normally, when crossing campus, I take time to admire the structures that have stood for, in many cases, well over two centuries. After the Seven Stages of War came to an end, the surviving population of the former United States had the courage to begin the overwhelming process of rebuilding. Leaders chose the city of Wichita, renamed Tosu City, in what used to be the state of Kansas as the starting point in the revitalisation process. While major cities like Chicago, New York and Denver had been destroyed during the war, Wichita – with its lack of strategic placement – remained intact. The earth's reaction to man-made warfare destroyed many buildings, but the vast majority could be repaired and used.

Most days, I admire the architecture and think of the hope the buildings represent. Today, I keep my head down in an effort not to be noticed by the students and faculty crossing campus. I cast glances at Obidiah and the officials to make sure they are still in sight. No one has forbidden passing students from walking around campus today, but I am not naïve enough to believe my presence would be welcomed by Obidiah or the administrators.

Sunlight gleams on glass windows as I pass behind buildings. Obidiah and his escorts walk quickly, and I have to move faster to see which direction they travel in. After passing several large structures, the escorts turn down a walkway that heads in my direction.

There are no trees large enough to hide behind. A group of older students stroll across the grass a hundred feet to my left. Too far away for me to look like I am with them. The closest building entrance is at least fifty feet away. If I run, someone will see me and wonder why I am in such a hurry. Despite the quickening of my pulse and the desire to flee before the officials can spot me, I do the only thing I can think of. I take a seat on the cold ground, open my book and let my hair fall over my face as I feign interest in the history contained on its pages.

I hear footsteps growing closer. Each one makes my nerves jump and my breath catch. The sounds tell me the officials and Obidiah are now passing only ten feet from where I sit. I flip a page and keep my eyes on the words swimming in front of me. I pretend to be absorbed in my reading, even though I am aware of every second that passes. The footsteps grow fainter. I brave a look up from my book and see the officials head north at the next walkway. Obidiah follows, but his gait slows as he turns his head. For a moment, our eyes lock. I see confusion and other emotions I can't put names to cross his face. Is he happy to see a fellow first-year student? Does he remember that I wanted us to be friends and now regrets not making that connection?

Our gaze meets one last time before Obidiah starts walking again. I scramble to my feet and slowly follow behind. Twice I see Obidiah turn his head. If he sees me hiding behind bushes or walking in the shadows of trees, he doesn't give any indication. He just follows the officials as they lead him towards a brick building surrounded by a large black fence located at the north-east border of the campus. It sits alone. Far from the residence and the other University buildings designated for student use. Behind the building, the grass looks sicker. The soil poorer. Less revitalised than the rest of campus. This structure was not among the ones we toured on our University orientation, but during the tour, our guide told us the University sits on the northern edge of Tosu City. Until this moment, I didn't realise how close to the boundary we really were. A plaque on the fence next to the open gate reads TU ADMINISTRATION.

I watch Obidiah and his escorts disappear inside the large white doors and try to decide what to do next. Unlike on the rest of the University campus, there are no people wandering this area. No one sits on benches or debates with fellow students under trees. Whatever this building is, it doesn't appear to get a lot of visitors. I wait for several minutes to see if anyone else approaches. When no one does, I slip inside the fence and walk confidently to the front door as though I have every right to be here. If someone stops me, I can say I decided to celebrate passing my test by learning more about the University.

Glancing through the front door's long, narrow window, I look for signs of Obidiah and see no one.

Now what? Do I go inside and risk running into a University official or wait out here for Obidiah to be escorted out? I am about to open the door when I see Dr Barnes, who is in charge of The Testing, and a petite, dark-haired woman come out of a room and walk to the back of the building. They must be going to meet Obidiah. I watch as they disappear through a room at the very end of the hall, and I hurry around the building to the other side to look for a window to observe the meeting through.

I reach the back of the building and feel a stab of disappointment. In the middle of the wall is a large metal door and a keypad but no windows. Probably because no one wants to look out on the lone vehicle-storage outbuilding that sits thirty yards from the back door or the unrevitalised expanse of grass and cracked roads beyond it. The fence does not enclose this side. Probably to allow for the arrival of vehicles. The rest of the area beyond is barren, albeit cleared of debris. To prepare it for revitalisation or to make sure this building stays isolated?

Since I cannot see anything, I start back towards the front of the building. The sounds of grinding gears and a revving engine still my feet. When I turn back, I see a large black skimmer coming out of the outbuilding. I race to the side of the building and flatten myself against the wall behind a scrawny bush to keep out of the skimmer pilot's sight. The roar of the engine comes closer and then goes quiet, telling me it stopped somewhere nearby. I hear a door open, followed by the sound of a female voice.

"It's such a waste. He should have been one of the stars of this class. There should be another way."

"Procedures are in place for a reason, MayLin." My heart leaps into my throat. That voice belongs to Dr Jedidiah Barnes. "The country can't afford to change course now. Not when we are finally beginning to make real progress. You know what to do with him."

A male voice answers, "Yes, sir."

I peer around the corner of the building and my knees give way. My fingers dig into the brick wall to keep me from falling as I see two officials carrying Obidiah towards the skimmer. His head lolls back. His braids drag on the ground. When they reach the vehicle, the officials set him on the skimmer's floor and climb into the pilot's cabin. I wait for Obidiah to sit up. He doesn't. I look for the rise and fall of his chest, but there is nothing.

The female official who escorted Obidiah appears with a black bag and Obidiah's guitar. She throws them both into the skimmer before climbing in. The skimmer lifts off the ground and travels across the barren landscape. Before I can understand what I have just seen, the skimmer and Obidiah are gone.

CHAPTER 3

Tears build behind my eyes. My breath comes short and fast as I flatten myself against the cold, hard wall. Obidiah is gone. Redirected. Dead. If I am not careful, I will be too.

Dr Barnes is still talking. "You know how disappointed I am every time a student with such promise is Redirected, but this is the only option. Revitalisation requires unity. Students with Obidiah's potential cannot be allowed to work outside the framework of the Commonwealth. People could start turning to them for leadersh ip instead of following the course our current leaders have set out for us. That kind of disharmony would undermine everything we have done for the last one hundred years."

"I know," MayLin says. "But Redirection may no longer be the answer. The president is becoming more vocal in her concerns about the number of students who fail to make it to graduation."

"The president can express concern, but unless the law

is changed, the testing and education of our leaders are in my hands. It is better for our country to learn early on that a student is not capable of dealing with the kinds of pressure he or she would have to face in the future."

Something about Dr Barnes's words feels familiar. My stomach roils as I see a flash of my Testing roommate, Ryme Reynald. Her blonde hair. A yellow dress. I try to hold on to the memory, but it vanishes like smoke as Dr Barnes's voice booms, "Removal now is preferable to the damage that could be caused later. If the president doesn't understand that, she will have to be persuaded. We have come too far—"

The slam of a door cuts off the rest of his words. Taking a deep breath, I look around the corner to make sure he and MayLin are gone. Then I run.

Finally, when I reach the stadium at the far north-west side of campus, I slow my pace, gulp in air and try to think.

In the distance I see people strolling through the late-winter grass. No one is looking my way. Still, I put a smile on my face and pretend my heart isn't racing as I pull my jacket tight around me and walk across the lawn, all the while fighting the urge to let the tears burning my eyes fall.

I walk in the direction of my residence even though I can't go there. Not yet. My friends will be packing. Celebrating. Getting ready for tomorrow, when we move to our new residences and begin the next phase of our studies.

Only, after today – after seeing Obidiah's unmoving body – I am not sure I can. I close my eyes and hear the words on the recorder talk of those who died. My friends from Five Lakes Colony: Malachi Rourke and Zandri Hicks. My roommate, Ryme Reynald. Will's twin brother, Gill Donovan. I can no longer deny the truth of those whispered words. How can I stay and study, knowing so many have died or disappeared? To do so would be like saying their deaths don't matter. That Dr Barnes and his people have the right to select not only who leads but who lives and dies.

He doesn't.

They don't.

No one does.

Over a century ago, other leaders felt they had that right. We are still paying the price for their actions. Our current leaders should have learned from those mistakes.

Picking a shaded spot under a tree, I sink to the ground and pull my legs tight against my chest. The ground underneath me is cold, but the green buds on a nearby bush speak of the spring that is on the cusp of bloom. A bird whistles from a branch above my head. All around me are signs of a world on its way back from disaster and decay. Signs the University has chosen people with talent and skill who, with their knowledge, have brought hope to our country. Looking now at the healthy plant life, I have to ask – was it worth it? Yes, lives were saved, but what about the lives taken? History says that progress often requires sacrifice, but what kind of progress can we claim when it is built on the lives of the citizens it is supposed to aid?

I look at the sun's position in the sky. In a matter of hours, the sun will set. While I have learned much about Tosu City during the past several months, I do not know it well enough to feel secure roaming the streets after dark. If I am to leave and have a chance at escape, I have to do it now.

I push to my feet and walk to the Early Studies residence. Sounds of laughter greet me. Shouts of happiness. I wave at a girl named Naomy as she races by. My hand shakes as I put the key in the lock and open my door. Somewhere deep inside, I must have always known I would run, because when I shut the door behind me, I know exactly what to bring.

Just like for The Testing, I allow myself one bag. Two changes of clothing. Two personal items and my undergarments. Boots that were handed down to me from my brothers. Socks. The pocket-knife my father gave to me and my brothers years ago and Zeen's Transit Communicator. Though they are unnecessary for survival, I ache to bring along the dried flowers. The vase. There is room in the bag for them, but that extra space must be used for food, water and any items I find along the way that will aid in my survival.

As I slide the pocket-knife into the side pocket of my bag, my eyes settle on a small stack of notes from Tomas filled with words of support and love. My fingers brush the top scrap of paper – paper that should have been recycled but that I could not bear the thought of destroying. I ache to talk to Tomas now. To beg him to go with me. To leave the University, our futures and the shadows of The Testing far behind. Maybe the further away we go, the easier it will be to bury the memories that threaten everything and to forgive. To rebuild the trust that once was real.

I jump at the sound of the doorknob turning behind me. "Hey, Cia. I know you're in there. Open the door."

Stacia.

The minute I turn the lock, she pushes through the door, strides into the room and flops on my bed next to my opened bag. "Well, today has been interesting. Everyone is either celebrating or wallowing in the depths of despair. You're smart to have cleared out for a while to avoid the emotional tidal wave. Considering this crowd is supposed to be the best and brightest, I'd have thought they'd have figured out how things work by now."

The way Stacia is sprawled out with her hands tucked under her head suggests she plans on staying here for some time. Time I don't have. But I can't just ask her to leave. We've spent enough time together for her to realise such a request isn't typical, and she'll wonder why I made it. If I manage to escape, Dr Barnes and his team might question those who had any knowledge of my plans. I don't want Stacia to be punished for the choices I alone have made.

Tamping down my anxiety, I ask, "You're not upset about being assigned to Medicine?"

Stacia shrugs. "I would be lying if I said I wasn't upset at first. Over the past few months, I'd almost convinced myself I could control my future through hard work. I forgot what I learned growing up in Tulsa Colony. Control is an illusion. Only a handful of people have the ability to shape their lives and the lives of those around them. To become one of those people, I have to prove I can do whatever is necessary to succeed." She laughs. "So I will."

Her laugh makes me flinch. It's cold and practical. Hard. Determined. Stacia is smart, but I've often wondered if it's these other traits that helped her survive The Testing. I have to admire her ability to strip aside emotion and find the most direct solution to a situation, even if I don't agree with her assessment. Guilt tugs at me when I think of leaving her behind. But while part of me wants to ask Stacia to abandon the University and come with me, the words do not pass my lips. Stacia is not one to run from a challenge, even one that might result in her death.

For the next hour, Stacia speculates on what our class schedules will look like once we start our courses of study and makes me promise to share everything that happens in the Government Studies residence. No doubt she thinks the information will come in handy when she has achieved the control she so desperately seeks. I make Stacia promise the same, even as the lie makes my insides curl. I will not be here to follow through, and if I want to escape without notice, I cannot even say goodbye.

By the time Stacia heads back to her own room, the sun is low in the sky. Danger will be harder to spot as the light fades, but I have no choice. It is time to go. I fasten my coat and slide my bag onto my shoulder. When I reach for the doorknob, I notice the bracelet peeking out from under my sleeve. The one-starred band that defines who the United Commonwealth government and Dr Barnes want me to be. I remove the silver bracelet from my arm and place it in the centre of the bed. It is time to leave everything it represents behind.

Or it will be if I can find Tomas. When I get to his room, he doesn't answer my knock. Thinking he must have gone to the dining hall without coming to get me, I leave the building and hurry across the grass. If I can find Tomas, I can convince him to come with me. It will be easier for the two of us to survive outside the city limits. Together we can get home.

So focused am I on finding Tomas that I never notice the person in the shadows of the grey-stone Earth Science building until I hear a voice call, "Going somewhere?"

I spin and see Tosu official Michal Gallen standing thirty feet away. His shaggy brown curls have grown longer in the weeks since I last saw him. That, combined with the informal brown pants and billowy white shirt he wears today, makes him look more like a student than a graduate. Michal was the official who escorted me and the other Five Lakes Colony Testing candidates to Tosu City. For some reason, he chose to offer me assistance during that process, and once I was accepted to the University as a student, Michal found ways to bring news of my family. Both made me think he had my best interests at heart. But now that I know about Obidiah, I have to wonder if anything I believe is true.

Nodding, I say, "I need to grab a quick dinner so I can go back to the residence and pack. We're all getting ready for tomorrow's move."

I wait for Michal to congratulate me on passing the examination or on my designated field of study. Instead, he pushes away from the building and takes a step towards me. "I'm surprised you haven't already finished preparing. Visiting the north side of campus today must have taken time away from packing."

The set of his jaw. The warning in his eyes. Michal knows

what I did. Before I can come up with a plausible lie, Michal says, "You shouldn't have gone there today, Cia."

"I was celebrating passing the examination by touring the campus."

"You followed Obidiah." His eyes meet mine. "I saw you go to the TU Administration building. I watched you run away."

"Why?" The single syllable slips out. Given the implications of Michal's words, I should be worried about bigger things. But I need to know.

"I'll tell you after you answer one question." He walks closer and looks up and down the walkways before asking, "Why did you follow Obidiah and his escorts? None of the other students did."

It's a harder question to answer than any of the ones on yesterday's exam. I pause and choose my words carefully. "I wanted to better understand what Redirection meant."

"A student didn't pass the examination. He was Redirected to a different area. End of story." In his eyes is a challenge. One I accept.

"No. It isn't."

"You're right. It isn't." He closes his eyes and nods. "You saw Obidiah after his meeting with Dr Barnes?"

I see the image of Obidiah's hair dragging against the ground as the officials carry him by his hands and feet.

"Yes."

"And now you are planning to run."

It isn't a question, so I don't bother to answer. Instead, I cross my arms, allowing my unadorned wrist to show, and wait.

He blows a curl of hair off his forehead and sighs. "It's time for us to talk."

Warily, I follow him to the shadows of the building. I wrap my arms around myself and try to pretend my heart isn't slamming in my chest as I notice the temperature has started to drop. Darkness will be here soon, taking with it my best chance to escape. If I even can escape. Michal's presence has put that plan, not to mention my entire future, in jeopardy.

Michal leans against the cold stone of the building and sighs. "As your Testing escort, I'm tasked with watching for any behaviour that suggests the memory-altering procedure used after The Testing didn't work and reporting that behaviour to Dr Barnes. In order to fulfil my assignment, I've been required to follow you."

Betrayal punches through my heart. I grab the wall before shock sends me to my knees. "You've been spying on me?"

"I've been verifying that the memory procedure was successfully performed on you and Tomas. I thought it had been. During orientation, you and your friends made the typical jokes we always hear from students who have had those memories removed. However, over the last six months I've noticed little things that make me believe the memories have returned. Your actions today confirmed it. You remember."

"I don't." My voice is low. Breathy. Scared. My eyes scan the walkways, the buildings, the grass, looking for officials coming to Redirect me. "My memories haven't returned."

"But you know something about your time at The Testing. Enough to question what Redirection might mean for Obidiah."

"What does it mean?" I ask, hoping I was mistaken. That Obidiah was still alive when the skimmer drove away.

"You know, Cia." Michal's eyes meet mine. In their depths, I see a simmering rage that reflects my own. "Dr Barnes will not accept failure."

Obidiah failed. By preserving my Testing memories and searching for the truth, I have become a failure for Dr Barnes as well. Unless I want to be Redirected too, I have to run. Now. Michal's hand reaches out and snatches my arm. His fingers clamp onto my flesh like a vice and shove me back against the wall. The contact combined with my fear steals my breath.

"Where do you think you're going?" he asks.

"Anywhere else but here." I struggle against Michal's hold,

but he's bigger and stronger.

"Don't be a fool. You can't run. They'll find you. And if they don't, they know where to find your family. What do you think Dr Barnes will do when he talks to your father and your brothers? Do you think he'll believe your brothers weren't smart enough to be chosen for The Testing? What happens when he starts to wonder why your colony was without candidates for a decade? Who will pay the price for their deception?"

My family. My friends. My colony.

The strength my anger gave me is leached away and replaced by despair. "So now what?"

"Now you tell me what you remember, and I help you figure out how to keep safe from Dr Barnes." When I say nothing, he says, "You don't trust me."

"Why should I?"

"Because I'm trying to help you." Michal lowers his voice. "And because I remember my Testing too."

My eyes find his and look for the truth. He has the same haunted look I see in my own reflector. Can I trust that?

I realise it doesn't matter what I trust, because, regardless of my choice, Michal Gallen holds my fate in his hands.

"I don't remember my Testing," I admit. "Not exactly. I get flashes of images. Things I think I should remember."

Michal nods and leans back. He doesn't ask questions.

He just waits for me to continue.

After taking a deep breath, I do. "The night before I left for The Testing, my father told me that his memories from that time in his life had been erased. Sometime during The Testing, I must have become determined to keep my memories. So I left myself a message. I found it on my birthday." I'd been so happy. Tomas had told me he thought he was falling in love with me. I'd gotten a gift from my family. When I found my Testing symbol etched onto the Transit Communicator, I was giddy with delight at uncovering a secret. Then I pushed Play.

"I tried to convince myself it was another kind of test. I didn't want to believe that The Testing killed candidates who failed or that people I considered my friends could be capable of murder." My throat tightens, making it hard to speak. But now that I've started talking, I have to tell it all. In a way, it is a relief to speak my doubts and my worries after months of shouldering the burden alone. "But the message I left is real. Isn't it? Will murdered a girl named Nina. He tried to kill me. And Tomas..." Words fail. Now that I believe the truth of the recorder, I must accept that Tomas deceived me. That he was involved in Zandri's death, although I have no idea what part he played. But Michal might. "What did Tomas do to Zandri?" I ask.

"I don't know." Sympathy shines in his eyes. "Only top-level officials are permitted to read the detailed examination files."

Disappointment fills me, although I'm not surprised. "So now what?"

"Now you're going to pretend that none of this happened."

"I don't understand."

Michal looks off in the distance. "Six years ago, I passed The Testing. Only, when they performed the memory-elimination procedure, something went wrong. Two months after I started classes here at the University, my memories returned. I remembered watching my best friend die during The Testing and that the University student I had a crush on was the one who'd slit his throat. I learned that I too had killed. It was self-defence, but knowing I'd taken a life, even to save mine..."

I touch my scars – the five lines made by five fingernails – and hear my voice whisper. I didn't have a choice. I had to shoot. But when I fired my gun, I saw its eyes and realised it wasn't an animal I'd killed.

"I started having nightmares. I watched my friend die over and over at night and had to pretend during the day that none of it had happened. One night, I decided I couldn't take it any more. I grabbed my things and ran. As soon as I stepped off campus, I realised I had nowhere to go. My family would be in danger if I could get back to Boulder Colony, and since I didn't have enough food or water for the journey, it was doubtful I'd get back there at all. That's when I saw him."

"Who?"

"A man I remembered meeting during The Testing. You met him too."

A shadow of a memory flickers, but just as quickly vanishes like smoke.

"His name is Symon Dean. During the fourth test, he appeared out of nowhere and offered me help when I needed it most. He did the same thing the night I fled the University. He knew why I was running and asked if I'd be interested in working with him to put an end to The Testing once and for all. The only catch was I had to stay at the University in order to do it." Michal's smile is grim. "How could I say no?"

"What happened? Why didn't his plan work?"

"The plan still hasn't been put into effect. Symon is slowly building a network of people like me to help bring down The Testing. It's going slower than he'd like, but we have to be careful, even though some have grown tired of waiting and are demanding action now."

I stand up straighter. "So what's the plan?"

"Most of Symon's network lives in a non-sanctioned colony south of Tosu. They're passionate about changing the system, but they need people on the inside who can collect information and rally support when the time is right."

"Right for what?"

"A rebellion." Michal smiles. "That sounds more dramatic than it will be. If things go as Symon has outlined, most of the United Commonwealth will never realise anything has changed. We will remove Dr Barnes as the head of The Testing. Once that is done, The Testing will once again be the process the founders of the Commonwealth intended."

"That sounds simple enough."

"Not as simple as you might think. When The Testing was established, it was argued that the only way to select the country's leaders objectively was to make the system separate from the central governing body. The founders wanted to ensure that no one, not even the president, could manipulate the process. It was believed this separation of powers would prevent the detrimental politics of the past from intruding on the government of the future. Instead, it gave the head of Testing and his staff autonomy to run The Testing without oversight or retribution from the central government. In short, Dr Barnes is free to run The Testing as he sees fit, and under the current law, those who challenge him could be arrested for treason."

And the penalty for treason is death.

"How does Symon plan on removing Dr Barnes?"

"Symon's people are trying to convince the president and the members of the Debate Chamber to propose a new law that will authorise them to remove Dr Barnes and his team from power. Once that is done, officials sympathetic to our cause can lobby to appoint someone we approve as the head of The Testing. We'll then be able to implement a new method of picking University students. One that doesn't advocate murder."

Frustration furrows Michal's handsome face. "Things have moved more slowly than I'd like, but I prefer Symon's cautious approach to the option the other rebel faction is pushing for."

Other faction? "I don't understand. Aren't all the rebels working for the same goal?"

"Yes, but not everyone is content to wait for The Testing to end peacefully. Some want to employ any method necessary, even if it means the same kind of bloodshed we oppose."

My parents taught me that life is precious. I should recoil at the second rebel faction's plot to kill. But I don't. "If one person's death will end The Testing before more candidates die—"

"Dr Barnes's death alone will not end The Testing. The system has been designed to continue in the event of the leader's death. The only way the rebel faction can ensure the end of The Testing through violent means is if Dr Barnes and all his top administrators die."

How many are involved in planning The Testing? Dozens?

Maybe more? Would the ends justify those means? I don't know.

Neither does Michal. "One death can be kept quiet, but that many could induce panic and upset the balance of this city – perhaps even the country. The last thing we want to do is start a civil war."

I swallow hard and say, "I'm assuming you aren't telling every first-year student about this."

"No and technically, I'm not authorised to tell you. At least, not at this time." Michal frowns. "Symon has always planned to approach you about joining him, but not this soon. He doesn't want to bring any more University students into the rebellion until the divide between his faction and the faction led by Ranetta Janke has been mended. Your actions today gave me no choice but to move up that timeline. Which is something I'd prefer Symon to not know about."

"Why?"

Michal shifts uncomfortably. "Things are tense right now between the two factions. Symon has become more careful about who he can trust. I don't want him to think he has misplaced his faith in me."

"You can't expect me to go back to my room and pretend I don't know any of this! There has to be something I can do to help." I see Michal weighing the merits of my request, and I bite my lip and force myself to stay still.

I swallow hard as I wait for Michal to render his verdict. "Okay."

My heart leaps at the word.

"But you have to do exactly what I tell you. Deal?" When he holds out his hand, I don't have to think before I take it.

"What do you need me to do?"

Michal leans forward. "First thing is to move into the Government Studies residence and make friends." I let out an exasperated sigh, but Michal shakes his head. "You think I'm not giving you a real assignment, but I am. Some of the upper-level students are rebel members. There is concern that many have been won over and armed by Ranetta's faction. Symon has a person he trusts looking into the matter, but I'd feel better knowing someone else is watching out for us."

The thought that students living near me might be armed makes me break out in a cold sweat. The words on the Communicator warned me that my fellow students have not shied away from violence. My dreams are filled with their faces behind guns raised to kill. It is not hard to imagine those nightmares turned into reality.

"Also, Government students are required to do both classwork and a practical internship from the start of their studies. Those internships will determine the course of your entire adult life but will also potentially put you in a position to help the rebellion."

This is the first I've heard of the internships. Although, over the past few months, I've noticed some students leaving campus more regularly than others. Now I know why.

"In the next couple of weeks, the older students will help Dr Barnes and the residence advisers assign internships. Those internships allow students to get practical experience that complements their studies. It also gives you a chance to help us find information that might help Symon convince the president and other high-ranking officials to remove Dr Barnes from power."

"How hard can getting a good internship be?" I ask. "There are only three of us assigned to Government this year."

"Only three of you from the colonies. Add in the Tosu City students, and there will be a whole lot more."

"Tosu City students?" Icy shock is replaced by frustration at my lack of perception. With a hundred thousand people, Tosu City and the surrounding boroughs contain the largest concentration of the United Commonwealth's population. It only makes sense that the University trains students from that pool. I should have known they would be included, even though they have not been a part of the Early Studies classes my fellow colony students and I just completed.

During orientation, our guide pointed out some of the

Tosu City schools. The buildings were large and made of glass and steel and wood that gleamed in the sunlight. The kids walking into those buildings were no less polished. Healthy. Strong. And no doubt prepared for whatever a future at the University holds. But one thought stands out above all others, making my blood heat and my emotions flare. "They didn't report for The Testing."

They didn't watch friends die. They are not plagued by nightmares or doubts. They are safe. Whole. Unscarred.

"No. The selection process for Tosu students is different. Most of the students are the sons and daughters of past University graduates. Those who wish to attend the University are required to submit an application and sit for an interview. Fifty applicants take the same examination you took yesterday. Those who pass are welcomed into the University."

"And those who fail?"

"We're told that they get reassigned to jobs outside of Tosu, but no one who visits the colonies has seen proof of that. Symon is certain those students are Redirected."

I feel a stab of satisfaction that is immediately replaced by a wave of shame. Just because a Tosu City candidate's path to the University is easier doesn't mean he deserves to be punished in that way. None of us do.

"Of the fifty, how many passed?"

"Forty-two. Including the three from the colonies, sixteen students have been selected for Government. It's the largest Government class in decades. Which is why they don't have enough internships for everyone."

"How many internships do they have?"

"The last I heard, there were twelve."

If thirteen students have ties to Tosu City, the math doesn't work in my favour. "What happens if a student doesn't get assigned to one of those internships? Do they get... killed? Redirected?"

"We believe the Tosu City students get shipped to mid-level jobs outside the city."

"And the colony students?"

Eyes filled with sadness and concern meet mine. "None of them have been heard from since."

CHAPTER 4

Panic burns my throat, but I swallow down the fear and force myself to think. Worrying about an unknown penalty is pointless. The best way to avoid the problem is to make certain there is no need to be penalised. Taking a deep breath, I ask, "How and when are the internships assigned?"

"The faculty member in charge of Government, Professor Holt, will assign internships two weeks after classes begin, once the final-year students give her their assessments of the incoming class. Be careful when dealing with the first years from Tosu. Many of them have the ear of the professors or high-ranking United Commonwealth officials. If they think you are asking questions you shouldn't or doing something suspicious, they'll report you. They aren't above destroying your life or one another's in order to get ahead."

Michal glances at his watch and mutters a curse. "I have to make my final report to the University officials. Now that you've been placed in your designated field of study, my assignment to watch you is complete. Symon's asked some of his allies within the Commonwealth Government to shift me to a job that will help influence change, so I might not be around to help, but I'll get word to someone who can."

I start to ask who, but Michal starts walking towards my rooms and I have to hurry to catch up.

As we walk, he quietly explains, "During the first couple of days, the upper-year Government students are going to put you through what they call an Induction. They will be watching how you react to certain challenges. They might try to intimidate you or make you feel weak just to see if you are. Some challenges will be mental. Others, more physical. All are intended to see whether you can handle the pressure of leading a country. Remember that the Tosu City students haven't been through the rigorous Testing process. This is the University's way of exposing them to the same pressures. Once in a while, a first-year student gets angry and reports the initiation tactics to his head professor. Don't. As a colony student, you already have one strike against you. They expect you to be weak. They expect you to be less than they are. Show them they're wrong."

Fear shivers up my spine. "What if I can't?"

Michal stops walking and puts his hands on my shoulders. "You can. Everything you did in The Testing proves it. You may not remember what happened then, but I do. You're smart. You're fast, and you're strong."

"I'm the youngest student here."

"Use that." He nods. "The Tosu students are going to look at your size and pretty face and assume you aren't a threat, but I know different. They have no idea what you are capable of. I, for one, can't wait for you to show them."

I tamp down my anxiety and force myself to concentrate as Michal gives me all the information he can. Since the final-year students are the ones who orchestrate and execute the Inductions, no one can predict what exactly will happen – teamwork evaluations, trivia tests, exercises that push the boundaries of physical endurance.

"Memorise every face. Every name. Every detail. Learn where they come from and who they are related to. You never know what information will help you or the rebellion. Most students come from the families of high-ranking officials. But every year, there are a few from the less influential neighbourhoods. They can be the most dangerous. They fought hard to get where they are. They won't be pushed aside without a fight. More importantly, don't show anyone if you are afraid. Government professors value students who can push aside their fear. Everyone at some point is afraid of making the wrong choice. The programme's faculty believes the difference between Government students and the rest of the University student body is the ability to rise above that fear."

Thank goodness Michal doesn't say I'm not allowed to feel fear. Minutes later, as I replace my bracelet on my wrist and follow the sound of conversation and laughter to the common room, fear consumes me. Fear that I have made the wrong choice. That I should have run far and fast. That my fellow Government students will see the horror of what I know in my eyes. That they will pass judgement. That I will fail.

Only the warmth of Tomas's hand in mine and the hope that Symon's plan will put an end to a system that goes against the principles our rebuilt country stands for keep me in this seat, in this room, at this University. Stacia glances at Tomas and me and rolls her eyes. I pretend to laugh as I look around the room at the faces of those who might have killed to get here as they celebrate. As we say our last goodnights in this building and head off to our beds, my fellow colony students are unaware that a new test begins tomorrow. They do not know they should be as afraid as I am.

When Tomas walks me to my door, I consider passing along Michal's warning, but stop. Trust wars with love. The knowledge that the Transit Communicator's recording is real doesn't stop my heart from wanting to believe in Tomas's innate kindness. But something happened. Something he then lied about. Something involving Zandri. Then Tomas's arms pull me close. His lips touch mine, and all thoughts of the Tosu City students fade. I let myself forget the world around me and revel in this instant when I feel safe.

When Tomas steps back, he whispers that he will see me in the morning. That he loves me and that no matter what our fields of study are, we are still a team. We will always be a team. With one last gentle kiss, he disappears down the hall to find sleep. I turn to do the same.

A stunning girl with deep red hair appears out of the darkness. Anger pours from her blue eyes. Anger at me because I wasn't smart enough. Fast enough. Observant enough. I realised too late that our team was betrayed. She was punished. I was not.

A door appears beside her. I yell for her not to open it, but it's too late. Just like it was then. Her body goes still. Her skin turns grey. Her eyes roll back in her head. The door swings open just in time for her body to pitch forward into the darkness. The minute the door slams shut, I bolt upright in bed.

"Annalise." The name passes my lips, and though there is no mention of a girl named Annalise on the recorder, I can close my eyes now and picture her. Not angry as she was in the dream, but flashes of her laughing in the hallway of The Testing building. Confident in her abilities. Friendly.

Real? Imagined? I search inside myself for the truth, but find only the slamming of my heart and the lingering taste of fear.

I turn on the lights, walk to the bath and use the water to wash the terror from my face and mouth. Through the bedroom window, I can see dawn has yet to break. Hours yet before I start the next phase of my studies. I climb back into bed, hoping to find much-needed rest. Finally, I do.

The sound of doors slamming pulls me out of sleep. Raised voices are filled with excitement. Everyone is up and ready to relocate to the new residences. If I want people to continue to believe I am enthusiastic about being here, I need to get ready too.

I have just finished dressing when I hear a knock on my door. I open it expecting to find Tomas and instead come face-to-face with a tall, imposing woman with a cap of orange hair that matches the frames of her glasses.

"Malencia Vale?" When I nod, she smiles. "I'm Professor Verna Holt. The head professor of Government Studies." While her voice is warm, it feels calculated. Practised. The tone my mother uses when she trades with arrogant Mrs Pitzler for wool yarn. Professor Holt's dark, almond-shaped eyes don't blink as she looks down at me. Had I not talked to Michal, I might have shown surprise. Most likely, I would have assumed I'd missed a meeting time and offered my apologies. Instead, I hear Michal saying I will be tested. As a colony student, I'm expected to be weak. I vow to show

Professor Holt and her team that I am strong.

Straightening my shoulders, I give my most confident smile. "It's an honour to meet you. I'm looking forward to moving into the Government Studies residence later today."

Professor Holt's eyebrows rise. "If you are packed and ready, I'll walk you outside, where a final-year student is waiting to show you to your new home."

I glance at the clock. It's two hours before the time we were instructed to be ready. Good thing I'm prepared to leave now. I sling two bags containing my clothes, personal possessions and books over my shoulder and exit through the door without a backward glance.

The sky is overcast. Outside, a male student with close-cropped brown hair and an intense expression is waiting alongside two of my fellow first years, Will and the dark-haired Rawson. I take a step back when Will turns towards me. I know he's a murderer. Has Rawson also killed? My recorder never mentions him, but so much of what happened is missing. Should I believe that every candidate is capable of taking a life?

"This is Ian," Professor Holt says. "He will see you to the Government Studies residence. I trust you will be comfortable there." With a curt nod, she turns on her heel and strides away.

We all look at Ian. In his fitted black pants, shiny black

boots and deep purple shirt, Ian is more than a little imposing. Until he grins. The sternness disappears, replaced by an exuberance that makes me think of my brother Win. In a rich baritone voice, he says, "Congratulations on being selected for Government Studies. Not only are we the smartest students on campus, our house is the largest, which means we all get our own room."

I see Tomas come out of the building as Ian asks us to follow him. Tomas turns towards us. While I want to run to him and tell him where I'm going and what possibly lies ahead for both of us, I see Ian watching me. Waiting.

Over the years, my father complained several times that University graduates rarely had friends outside their designated fields of study. Part of me always thought he was exaggerating, since none of the graduates in Five Lakes behaved in that manner. But the way Ian's gaze shifts from me to Tomas makes me pause. If my father is correct, the students in my field of study might not appreciate my relationship with someone outside our career path.

Tomas comes closer. His eyes are bright. Happy. Seeing him warms my heart, but I do not return his grin with one of my own. Instead, I give a tiny shake of my head. I hope he sees the apology, love and warning in my expression before I turn and walk away.

Ian glances up at the rumbling sky as he leads us

across campus. "If we hurry, we should make it to the residence before the rain starts. The one downside to being part of Government Studies is the distance you have to walk to class. Professor Holt says exercise moves the blood in the brain, which helps us think." Ian laughs. "I'd be more impressed by that reasoning if Professor Holt didn't use a skimmer to get around campus."

We laugh. After a moment, Ian asks, "So, did any of you actually want to be chosen for Government Studies?"

Will looks down at the stone walkway. Rawson's cheeks tinge red. It's clear none of us want to be taking this walk today. Ian must know that.

Since I have not made any attempt to hide my desired course of study, I confess, "I wanted Mechanical Engineering. Government was the last choice on my list."

"Cia." Will nudges me with his elbow. I probably should stay quiet, but instead I smile at Ian and ask, "Was Government Studies your first choice?"

Ian frowns. My shoulders tense until I notice the corners of Ian's mouth twitch. Finally, he laughs. "I wanted Education and was pretty steamed when they stuck me here. It didn't take me long to realise very few students who want to be placed in Government Studies actually are."

"Why is that?" I ask.

Ian stops. "Because sometimes the best leaders are the

ones who have no interest in leading. Those are often the ones who are most interested in doing what is right, not what is popular." He gives an embarrassed shrug and starts walking again. "Sorry about the lecture. The last thing I want to do is sound like one of the professors. But in this case, I think they're right."

Ian falls silent. For the next few minutes, thunder is the only accompaniment to our journey. It isn't until we pass the History building that I realise we are going into a section of campus I have only walked through once, during the University tour after passing The Testing. It's a section less utilised because it was hit harder than the rest by the earthquakes that shook the country during the Sixth Stage of War.

Here trees are less abundant. The grass has been revitalised, but is a shade yellower. Ian leads us across a bridge that was erected after Tosu City was named. The bridge spans a gap over twenty feet wide and hundreds of feet deep. In the distance, I see a massive, three-storey structure constructed of dark-grey stone. Atop the structure is a clock tower. As we step off the bridge, I spot a small stone sign engraved with the words GOVERNMENT STUDIES.

"The clock tower is several hundred years old." Ian's voice breaks the silence. "The earthquake that caused the fissure we just passed tore apart several buildings, including the one with that tower. While most of the tower's original building was reduced to rubble, the clock portion survived. When the founders of the University decided to construct the Government Studies residence, they had the architects include the tower as a homage to the past."

I look at the tower with new appreciation, but can't help wishing the builders had made the rest of the residence more hospitable. Aside from the lovely tower, the building is all hard lines and massive stone. Tall, narrow windows line the second and third floors. A large black door at the end of the building looks to be the only entrance or exit. A small sign next to the door says WELCOME, which is almost funny, since I feel anything but.

"Don't worry," Ian says. "It's homier than it looks."

"It would almost have to be." I laugh as a drop of rain hits me.

The sky rumbles, and rain falls faster as we race for cover. Ian pushes open the heavy wooden door, waits until all of us step inside and then closes it behind us. Lights blaze in the foyer, giving me a clear view of the framed portraits that line the room. The first president of the United States, George Washington. The last United States president, Nicholas Dalton. The five presidents that have served the United Commonwealth. A few others, whose faces I don't recognise but whose names I'd probably know from my history lessons. People who ran our country. Did their best to change the world for the better.

"As you can probably guess, the students have no say in decorating the common rooms. Otherwise, the portraits would have been used for firewood years ago." Ian gives our current president's face a pat as he passes through the doorway and beckons us to follow him into a wide room filled with cushioned benches, faded armchairs, an enormous fireplace with a burning fire and people. At least two dozen of them. Whispering. Eyes wide with curiosity as they study us.

I scan the faces. Most appear close to my age, but a handful look like Ian – older, more experienced, watching our every move.

Ian tells us to take a seat. A girl with short curly blonde hair and cheeks filled with freckles shifts to the end of her bench, giving Will, Rawson and me room to sit. Once we do, Ian walks across the room, stands in front of the arched stone fireplace and says, "For those of you who don't know me, my name is Ian Maass. I'm a final-year Government student. For the next few weeks, I'll be serving as one of your designated study's guides. Each first-year student will be assigned to a guide who will show you around, help you figure out where your classes are and answer whatever questions you might have. This year, there are sixteen of you in the first-year class."

Will sucks in air. Rawson blinks. Even knowing the Tosu City students would be here, I feel my heart race at the sight of the faces turned towards us. Some look smug. Others are curious. Many snicker, which says that while we did not know of their presence, they have not been unaware of us. I don't know where they have been studying these past months, but no matter where they have been, they are here now and ready to do what it takes to make top grades.

I see Ian assessing our reactions from across the room. His eyebrows shift upward as he looks at me. Then he continues to speak. "Adjusting to University life and to your new residence is always a challenge. The guides are here to make that easier. Think of us as a big brother or sister and come to us with any questions, concerns or fears. We can't help you if we don't know there's a problem."

The older students smile.

"When I announce your name, please stand so your guide can identify you. Once all assignments are complete, your guide will show you to your room and help get you settled in. And since I'm already standing, I'll announce my little siblings first." Ian takes a clipboard from a dark-skinned girl who gives him a flirty smile.

"Kaleigh Cline." The freckled girl at the end of our bench swallows hard and stands. "Raffe Jeffries." A tall, broad-shouldered boy with bushy eyebrows stands to my left.

"Last, but by no means least, Malencia Vale."

Most eyes in the room swing towards me when I stand, but I can't help noticing the quizzical look the dark-skinned girl gives Ian. She had the clipboard with the list of first years and the guides they were assigned. Did Ian alter the assignments?

I continue to wonder as Ian announces the rest of the mentoring assignments. Three Tosu City boys are assigned to the dark-skinned girl, whose name turns out to be Himani Biseck. If I was supposed to be placed with her, I'm grateful to Ian for the change. Himani's smile is bright, but something about the narrowing of her eyes reminds me of a cat stalking a field mouse.

As Michal suggested, I try to memorise names and faces. Will is called next, along with a slightly rounded girl named Olive and a boy with no hair named Griffin. The three are assigned to a big brother with large black-rimmed glasses who I think is named Sam. Rawson's trio is completed by a sweet-faced boy named Enzo and a girl with sharp features called Juliet. They are assigned to a hulking final year Ian introduces as Lazar. The last four first years, three boys and a girl, are assigned to a tall, brown-haired girl with wide-set eyes. Due to the murmurs in the room, I have a hard time catching their names. I can't help noticing that first-year girls are outnumbered at least three to one.

Before I can decide whether those odds put me at a disadvantage, Ian lays down the clipboard, grabs something from the girl next to him and says, "Your guides will now show you to your rooms and help you settle in. Kaleigh, Raffe, Malencia, you're with me." Ian heads through a door to his left. I grab my bags and hurry after him, dodging other students looking for their guides. For once, my height and small build are an advantage as I zigzag under and around and reach the doorway first. Ian is standing in the middle of a dimly lit room filled with shelf after shelf of books. He grins as I cross the threshold, but says nothing until the other two first years arrive. Moments later, Raffe strides through the doorway. He stands at least a foot taller than I and scowls when he is bumped into from behind by the third member of our group.

"First things first," Ian says with a grin. "I'm going to take you on a quick tour of the place before showing you to your personal quarters. This is one of three library rooms in the building. All the books stored in our libraries can also be found in the main campus library. The main library's books are in better shape than these, but we're willing to put up with faded ink, broken bindings and water-damaged pages, especially when it's raining outside. Just make sure you put the books back where you found them when you're done, or your fellow students will get testy. Follow me."

He leads us through a door in the back of the room that empties out into a large space illuminated by the light trickling in from four square windows. Eight long wooden tables with long benches on either side fill the room. "This is the dining hall. The kitchen is through the doors back there. They turn the lights on during meals. If you come in after the lights have dimmed, it means mealtime is over and you'll have to make your own dinner."

We head back through the library to the room with the fireplace. "This is the hangout room. Just about everyone uses it for studying or just kicking back. Almost all the upper years are currently at class. That's the only reason no one is in here now. On the occasions our faculty adviser, Professor Holt, asks to speak to us all, this is the room we use. It can get kind of crowded during those meetings, so get here early if you want to catch a seat."

I can hear the sounds of feet tromping above us as the others settle into their rooms. Kaleigh complains that her bags are getting heavy, but Ian isn't done playing tour guide. He shows us the other two libraries, as well as three labs that we can use if we don't have time to finish an assignment on campus. Etched on all the doors is the symbol of the balanced scales.

When I ask about the design, Ian explains, "The balanced scales represent all Government Studies students." He holds out his wrist, and I see he is wearing a thick bracelet engraved with a design that features the same scales. Below the scales is a crescent shape. "The symbol was chosen to remind us that government is supposed to balance humanity and kindness with law and justice. The imbalance of these principles caused the Seven Stages of War. It is our job and the job of all United Commonwealth officials to restore that balance and see that it is never allowed to shift again." In a teasing tone, he adds, "And, of course, it looks way cooler than the other symbols. So we have that going for us, right?"

The other two first years laugh. I study the symbol again, wondering if anyone realises that The Testing process has already upset that balance we are supposed to seek. With any luck, the rebellion will restore the balance and I will be a part of that process.

"Now, time to see where you're going to be sleeping. If you get to sleep." He winks and heads up a wide wooden staircase. The wood is scarred but polished to a shine. "The top two floors are personal quarters. Boys are assigned rooms on the second floor. Girls on the third. Raffe – your room is this way."

"You have two hours before lunch to unpack," Ian explains as we stop in front of a door on the second floor marked with the symbol of a coiled spring. "After lunch, Dr Holt will meet with each of you to talk about your class schedules and answer any questions you have."

Raffe enters the room, and Kaleigh and I follow Ian to the third floor. There is no one in the hallway as Ian heads to the right and stops in front of a door marked with a key. When Kaleigh opens the door, Ian leads me to the door at the end. A lightning bolt says the room now belongs to me.

I switch on the light and step into a sitting room. A table with two chairs sits against one wall. A small sofa rests against another. Straight ahead is a doorway that leads to sleeping quarters, complete with a bed covered with a dark red quilt, a trunk for personal items and a small wooden wardrobe for clothes. Under the one narrow window is a scarred wooden desk with several drawers. Off the bedroom is a small bathroom. The rooms are almost identical in style to the ones I left this morning.

"Are the rooms big enough?" Ian asks from the doorway.

"Are you kidding?" I laugh. "I used to share a bedroom not much larger than this with my four brothers."

He smiles. "I know what you mean. There are six of us in my family. My being selected for The Testing meant my youngest sister's getting her own bed."

"You're not from Tosu City?" I know the answer before he shakes his head. The Testing is only for candidates from the colonies. And in the corner of my heart I find myself wondering – what did Ian have to do to pass The Testing?

"Is that why you decided to be my guide instead of taking whoever you were supposed to be assigned?"

"I'm not sure what you mean," he says, but the gleam in his eyes says different. "Remember, you have just shy of two hours before you need to be downstairs. No matter what happens, don't be late."

Before I can ask what could possibly happen, Ian closes the door behind him. By the time I open the door and look down the hall, he's gone.

Carefully, I unpack the vase with my father's dried flowers. I place the flowers on the table in the sitting room to remind me of where I came from and what I am fighting for. Bit by bit, I empty my bags. Clothes in the wardrobe. Zeen's Transit Communicator under the mattress. My few books, pencils and stray odds and ends get neatly stored in desk drawers. While I unpack, I check the room for signs that someone is observing me. While there weren't any at the Early Studies residence, I still remember the glint of the camera lens in the skimmer as we travelled to The Testing and am relieved when I don't find cameras here.

As I place the now-empty bags next to the desk, I hear a loud metallic click from the sitting room. I start towards the sound and hear another click from the bedroom behind me a moment before the lights go out.

CHAPTER 5

I blink, trying to clear the inky darkness from my eyes, but to no avail. Whatever light the narrow bedroom window provided is now gone. I can see nothing.

My heart pounds. Michal said the upper-level students would challenge us to assess our skills and our personalities. An Induction he called it. Well, let the Induction begin.

In the darkness, I can hear female voices calling for help. I stretch my hands out in front of me as I creep across the unfamiliar sitting room, looking for the exit. Pain sings up my leg as my shin connects with something hard. Probably the bottom of a chair. My hands rub the injured area, but at least now I know where I am.

Cautiously, I inch my way across the room. The wall greets my fingers, and I slide them across the smooth surface until they find the door. My hand closes around the knob. Locked. I try to flip the deadbolt. It won't budge. Disappointment is quickly replaced by chagrin. Surely I didn't expect this test to be that easy.

Leaning against the wall, I think through the goal of this challenge. Ian's final instructions were that we must be downstairs in time for lunch. So, while I might be able to splice wires and use the Transit Communicator's solar cells to illuminate the room, creating a light source isn't the point. Escape is. To escape I need to open the door. To open the door I need... what?

Once again, my fingers probe the area around the doorknob as I try to learn what I can about the lock. I'd been too focused on the rooms themselves to notice how the door was constructed. If I make it past this test, I vow, I won't make that same careless mistake again.

The wood is scarred but smooth. My fingers run over the lock. I think it's a single-cylinder deadbolt. A key opens the lock from the outside. The latch mechanism opens it from here – only the lock isn't working. For a moment, I wonder if the deadbolt is the only lock holding this door in place or if something more is keeping it shut. Ian warned me not to be late for lunch. That warning implies the possibility of an on-time arrival. Since the lights went out about an hour before we need to be downstairs, I assume the locking mechanism must be simple in order for me to meet that expectation.

The rumble of thunder makes me jump. Taking a deep breath, I search the other side of the door with my hands and smile into the darkness. The door is hung with old-fashioned pin hinges. The same kind my family uses back in Five Lakes. Five years ago, my brothers locked me into our bedroom. They said I had to tell them all how smart and handsome they were before they let me out. While they made jokes on the other side of the door, I popped the hinge pins and came strolling out with the threat that I'd tell Mom if they didn't do my chores for seven days. If I have my way, today will be no less triumphant.

Careful to avoid getting another bruise, I inch my way to the bedroom and picture the layout of the space. I walk to where I think the desk should be. There. I yank open the top-right drawer and close my fingers over the pocket-knife given to me by my father. The knife is complete with a blade, file, screwdriver and other tools. Several of those should come in handy now.

I make my way back to the door and flip open the pocket-knife, feeling for the right tool. The file, with its flat pointed edge, worked when I was twelve, and it does the trick now. I work the tip of the tool under the pin and use the file as a lever to pry up the metal rod. One down. I climb on a chair to get a better angle on the top hinge, and it isn't long before I am placing the pin in my pocket and hopping down. Wedging the file between the door and the frame, I wince as a splinter lodges into my thumb.

But within minutes, I work the door free.

The hallway lights are off, probably to ensure we couldn't use the sliver of light they'd provide under the door to aid us in our task. However, the dim glow near the staircase, probably light from the first floor, makes it easy to navigate the path to the steps. Aside from my own, no doors are open. Banging and the sounds of muffled cries tell me my fellow female students are still working to pass this Induction.

I stop at the second floor and glance up and down the hall. Two doors open. The rest are closed – although, judging by the sound of cracking wood, one more will be open soon. Not sure how much time remains before the deadline, I make my way to the brightly lit first floor. A fire still crackles in the hearth of the hangout room, but no one is there to enjoy the warmth. Rain pelts the windows, and for an instant, lightning brightens the world outside. A clock over the mantel tells me I have arrived with ten minutes to spare. I take a minute to run my fingers through my hair and smooth down my shirt before straightening my shoulders and walking to the dining room. When my feet hit the threshold, dozens of people applaud.

Near the back, Ian is standing and gesturing me towards him. I weave around tables while looking for familiar faces. Will is not here. Neither is Rawson. But I spot two faces I recognise from the meeting where we were assigned our guides: the first-year student with no hair named Griffin, who watches me with a fierce intensity, and the slight, curly-haired boy named Enzo. His face is thin and narrow. His smile warm and angelic. Trustworthy. Since both he and Griffin finished this test before me, I plan on keeping a close eye on both of them. Just in case.

Ian tells me to take a seat between him and a pretty girl with a sleek braid running down her back. When I'm seated, the room falls quiet and all eyes shift from me to the door as they await the next successful first year. All eyes but Ian's. His are still fixed on me. Leaning close he whispers, "Thank you."

"For what?" I whisper back.

"I bet Jenny you'd be the first female student to arrive." Ian grins over my head at the girl seated beside me. "She's got to do my laundry for the next two weeks."

"I suck at laundry," Jenny says under her breath. "He'll be lucky if his underwear comes back in one piece."

"As long as I don't have to clean them, it doesn't matter to me." Ian looks at the clock. "Seven minutes left. I have to think at least one or two more first years will make it downstairs before the limit."

Jenny smiles. "You want to go double or nothing on that?"

Before Ian can take her up on the offer, a red-faced

blonde boy appears in the entrance, and the room breaks out in applause. From the hulking girth of the boy and the way sweat pours down his face, I'm guessing he was the one using brute force, not guile, to get through his door. Just before time expires, two more first years make it through the door – one boy, one girl. They come in together, both looking winded and dishevelled.

A buzzer goes off as the clock strikes noon. The first challenge is over.

"What happens to the first years who didn't make it out of their rooms?" Ten are missing, including Will and Rawson. Too many to warrant an extreme punishment. I hope.

"We starve them," Ian says with a serious expression as the kitchen staff bring out platters of food. The smell of roasted meat fills the air, making my stomach yearn for sustenance even as it swirls with anxiety. The concern I feel must show in my face, because Ian laughs and says, "Don't worry – it isn't for very long. As soon as everyone down here is served, the locks on their doors will open." Ian stabs at a chicken leg and passes the platter to me.

"So, they just have to wait for us to start eating?" Not such a bad punishment, I think as I put a slice of meat in front of me.

"They also have to clean the dishes after everyone is done." This from Jenny, who takes the plate of chicken.

"You should be glad you got here before time was out. When motivated, we can make quite a mess."

The other students sitting at the table laugh, but the amusement isn't malicious. They remind me of my brothers, teasing me and my friends whenever they got the chance. Which always seemed to coincide with my mother being out of the room. Aside from the kitchen staff, I don't see anyone who isn't a student in the dining hall. While most things here in Tosu City are different from what I grew up with, it's nice to know that some are the same.

Ian nudges me and hands me a plate filled with some kind of cooked greens. "You'll also be meeting with Dr Holt in the order you arrived in the dining hall." The tone Ian uses is light, but the way he holds my gaze tells me this is an important advantage. One I should not discount.

Aside from Jenny and Ian, four other students are seated at our table – three male, one female. Despite my success with the first Induction test, none of them gives me more than a fleeting glance. I'm starting to ask Ian for an introduction when the rest of the first years arrive.

Some look angry. Others appear nervous as they walk to the seats their guides have reserved for them. Will catches my eye and gives me a wide grin before taking his seat. Of all of the students, he looks the least flustered by the day's developments. His hair is perfectly slicked back. His shirt is tucked in. Not a hint of strain shows around his bright green eyes. Perhaps it is his ability to mask his true feelings that prompted University administrators to direct Will into Government Studies.

It's a skill the two first years at my table could learn from. The puffy redness around Kaleigh's eyes speaks volumes about the distress she experienced during the blackout. Raffe is better at keeping his emotions off his face, but his clenched fists tell their own story. A scan of the room tells me that all unsuccessful Tosu City first years are still working to regain their composure. Though the inequality between the different methods used to choose Tosu City and colony students for the University still grates, I'm forced to admit that those of us from the colonies have an advantage over the others. Our Testing memories might have been erased, but we are still the same people who used our skills, intelligence and wits to survive.

Conversation gets louder. Older students lament cramming for examinations or difficult assignments. Others quip that they're thankful they don't have to do the dishes as they smear the last vestiges of their meals around on their plates. From the mess I see at my table, I'm thankful too. The first years at my table don't talk. We eat. We watch. We listen.

"Enzo Laznar."

Conversation ceases, and we all turn towards a young,

purple-clad University official who stands in the doorway. Enzo rises. Here and there, I see Tosu City first years whispering to one another. Enzo is stopped by the massive-looking boy next to him, who says something I can't make out. Whatever he says has Enzo nodding before he heads out the door with the official. A moment later, the dining hall once again buzzes with laughter.

"Was Enzo the first to come downstairs?" I ask Ian. Because of his size and intimidating demeanour, I had assumed Griffin was the first.

"Enzo arrived two minutes ahead of Griffin. You came in five minutes after that. You'll be called to meet with Professor Holt after Griffin has talked to her."

Turning towards Raffe and Kaleigh, Ian adds, "The students who didn't make the time deadline will be called at the end in alphabetical order. Professor Holt will ask all three of you a few questions. Then she'll hand you your class schedule. No big deal."

I hope not, because fifteen minutes later, my name is called. I follow the purple-clad official to one of the small libraries. Two grey armchairs face each other. Professor Holt is seated in one. She gestures for me to sit opposite. When the man in purple leaves, she says, "It's a pleasure to see you again, Malencia. Although, I've heard people call you Cia. Which do you prefer?"

"My friends call me Cia."

Professor Holt smiles. "Well, first let me congratulate you on your performance in the final Early Studies examination. Your scores were quite impressive. I hope you do as well in your regular classes when they begin next week." She takes a sheet of grey recycled paper off the table next to her. "Because of your high examination marks, your class list is more challenging than the others. Please let me, your guide or one of the other faculty know if you feel overwhelmed by the work you are being given. We are here to teach, but, more importantly, we are here to help."

Professor Holt pauses. Since no question has been asked, I simply nod my understanding. Giving me another smile, the professor says, "In addition to your classroom studies, you'll also be assigned an internship that will, alongside your book learning, teach you how best to achieve success in your future career. Juggling both can be a challenge. Once again, if you have any difficulties handling that challenge, please let us know so we can alter your workload in a manner that will best benefit you, the University and the United Commonwealth."

If I hadn't seen Obidiah after Redirection, if I hadn't listened to my own recollections of The Testing, I'd feel reassured by her words. I would believe the expression of maternal concern on Professor Holt's face. But I did see, and the words on the recorder are etched in my memory. No matter what the course load, I will not complain. More, I will not fail.

My resolve almost cracks as Professor Holt hands me my schedule. During our Early Studies semester, every student was assigned five courses. This schedule has me attending nine.

Professor Holt leans forward. "I know the schedule looks intimidating."

Yes. But I'm not foolish enough to admit my concern. "I'm excited to see science and math classes. I assumed those were courses reserved for Biological and Mechanical Engineering students."

Professor Holt's eyes meet mine. "Those who depend fully on another person's knowledge to decide what is possible are easily manipulated. The most effective leaders utilise experts from all fields, but rely on none when it comes to making a decision. I think you will find your excellence in math and science will be more useful in your selected career path than you might have believed."

The thought makes me smile.

"Do you have any other questions?" she asks. When I shake my head no, the professor reaches for an ornate gold bell on the small table next to her and gives it a ring. "I hope you enjoy your new residence and class schedule,

Ms Vale. And please remember, I am always here if ever you need assistance."

The purple-clad official appears at the doorway, signalling more clearly than the bell that the meeting is at an end. After thanking the professor for her time, I head for the door. It isn't until I'm headed back up the stairs to my rooms that I realise that Professor Holt used only my last name as she said goodbye. Not Cia. Was that a deliberate choice? I believe so. Professor Holt is leaving it to me to determine whether she is a friend or if she is my foe.

The door to my rooms is back on its hinges. Whatever they used to cover my window is gone. The Transit Communicator and the rest of my belongings are where I put them before the lights went out. The only difference is the envelope, stamped with my symbol, lying on the sitting-room table. Inside the envelope are two pieces of paper, a small solar watch and a gold key. One paper is a schedule that tells us what times the dining hall opens and closes for meals. It also says the kitchen has snacks and water available throughout the day for those who cannot make it to mealtimes.

I put the schedule on the table, unfold the second piece of paper and read:

GOVERNMENT LEADERS MUST BE PREPARED FOR ALL

Joelle Charbonneau

THINGS AT ALL TIMES. FOR THE NEXT WEEK, YOUR
SUITABILITY FOR THIS FIELD OF STUDY WILL BE TESTED.
WE HOPE YOU ARE READY TO BECOME ONE OF US. —
The final year Government Studies students

I try the key on the outside door lock and find it to be a perfect fit. Putting the key in my pocket, I pick up the black solar watch. It is two inches in diameter. Silver solar storage panels around the face of the watch power the glowing hands in the centre. A button on the back allows the user to change the time. Another operates an alarm. I compare the time on the watch to the clock in my rooms. They are a perfect match.

As long as I keep the solar cells charged, I will have the correct time, no matter what test the final years throw at us.

Turning the watch over in my hands, I try to guess what those tests could be. Michal said they change from year to year, so using his experience will not help me, but thinking of him brings back a memory from just before the start of The Testing, when we first arrived in Tosu City. Michal warned me to keep my things with me at all times. Advice I heeded. Since the note suggests I be prepared for anything at any time, I decide to follow that same advice now.

Walking into the bedroom, I put my class list on the desk and grab my University bag. I attach the watch to the strap of the bag so the solar cells will be more likely to collect power. Inside the bag I place a change of clothes, an extra pair of socks and Zeen's Transit Communicator. Then I try to decide what else I might need. My pocket-knife. A towel. Finally, a pencil and the note find their way into my bag. Then I hoist the bag onto my shoulder and head downstairs. It is time to do what Ian suggested earlier. If I want to be as prepared as possible, I have to get to know my fellow students. It's time to make friends.

A dozen students are in the fireplace room. Only a few of them are first years. The rest must still be cleaning up from lunch. Those first years present are holding class schedules in their hands, which makes me think they've yet to return to their rooms. I wonder if it is the desire for company or the fear of containment that has them seated here now. Looking around, I spot a solitary figure seated on a faded yellow sofa in the back corner and walk over.

"Do you mind if I sit here?" I ask.

Enzo's dark eyes rise up to meet mine. "It doesn't matter to me."

Not exactly a warm reception, but I sit anyway and notice a bandage on his left thumb. "I'm Cia Vale."

"I know." Enzo glances around the room and looks down at his class schedule.

A quick scan of the room tells me why. All the Tosu City

first years are watching with narrowed eyes. Maybe making friends isn't going to be as easy as I'd hoped. Still, the fact that Enzo is sitting here in the corner by himself leads me to believe he is not close with his Tosu compatriots. If I can get him alone, he might be willing to chat.

Standing, I lift my bag onto my shoulder and look at the paper in his hand. "The rain has stopped. I'm going to go out for some fresh air." Lowering my voice, I add, "They left notes in everyone's room. The message doesn't give much of a clue as to what they plan on doing with us for the next week, but you might want to check it out."

Without waiting for a response, I head for the exit, feeling everyone's eyes on me as I walk out. While I have only been at the Government Studies residence for a few hours, escaping the pressure-filled building makes me sag with relief. The sky is tinged with grey and yellow – signs the storms are not over quite yet. I close my eyes, breathe in the damp air and smile. The smell of the wet earth and trees helps me imagine that I am home in Five Lakes. In our backyard, sitting on my mother's wooden bench, listening to the sound of the wind through the trees.

Longing and hopelessness snake through me. Tears prick the backs of my eyes. The desire to be with my family, to return to a time before I was selected for The Testing and still believed that our leaders were kind and fair, is overwhelming.

I walk across the wet grass to a small grove of weeping willows. The trees are tall. Old. The bark under my fingers, rough and brittle. The branches more twisted than those on the trees my father and brothers have planted back home. By their size, I would guess several of these are at least fifty years old, which means they were planted before the new strain of willow was created. The most recent version bettered the tree's absorption of nutrients from the blighted soil. But even before that improvement, the willows thrived. Of all the trees, they were the most resilient after the Seven Stages of War. Even where the soil was most corrupt, the willow found a way to survive.

After taking the knife out of my bag, I strip part of the bark away from the tree and shove it into the side pocket of my bag. The salicylic acid in the bark can be used to help reduce headaches. After seeing my class list, I have a feeling I am going to need it.

"Why did you tell me about the note?"

I jump and spin around to face a belligerent-looking Enzo. So immersed was I in the memories of home, I missed the sounds of his approach. Or maybe he is just that light on his feet.

"I thought you might want to know it was there." The suspicion narrowing his eyes makes me add, "It's not like you weren't going to find it at some point." Enzo concedes the idea with a shrug, and I notice the bag hanging from his shoulder. Giving him a smile, I ask, "How did you get out of your locked room so fast today? My guide said you beat me by seven minutes."

This makes Enzo smile. "I detached the hinges with this." He reaches into his bag and pulls out a thin, sharp knife. Dr Flint is the only person I've ever witnessed using one. A scalpel. Clearly, Government wasn't Enzo's first choice either.

"Is that how you cut yourself?"

He looks down at his hand and frowns. "Yeah. I was reaching up to detach the top hinge. I figured moving a chair would take too much time."

Time I had to take because of my short stature. While Enzo isn't tall, he stands five inches above me. "Were your friends upset with you for getting through the locked door first? They didn't seem all that social."

Enzo stiffens. "Just because we all come from Tosu City doesn't make us friends. Are you friends with everyone in your colony?"

I laugh. "We might not all be best friends in Five Lakes Colony, but we are cordial. When you only have a thousand people, it's easier if you all at least act like you get along." I wait for the surprise I normally see when someone hears what colony I'm from, but it doesn't come. "You already knew I was from Five Lakes."

"Part of our Early Studies was to study not only the colonies but the students they sent to Tosu who would be attending the University with us." His smile is grim. "We may not have set foot onto campus until today, but our instructors have made sure we know about you."

"Why? And where were you studying?" Were they kept away from campus because we would have wondered why they weren't part of The Testing? Or did the University officials want us separated for as long as possible to keep us off balance when we finally met?

"We met for test preparation and our entrance exam at a school near the Central Government Building. And we studied you because our instructors wanted us to know our competition."

"I thought the point of being here was to learn for ourselves, and to learn how best to work together to help our country. Where a person comes from doesn't matter."

"If you believe that, you're not as smart as our instructor thought." I see anger flash in Enzo's eyes before he looks off towards the clouds that are darkening once again. And I find myself wondering what part of Tosu City Enzo is from. The clean, repaired section United Commonwealth officials helped us explore during the weeks immediately after The Testing, or the side streets filled with shadows that I caught glimpses of. Is he one of the students Michal said is more dangerous because he had to fight harder to get here?

Rain continues throughout the day and evening, which keeps all but those who have to attend class inside where it is dry. While I make attempts to converse with several other Tosu City first years, no one gives me more than monosyllabic answers before turning away. The older students aren't much friendlier, claiming they don't have time to talk. Michal's directives to make friends and identify potential upper-year rebels aren't going to be as easy to follow as he made them seem.

During dinner, Ian asks Raffe, Kaleigh and me about our class schedules. Raffe has six classes. Kaleigh five. When I say nine, the conversation at our table stops. The upper-level students give me speculative looks before resuming their dinners. Ian just smiles and tells us all to let him know if we have problems with our class load, but I catch the concern on his face in the glances he casts at me throughout dinner. No longer hungry, I push my plate away.

Will finds me in my room after dinner. He too has found conversation difficult among the other first years, but it doesn't appear to bother him.

"If they want to be jerks about it, so much the better." He laughs and settles into one of the chairs in my sitting room. "It'll make it more satisfying when we get better jobs after graduation."

Will has six classes on his schedule and has sneaked glimpses of several other students' course loads. Thus far, the highest number he's seen is seven, which doesn't do anything to still the growing sense of dread I feel as we wait for whatever task the final years have planned next.

Will also tells me what he's learned about the other first years assigned to his guide, Sam. "Olive thinks a whole lot of herself. Probably because she's the daughter of Tosu City's Power and Efficiency manager. A fact she's reminded everyone at our table of at least a dozen times." Will rolls his eyes, and I can't help but laugh. In Five Lakes, there isn't much call for power management.

"Griffin doesn't say a whole lot," Will continues. "But I'm guessing his family must be pretty connected. Olive giggles at anything he says, and the upper years make a point to say hello whenever they come near."

I wonder if Ian knows who Griffin is related to and if he'd be willing to share that information. When Will asks about Ian's other two first years, I admit I don't know much. "I think Kaleigh's mother might be a University administrator." During dinner Kaleigh complained about her class assignments, but assured everyone that the mistake would be dealt with the minute she could visit her mother's office. Whoever made the error was going to be sorry. "Raffe's father works in the

Department of Education." Which I only learned because two of the other students at our table mentioned it. From the way they talked, it was clear they were scared of whatever power Raffe's father wields.

When Will leaves, I go to sleep without changing clothes and dream of home. My mother bakes my favourite cinnamon bread. My brothers and I play cards at the kitchen table while my father sits nearby, poring over reports. Zeen wins a hand, opens his mouth and shrieks. I jolt awake to the sound of sirens and a voice yelling down the hall for everyone to get out of bed. We need to be downstairs, ready to go, in five minutes. The next phase of our Induction is about to begin.

CHAPTER 6

The cry of the siren drills my eardrums as I climb out of bed. I pull on my hand-me-down boots and my warmest jacket before slinging my bag over my shoulder. The watch on my bag reads four in the morning as I lock the door and hurry down the stairs to whatever awaits.

Doors slam. Feet pound the halls above me as I step onto the first floor. Ian and the other guides are standing at the base of the stairs. Two of my fellow first years, Griffin and a boy named Lars, stand beside them. I was quick. They were faster.

Standing beside Ian, I watch other first years race down the stairway. The siren goes silent as the last student arrives. Only five of them have brought their bags, but all have enough wits to have worn coats.

"Good morning," Ian announces. He climbs three steps, turns and faces us. "There are two skimmers waiting across the bridge. They will transport you to your next challenge. Once we arrive at our destination, I will explain what is expected of you."

Ian turns on a flashlight and leads the way out the door. The hazy moon and Ian's circle of light help us navigate our way down the wet path. I am careful to keep to the centre of the bridge as I cross. While there are rails on either side, I do not want to risk a misstep.

As promised, two skimmers like the one that brought me and my fellow Five Lakes Testing candidates to Tosu City are waiting on the other side. They are long and sleek and designed to skim above the earth, making them perfect for travelling across terrain broken and scarred by the Seven Stages of War.

Since most of the first years pile into the front skimmer, I climb into the one in the back. Soft lights along the ceiling illuminate the interior, which is tall enough for me to stand upright. Plush grey cushions line both sides of the passenger cabin. Near the back is a cabinet that in the skimmer Michal piloted over half a year ago was filled with snacks. To the left of the cabinet is a door that past experience tells me leads to a small bathroom. The one surprise is the windows. They are fitted with a black, opaque material that prevents anyone in the cabin from seeing out. Wherever the skimmer takes us will be a complete surprise.

With that mystery in mind, I take the opportunity to slip into the small bathroom and close the door. On the other side I hear murmurs as students climb inside. Pulling open my bag, I take out the Transit Communicator and flick on the compass and positioning locator. The small machine hums and two green numbers light up the screen, giving me the precise longitude and latitude of my current location. I hit the Save button, turn off the device, and slip it back into my bag. The note warned me to be prepared. I am doing my best to comply.

Hoisting the bag's strap onto my shoulder again, I slip back into the passenger compartment and take a seat in the rear next to Will. Across the aisle is Rawson. While his hair looks as though it hasn't seen a comb in the last twenty-four hours, his eyes are alert. Enzo sits next to him, looking down at the University bag balanced on his lap. He makes eye contact with no one as the skimmer begins to move.

I can almost imagine the outlines of trees and the shapes of the buildings as the skimmer crosses from the University campus into the city. The door to the pilot's compartment is closed, but the smooth movements of the skimmer tell me the pilot is seasoned at his job. The changes in direction are almost imperceptible. Some speculate on our destination, but despite the bravado, the cabin vibrates with nerves.

I check my solar watch frequently. Ten minutes. Twenty. Thirty. I open the cupboard and find a box of crackers, which we pass around. Forty-five. Just past the hour mark, the skimmer gives a slight bump and the hum of the engine stops. The skimmer door slides open. We have reached our destination.

Wind whips my hair as I step out of the skimmer onto crumbling asphalt. The sky is streaked with grey, announcing the approaching dawn. I step in several puddles, but am grateful no rain is falling from the sky. If nothing else, we will not be forced to battle a downpour as we begin this task. When we are all out of the vehicles, the skimmers' engines once again begin to hum. Several first years shout their surprise when the skimmers disappear into the mist of morning.

Once they are gone, Ian yells, "Everyone, please follow me."

The sky continues to lighten as we pick our way across the broken stone that must once have been a smooth surface intended for automobile travel. Before coming to Tosu City, I'd only seen automobiles pictured in books. Because Five Lakes' resources are mainly devoted to the earth's revitalisation, little time has been spent working on roadways that would accommodate motorised cars. Walking, bicycling and riding the occasional tractor or skimmer gets us from place to place just fine. However, the main roads in Tosu are repaired enough to allow automobile travel for those important enough to have extra power allotments for a working vehicle.

The condition of the road and the discolouration of the plants and trees growing up through the cracks speak of neglect. If this is still Tosu City, it is not a section that has been touched by the government's construction and revitalisation crews.

Ian stops in front of two wooden bridges. "Since your Government Studies classes don't begin until next week, my fellow guides and I think this is a wonderful time for you to blow off some steam and get to know your fellow first years better. It's also a great time for us upper years to have some fun." His amused expression gives his face a boyish quality.

"You'll be working in teams of four. Each team will get one of these." He holds up a large green bag. "In this is food, water and a list of locations your team needs to find. At each destination is a task you and your fellow team members must finish. Upon completion of the task, your team will receive a marker as proof of your success. Each team must have all four markers in its possession when it returns to the Government Studies residence. Any team that returns without one or more of the markers will be penalised."

In my head, I hear a voice whisper, "Wrong answers will be penalised."

Not Ian's cheerful voice. Dr Barnes's. I can see him dressed in purple, wearing a stern expression. If I close my eyes, I can picture Tomas seated on one side of me, looking strong and sure. Will on the other, looking frail and sad. The memory feels real. My heart pounded then the same as it does now. I taste the anxiety I felt and swallow it down as I shake free of the image. The past is important, but if I want to succeed, I have to focus on what is happening now.

"The first team to return with all its markers will win this Induction challenge and impress the rest of us. Those who return to the residence after the rest of their team have returned will automatically be asked to pack their bags and leave. So try to stay together. Okay?"

I look around and see several of my fellow students grin. Do they think Ian is joking or view this as an opportunity to eliminate the competition?

"To make things fair, I am going to pull four names out of this bag." Ian takes a small brown sack out of his pocket. "These four will act as captains and select the other members of their teams. Please come forward when your name is called." Ian reaches into the bag and pulls out a piece of paper. "Griffin Grey."

Griffin pushes forward with a confident smile. He receives a green bag from Ian and then steps to the left. Though Griffin has already proven to be smart enough to excel at one Induction test, I find myself hoping I do not end up on his team.

"Olive Andreson."

The dark-haired girl giggles as she walks to the front of the group. Once she has her green bag, the next name is announced.

"Malencia Vale."

The sound of my name makes me jolt. Straightening my shoulders, I avoid a puddle and walk up to Ian. As he hands me the bag, I feel his hand give mine a quick squeeze of encouragement. I take my place next to the still-giggling Olive, and Ian reaches into the bag and comes out with the name of the final team captain.

"Jacoby Martin."

A tall, lanky boy with deep-brown skin and even darker eyes takes his place beside me. While the rest look to Ian for the next set of instructions, I find myself scanning the faces of my fellow students. Ian said the captains will have to choose their teammates. That means the success or failure of my team rests squarely on my shoulders.

"Captains will choose one team member at a time in the order in which they were announced until all students have been placed on a team. Griffin will start."

Griffin wastes no time making his choice. Raffe. Not a surprise. I've seen the two of them hanging out in between meals. Their team will not lack strength or smarts. The giggle is gone as Olive announces her first team member. A tall blonde named Vance. My turn.

I look from face to face. This is a team challenge. To work effectively in a team, trust is essential. If only Tomas were here. No matter what he might or might not have done, I know he is on my side. Now I must decide who else is.

The obvious choices are the colony-born students, Will and Rawson. They are my natural allies. I may not trust them, but I have known them for months. Gone to class and studied with them. They are both smart and resourceful. But I don't call either name. Not yet. Though Will and Rawson will be more inclined to help me due to our shared colony status, this is also an opportunity to follow Michal's directive and make allies among the Tosu students. Allies will be essential long after Induction has ended. So, I opt for one my gut says is smarter, has worked harder to get here, and is less inclined to side with the others from his city than the rest.

"Enzo."

A number of students give Will and Rawson smug looks as Enzo walks towards me. Though the Tosu City students have not appeared friendly towards Enzo, this choice has no doubt confirmed their suspicions about my fellow colony natives' lack of abilities. Good.

Three Tosu City students are chosen in succession.

"Will," I announce. Do I trust Will? No. His actions during The Testing make it hard to place my faith in his hands. But he is smart and willing to do whatever it takes to get the job done. It's better to have those qualities on my team than working for another. Otherwise, I would be constantly watching over my shoulder to see what danger he might inflict on me.

"Kaleigh."

"Drake."

"Rawson."

Olive's choice makes me blink. I had been so certain the other captains would shun the colony students that I hadn't considered selecting anyone else. Rawson frowns as he takes his place at Olive's side, and I turn my attention to the two remaining students, whom I know next to nothing about. A girl named Juliet and a boy whose name I've never learned. I look from one to the other, hoping something in their expressions will help me decide. Both refuse to make eye contact. Neither has brought a University bag. Nothing I see aids my decision. If I want to avoid an uneducated choice, there is only one other option.

"Enzo will make the last choice for our team." I ignore the gasps around me and the anxiety that takes hold because of them. Do people think I am indecisive or weak because I passed the choosing to another? I tell myself it doesn't matter what they believe. This is the smart thing to do. Enzo might not be close friends with these two, but he has attended class with them. He is better suited to pass judgement on their collaboration skills.

Enzo doesn't hesitate in his selection, and we are joined by Damone, who stands at least a foot taller than me.

"The first location on your team's list is somewhere behind me," Ian says. "Waiting inside your bag is a clue to the specific spot where you'll find your first task. When you are done, return to this location for transportation to the next site. We wish you luck and look forward to seeing all of you back at the residence. Don't get lost. We'd really hate to have to come find you." With a wink, he and the other final years stride across the broken ground. A moment later, a skimmer appears and they hop inside.

Before the skimmer can clear the horizon, the other teams are racing across the weathered wood bridges towards a building partially hidden by yellow and brown trees.

"We need to get going," Will says, shifting his weight from foot to foot. Enzo and Damone are anxious to get moving too. My instinct is to go along with the others automatically – after all, I'm the youngest of my team. In Five Lakes Colony, I only raised my hand in class or took the lead in an assignment if I was one hundred per cent certain

I was correct. But as much as I want to get started, I am not going to run blindly into a situation I know nothing about. A mistake now will cost more than the time it will take to read the clue. So, I sit down on the ground, open the green bag and search for the information contained inside.

As I rummage through the contents, I do a quick inventory. Four bottles of water. Four bags of dried meat. Raisins. Apples. Not a lot of food or water, which means this Induction will either be quick or require us to find more sustenance along the way. My fingers dig to the bottom of the bag and close over a large grey envelope. Inside is the promised list, although what help it could be is hard to tell: Animals, Plane, Law, Learning.

After handing the list to Enzo, I pull out a second slip of paper and read, *"A silver treasure was brought here to eat, mate and rest. Can you now find what is left of this treasure's nest?"*

"We're supposed to find a bird's nest somewhere in that building?" Will asks.

Enzo takes the paper from me and frowns. "That seems like the obvious answer."

This adventure is being orchestrated by University students. They are the best and brightest of our country, which means anything obvious is most likely incorrect. "Why don't we head inside and see what's there?" I suggest. "The clue will probably make more sense once we figure out where we are."

After sliding both my University bag and the team's green one onto my shoulder, I head across one of the bridges. The bright rays of the early day make it easy to see where newer slats of wood have replaced old ones. Those repairs are the only signs of improvement. Whatever this place is, the United Commonwealth has not deemed it important enough to revitalise. At least, not yet.

The building peeking out from between overgrown trees and bushes is a dingy greyish green. There are holes in the roof and branches sticking out in places where animals have probably set up their homes. Dozens of sickly yellow- and brown-leafed trees grow around the structure. Though this area was not hit by the bombs that destroyed so many cities, this diseased ground demonstrates that nothing in our world was left untouched.

On the right side of the building is a tunnel strewn with leaves, branches and broken rock. As we pass through, I notice the ceiling of the tunnel has, like the bridges, undergone recent repairs. We emerge from the tunnel into an area filled with scraggly plants, more unhealthy trees and lots of buckled and uneven stone walkways jutting up in front of us in different directions. I can see other buildings off in the distance.

"Which way should we go?" Damone asks. Since we

don't know what kind of place this is, travelling along the stone pathways, as damaged as they might be, is the safest way to start exploring. Unfortunately, none of the walkways goes in a straight line. Instead, they bend and curve around the terrain. If we are not careful, instead of saving time, we could waste it getting lost or turned around.

With that in mind, I pull the Transit Communicator out of my bag and turn on the compass. At least we won't get lost. Will peers at the device and says, "If no one has a better idea, I say we go left."

He takes the lead, and we follow the path as it curves around an area to our right. This space must have been vibrant once, with green grass and colourful flowers. The plants that grow now are a sickly brown, although here and there, I see thriving patches of red clover. When the path forks, we follow the sharp turn to the left. The trees lining the path are more plentiful. The bushes fuller. The thicker foliage makes it hard to see what is ahead. The walkway curves again. My steps grow slower, more cautious, as I peer through the trees, trying to see if danger lurks around the next bend.

We come to a large building. The roof is collapsed in a number of places. Weather and animals have eaten away pieces of the dark grey walls. The doors look as though they haven't been touched in at least a decade. I am trying to decide if we should attempt to open them when a blood-chilling scream rips through the air.

Will.

Instinctively, I run to help. The scream came from somewhere through the foliage. Will must have decided to explore while the rest of us looked at the building. My foot catches on a piece of broken stone. I take the left path, which I hope will lead me to Will. The footsteps at my back tell me my teammates are close behind. And when I burst free of the trees, I am prepared for the worst. Which is why, when I spot Will dangling upside down, looking red-faced and very much alive inside a large metal structure, I begin to laugh.

"Don't just stand there," he yells. "Help me get down."

Will struggles to grab the rope holding his ankles. The movement makes him swing back and forth, making me laugh even harder. Next to me, Enzo and Damone are fighting their own amusement. Finally, when our laughter subsides, I move closer for a better look.

Standing at least twenty feet high, a rusty but still sturdy looking chain-link fence makes up three sides of a cage. The metal fence is attached to the building, which forms the fourth side. Metal bars spaced two to three feet apart make up a grid that forms the roof. More chain link covers the grid. The rope Will dangles from is attached to a roof support located in the middle of the enclosed space. On the far right side of the cage is an opened door. That must be how Will got inside. On the left of the cage is a door that leads into the attached structure.

"I might be tall enough to reach the rope around his ankle," Damone offers.

"Maybe," I say, although I doubt it. When Damone tries to reach, he proves me right. Drat. And from the looks of the knot around Will's ankle, working the rope free is going to take time. Meanwhile, other teams are getting closer to finding the nest and moving on to the next location. We need to get Will down and get moving – now.

I fish my pocket-knife out of my bag, climb through the cage door and eye Damone's lanky build with a frown. "Do you think you can lift me onto your shoulders, Damone?"

Damone is tall but slight. And while I'm not very big, my brothers used to say that carting me around was like lifting a cow. But Damone doesn't think I look too heavy and squats down so I can climb onto his shoulders. Moments later, I am high in the air, sawing the rope. Every time Damone shifts under my weight, I hold my breath and prepare to hit the deck. But Damone is stronger than he looks and doesn't falter as I run my blade back and forth until finally... snap. The last threads of rope break free, and Will tumbles to the hard grey stone ground.

When I am safely standing on my own two feet, I shove the knife into my pants pocket. Then, shrugging both of my bags onto my shoulder, I turn for the door in time to watch it slam closed. The distinctive clank of metal against metal announces loud and clear that the cage has been locked. Will, Damone and I are trapped inside.

CHAPTER 7

Will races past me to the door and yanks on the handle. Enzo tries opening it from the other side. I'm not surprised when neither is successful. Whoever rigged the rope and door traps did a good job. But we've already beaten one of the traps by getting Will free of the rope. Now we have to defeat the second and get out of here.

Damone and Will climb the fence, hoping to escape that way. Enzo tries to unlock the cage door while I walk to the one that leads into the building. The handle is missing, but it only takes a nudge of my foot for the door to creak open. I shove the door wider and wrinkle my nose at the musky smell of animal waste. The final years have created this scenario to test us. No doubt they will have something interesting in store. Hoping that whatever animals made that smell are harmless or gone, I turn back to my team and say, "We have to go this way."

"I'll go to the other door and yell into the building from there. You can use my voice as a guide." Enzo digs through his bag and comes up with a small metal flashlight. "You can use this, too."

He slips the flashlight through the fence. I take it and realise that while we are trapped inside this cage, Enzo is free to solve this part of the task and leave us behind. Will he be waiting for us when we find the exit? There is only one way to find out.

"Thanks," I say, turning on the light. "See you on the other side."

Taking one last breath of fresh air, I duck through the door. The smell of urine and decay makes me gag as I pan the light around the small room. I see rotting cabinets, counters strewn with dust and mouse droppings and an overturned metal stool. At the back of the room is another door. I push the stool out of the way and cross to the door, making sure Will and Damone are right behind.

I hear the sound of tiny feet scurrying across the cracked tiles of a long, narrow hallway. My father and his team have discovered several methods to limit the rat population in our area. I know other colonies and the city of Tosu have done the same. But the glow of dozens of pairs of eyes as they reflect my light tells me the rat population in this area has gone unchecked. Ick.

The smell of stagnant water and animal faeces grows stronger as I step into the next room and gasp. Most of the ceiling is gone. Light streams in, giving me a clear view. This room – if it can be called a room – is enormous. The ground grows uneven as I walk deeper into the cavernous space. The floor looks like rock, but when I run my fingers over it, it feels synthetic. Something man-made. The same can be said for some of the plants that appear to be growing out of the room's floor. Ten feet in front of my position are pieces of what must have once been a safety railing. And it is clear why it was needed. Beyond the railing is a drop of at least forty feet. At the very bottom is a river at least ten feet across. Beyond that is a large expanse of rocklike surfaces and greyish trees that stretches as high as the surface on which I currently stand. A foot placed wrong near the railing could mean a broken bone or worse.

"Don't step too close to the edge," I warn, and walk to my left. The floor slants upward and is slick with decayed leaves. A flutter of wings from above makes me jump, and I grab on to a nearby wall to keep myself steady. Looking up, I see a bird soar out of the room into the sky above. Too bad we can't escape the same way.

"What is this place?" Will's voice is hushed.

"Don't ask me," Damone says. "I've never seen anything like this."

None of us has. Now that the silence has been broken,

Damone adds, "I bet Enzo is long gone by the time we get out of this place. He's not stupid. He's going to try to find the task without us. I would."

"Remind me never to leave you alone for a minute, unless, of course, I want to get screwed," Will says.

"Leaders don't wait around for other people." Damone kicks a rock and sets it flying over the ledge.

"Cia would," Will says. "Real leaders do more than work to get ahead of everyone else."

"No one follows the person who comes in last. Would you?"

I don't know. Not being sure of my answer to that question makes me walk faster. Damone might be right about Enzo. If so, we need to get out of here as quickly as possible – otherwise, we might not have an opportunity to catch up with him.

Tuning out Damone and Will's sniping, I focus on the terrain around me and notice faded letters on the wall that spell the word RAINFOREST. Farther down I see the word DIET followed by LEAVES, FRUITS and several words that are too marked by time to make out. After a few more steps, I spot another word I recognise from a book my mother read to me when I was a child. The book was old and filled with faded pictures and told the story of children who went on a special trip to a place where they could see different kinds of animals. A place with the same name as the word next to me: ZOO.

When my mother read the book to me, I thought the idea of keeping wild animals in cages was mean. Most Five Lakes families don't own pets, but those who do allow the animals to come and go as they choose. For the most part, the pets stay close to home, but a few, like my friend Daileen's cat, disappear and never return.

Of course, from what I learned in that children's book, the animals put into cages at the zoos weren't domesticated. Wild animals from around the world were plucked from their homes and brought to places like this one. We have our share of wild animals prowling beyond, and sometimes across, the borders of Five Lakes. Some are small and relatively harmless, but there are breeds that can kill with one snap of their jaws. It's hard to conceive of a time when someone trapped those types of creatures and forced them into cages for entertainment.

Looking around the vast space, I try to imagine what it was like before the Seven Stages of War. Manufactured trees and rocks. Maybe some real ones mixed in. A river flowing around the rim of the rocks providing both a water source and a barrier between whatever animals were kept in here and the freedom of the path on which I now stand. Even if the animals could climb the trees – and the design of this place suggests they could – the trees are far enough back to prevent escape. The animals that lived inside this place were trapped just as Will, Damone and I are now.

Monkeys, maybe? Or, considering the size of this place, something larger, like chimpanzees. We studied the histories of other countries last year in school. During our studies, we covered the species that were indigenous to various regions prior to the end of the Seven Stages of War. It's impossible to say which species survived the wars, since earthquakes and windstorms destroyed previous methods of worldwide communication. I had hoped to be one of the mechanical engineers who would re-establish communication through the United Commonwealth and beyond our borders. Now—

"Cia, don't move."

Will's urgent whisper pulls me from my thoughts, and my foot stills. Have I ventured too close to the drop-off? No. The edge of the path is several feet to my right. The ground in front of me looks solid and secure. I turn to ask Will what the problem is, but the words die on my lips as he shakes his head and points up. My eyes follow the line of his finger to the branches of one of the man-made trees hanging to my right. For a moment, I don't understand. Then I see it. Black eyes. The shimmer of copper and gold scales wrapping around and around the branch all the way to the tree trunk. A red tongue that tastes the air with quick flicks.

A snake. At least a foot wide and more than a dozen feet long. And its head is a mere eight feet away from where I currently stand.

The snake's tongue flicks in my direction, and I hold my breath. Snakes are common in Five Lakes. For some reason, the chemicals that left so many species disfigured or dead didn't hurt the reptiles. Instead, the chemicals seemed to strengthen them. Scales that were once as vulnerable as human skin are now thicker. Tougher to penetrate. The bites of a number of species, once relatively harmless, are now fatal. Whatever poison transformed their scales also made them venomous. But since Five Lakes is in an area of the country less affected by the biological and nuclear bombs used in the Four Stages of War, the snakes I encountered there were easy to ignore or kill. The one dangling above me is neither.

Scales ripple as the reptile shifts position. The head drops slowly towards me. I fight to keep my feet firmly in place and force myself to think rationally as the snake's tongue sips the air just two feet from where I stand. My eyes dart to the path ahead. The rocky surface slants upward and is caked with dirt. About twenty feet from where I stand is a door. I shift my eyes back to the snake, which looks alert but calm. My father once mentioned that certain types of snakes are deaf. Also, that some of the larger snakes he encountered on the outskirts of other colonies were known to telegraph their upset or intent to strike by flattening out the ribs in their necks. Since the snake's eyes are fixed on me and it hasn't moved, I assume the snake knows I'm standing here and does not feel threatened or hungry. I can only hope that trend continues.

Clutching the flashlight tight in my hand, I take a small step forward while keeping my eyes firmly fixed on the threat. The snake's tongue flicks again, but the rest of it stays put. Considering that a good sign, I take another step. Then another.

My heart pounds with each agonisingly slow step. Inch by inch, I cross the uneven path, resisting the urge to look behind me in case that movement makes the creature attack. When I reach the door, I turn back. Both the snake and my teammates are exactly where they were when I saw them last. Slowly, I raise my hand and motion for Will to join me. His green eyes shift towards the snake, then back at me, before he takes his first step. The snake's scales shine in the sunlight as the head drops lower, until it is at the same level as Will's forehead. Sweat drips down Will's face as he creeps forward. The snake's tongue brushes Will's hair. I hold my breath, but Will doesn't flinch as he takes his next step. I watch him cross the floor. When he finally reaches my side, I grab his hand and hold it tight in mine. No matter what happened during The Testing, at this moment, I am glad Will is beside me and alive.

I glance back at the snake, which has once again shifted lower. It still appears unbothered by our presence, so I nod at Damone that it is time for him to start walking. But he doesn't.

Slowly, trying not to attract the snake's attention, I raise my hand and beckon him. His eyes are wide as his gaze shifts from the snake to me and Will and back to the snake. Both his hands are clenched at his sides. His face looks ashen. Even from this distance, I can feel the waves of terror emanating from him, and I wonder if the snake can feel them too. If so, Damone is in more danger than either Will or I had been. But I don't think he knows it. I doubt he has ever seen an animal that could cause him danger, let alone something like this.

Will tries to beckon Damone forward, but it's no use. Damone has been rendered immobile by fear. A fear that could drive the snake to attack at any moment. Damone has to get out of there now.

"Here," I whisper as I pull the two bags off my shoulder and shove them and the flashlight into Will's hands. Before he can ask what I plan to do, I slide my knife out of my pocket, flip open the blade and step through the doorway back into the cavernous room. While I doubt the blade will do any good against the scales, it's the only weapon I have. Someone has to help Damone to safety. Will is resourceful, but I am smaller and more agile.

Fear punches through my chest. Still, I force my feet forward. The distance back seems longer. Harder. More terrifying. Both Damone and the snake turn their heads and blink as I approach. One foot in front of the other. The small knife clutched in one hand. The other extended towards Damone, willing him to close the gap between us.

He doesn't move.

The snake does.

Its body skims around the tree branch. The head undulates. Damone stumbles backwards and the snake's eyes swing towards him. Its red tongue quivers in the air. It is the sound of scales rubbing against tree bark that urges me to run. I spot a foot-long piece of rotting wood on the ground near me and almost lose my balance as I race forward and pick it up. The snake's eyes don't shift from its target – Damone.

I come to a stop four feet from the shovel-sized head that is now at the same level as my forearms. One wrong move and the jaws of the snake will reach out. The fangs will clamp down, shooting poison into my bloodstream. My life will be over before I hit the ground.

Damone's eyes are glazed. His knees locked. He looks

ill-prepared to do what I plan, but I don't allow that to stop me. I throw the block of wood at the trunk of the tree near the end of the snake's tail. The wood clattering against the tree echoes in the cavernous space.

The snake's head whips towards the sound vibrations. Its body uncoils. The wood skips off the rail and plunges below. Scales scrape against tree bark as the snake lunges towards the rail, and I act. I dart forward, grab Damone's arm, and pull. Damone stumbles and kicks a rock across the path. The snake changes course, but I don't. I dig my fingers into Damone's wrist and half drag, half pull him as I run. Thank goodness the fear that rendered Damone immobile now propels his legs forward. His feet keep pace with mine as they pound the rocky ground. The path narrows near the door. I let Damone streak by me to what I hope will be safety.

That's when I hear the hiss. If it can be called a hiss. More a growl like the ones the wolves that lurk outside the Five Lakes borders make. The sound tingles down my spine, raises the hair on the back of my neck, and urges me forward. When my feet cross the threshold, I glance back and see a streak of copper and gold moving fast. Black eyes focused on me. Metallic and black scales flared on either side of the snake's neck, forming what looks like a hood. The mouth opens. A scream rips from my throat as a thick metal door screeches and slams between us.

I double over and try to catch my breath. The rasp of laboured breathing and the muted growl from the other side of the door are the only sounds. Finally, a beam of light cuts through the darkness.

"I'm glad the hinges on that door still work," Will says.

Hysteria bubbles up and out of my lips. "You're glad?"

Will grins. Damone looks at us like we're both crazy, which makes me laugh harder. I can't help it. I'm happy to be alive.

Still laughing, I take the flashlight from Will, sling the bags onto my shoulder, and say, "How about we find the exit out of here?"

The hallway is long, with a high ceiling, and is wide enough for the three of us to walk side by side. The walls are lined with faded photographs of animals. Chimpanzees. Orangutans. Monkeys. Gorillas. I'm pleased to know I was right about the former inhabitants of this structure, but I can't help wondering what happened to the animals when the world collapsed.

"Wait. Do you hear that?" I cock my head to the side. There. The sound is louder this time. Someone is yelling my name, and relief streaks through me as I recognise the voice.

"Enzo," Will says, shooting a grin at Damone. "I guess

not everyone at the University believes getting ahead is more important than real leadership."

Using Enzo's voice as a guide, we creep down the long hallway. As much as we want to hurry, we force ourselves to go slow. To watch for things that might be lurking in the shadows. We don't want to face another situation like the one we just escaped. We go through a door on the left. Another large hall. More faded placards and photos of animals. Signs about eating habits. Behaviour. Anatomy. Signs of a past society that caged animals for amusement and education.

Enzo's voice gets louder. Closer. I smell fresh air. The idea of freedom propels us faster. We take another left turn and see an open doorway. Sunlight. And Enzo standing near the threshold, looking relieved to see us. No more cages or synthetic trees. Freedom.

I want to sit on the ground and appreciate the moment, but we've already lost a great deal of time. Other teams have probably found the 'nest'. We have to get moving if we're to have a chance at winning. While the others might believe this is only a game created by the final-year students, I know better.

The good news is that our most recent adventure has given me an idea of where we need to go to find the first task. Handing the flashlight back to a curious Enzo, I say,

"We'll fill you in on what happened while we walk. We can't fall too far behind if we want to come in first."

As we head down the path, Will gives Enzo a rundown on the events that occurred inside the former monkey house. I let Will tell the story as I walk in front of the group, looking for anything that will give me a clue which direction we should go in. Enzo asks dozens of questions. Especially about the snake. Enzo thinks Will is exaggerating the reptile's size, which isn't surprising since Will tends to over-dramatise.

I'm about to say that when Damone speaks for the first time since we saw the animal. "Will's telling the truth. I've never seen anything like it." Damone stops walking. "How could the final years drop us in a place with a thing like that? How could the professors let them? They said this was supposed to be fun, but they could have killed us."

"I don't think the final years knew the snake was in that building," I say. "The snake probably got in through the roof after they set up their trap in the cage."

Will nods. "We have a lot of snakes in Madison Colony. They're always sliding into places without anyone seeing them. My mom found a six-foot snake in her closet, curled around a pair of her shoes. No one knows how it got in. Dad used my brother's crossbow to get it out."

The mention of the crossbow makes me flinch. Suddenly, I'm somewhere else. A bridge with a crossbow quarrel soaring through the air towards me. Then the image is gone.

Damone folds his arms across his chest. Though his stance is belligerent, I can see the fear lurking in his eyes. Rubbing my temples, I say, "This area hasn't been revitalised yet, which means we should keep our eyes open for tracks or droppings and steer clear if we can. If we're lucky, the next location will be somewhere snakes aren't interested in calling home. Of course, to figure that out, we have to find the location. And I think I might have an idea of where we need to go."

"Where?" Enzo asks as I turn and walk down the path.

I step over a large broken branch. "My father has a lot of books on animal biology. His team uses them when they're working on genetic modifications in some of our farm stock but the books include information on all kinds of animals, including their behaviours. Behaviours like nesting." Even though I never wanted to go into biological engineering, I flipped through each book, devouring the pictures and the words, fascinated with the idea that somewhere, some of these creatures might still walk the earth.

"We already decided we're looking for a bird's nest," Damone says.

"Birds aren't the only animals that build nests," I say. "I don't think the final years would make the answer to this puzzle so easy. Do you?"

Will smiles. "Not for a minute. Which means the silver

treasure is something we normally wouldn't think of. Something like a lion or a tiger."

"Or a gorilla." Enzo looks at me, and I nod.

"Silverback gorillas. I thought of them when I saw the writing on the walls of the building we were in. I don't know if this place used to house gorillas, but it if did, I'm pretty sure we'll find whatever it is we're supposed to be looking for there."

The path curves to the left. We pass more trees, a couple of rotting benches and areas that must have once been used to display animals. I spot a faded sign lying in front of one of the areas; it pictures an animal with a long neck. This must have been the section where they kept giraffes. The next pen doesn't have a sign, but further down, we find another placard covered in dirt. When Will scrapes away the grime, there's a picture of an elephant.

We walk by the broken fences and walls, looking at signs. Lions. Baboons. Zebras. Animals we have heard of but never seen. There are also pictures of animals we can't put names to. The path circles to the right. More animal pens. More less-than-healthy trees. Decayed buildings that none of us wish to venture near in case more traps are set. Somewhere in the distance, we hear a shout. Of dismay? Triumph? The only thing we can be sure of is that at least one other team is nearby.

We're about to follow the path to the right when Enzo spots a large sign on a collapsed fence to our left. The picture and words are faded, but despite time and dirt, we can see the letters: D ni Gor la For st. No one has a clue what the first word could be, but we all think it's a good bet the final two are Gorilla Forest.

The path to the left curves in between the broken walls of two buildings. The single-storey stone structure on the right still stands, although the way the walls are slanted makes me think it won't be upright for long. To our left is a cone-shaped roof sitting atop a pile of splintered wood and broken rock. We pass between them, scramble over a fallen tree that is blocking the path and come to a long suspension bridge that stretches over a river. On the other side is a mostly intact structure surrounded by a tall stone fence. Unlike the rest of the zoo, the bridge is in good repair. Strong metal cables. Thick wooden planks. Rope railings on either side.

Will looks at the bridge and back at me. "What do you think?"

I put my hand on the rope railing and push down to test its strength. "Someone went to a lot of trouble to make sure we could get to the other side."

"Probably the same people who set the trap in the monkey cage." Will cautiously places a foot onto the bridge. "Let's hope I don't end up dangling from my ankles this time."

Will takes several steps and then jumps up and down. When the bridge holds, the rest of us follow. The water below is a murky brown. Contaminated, but probably drinkable if we get desperate. I hope we finish this part of the Induction task and move on before we have to test that out.

We reach the end of the suspension bridge and hear voices. Several of them. Beyond the stone fence. And though I can't make out the words, I understand the tone. At least one team is still in the zoo, and whoever they are, they aren't happy.

I scale a tree next to the wall and peer over. The area behind the fence is filled with rocks, leafless trees and grey dirt. The lack of grass and the condition of the trees speak of more severe contamination. The final years must have picked this location for that reason. Knowing we have to finish this task quickly or risk illness adds to the pressure we'll be working under. Standing near one of the trees are Griffin, Raffe and their two other team members. Griffin's eyes are narrowed and his mouth curled in a snarl as he shouts something at the only girl on their team. He stands at least six inches taller, but the girl doesn't shrink from the confrontation. Instead, she points to a large wooden chest on the ground and shouts back. The chest is marked with a large white 1. Three more dark brown trunks marked with the numbers 2 through 4 sit nearby.

"This is the place," I say, and hoist myself up to the top of the wall. Griffin's team goes silent as my feet hit the ground. They say nothing as, one by one, my teammates jump down. Together, we cross to the chest marked **3**. When I nod at Enzo, he flips the lid open. Inside is another, smaller trunk. Sitting on top of that trunk is a grey envelope. Enzo hands me the envelope. I open it, slide out a folded piece of paper and read. *"Complete the puzzle to receive your team's marker and the clue to the next location."*

Enzo flips the lid on the next trunk and we peer inside. A small metal box. On the side of the box is a keypad. Next to the box is a piece of paper with instructions that read *Input the answers to the questions into the keypad to unlock the box. Answer carefully. A wrong answer will result in a sixty-minute time penalty before your team can attempt to answer again. Try not to be wrong twice.*

I glance at Griffin's team, who watch us from the little shade they find under a barren tree. They must have answered the question wrong and are now waiting for their chance to try again. And each second they wait, they increase their exposure to the contaminants that twist the trees and turn even the clover a sickly yellow. I wonder if they realise the danger. Growing up in the revitalised city might have made them less aware of the signs of chemical corruption. I consider warning them, but my team has already begun to work on the task: a physics problem in three parts.

The first part asks the time it takes for a stone thrown horizontally to hit the ground if thrown at a rate of 5 metres per second from a cliff 67.4 metres high. Part two wants to know the distance the stone will land from the base of the cliff. The last question asks us to calculate the stone's final velocity, both magnitude and direction, when it hits the ground.

We ignore the four sets of eyes staring sullenly at us, and using sticks for pencils and the ground to write on, we get to work. Immediately, it is clear advanced physics is not Will's or Damone's strongest subject. Still, they check and double-check Enzo's and my answers until all four of us agree. While the answers weren't easy, the trickiest part is how to type them into the keyboard. Should our answers use abbreviations for metres, per second, or should we spell out entire words? The wrong choice will mean keeping Griffin and his team company until we are allowed to try again.

Since all of our teachers have always used abbreviations in class, we opt to use them now. Enzo quietly reads the answers aloud, and I punch them in on the keyboard. When all three answers have been given, I hold my breath and press Enter.

There is a click and the box opens. Will and Enzo

exchange high-fives. Damone stands off to the side and smiles at Griffin and company as I remove a grey envelope and a red disk marked with the number 3 from the box. Glancing at the other team, I suggest we wait to read the next clue until we are alone. When no one objects, I slide both objects into my University bag and head back to the stone wall.

Will gives Enzo a boost and then scrambles over the wall. As Damone hoists himself up, I hear the sound of a bell. Griffin and his team are hurrying back to their box. Their time penalty must have come to an end.

My fingers cling to rock. My feet propel me upward. I am about to swing my leg over the top of the wall when Griffin shouts. I look over my shoulder in time to see a flash of light. Surprise loosens my grip as something explodes.

CHAPTER 8

Hitting the ground knocks the air from my lungs. Struggling to breathe, I roll to my side and peer through a haze of smoke towards the screams coming from behind me. Something is on fire.

No. Not something. Someone.

Pushing to my feet, I pull my bags up onto my shoulders and run. My heart pounds with each step. A female shriek for help cuts through the air. As I get closer, I see Raffe batting at flames streaking up his left arm. The girl keeps screaming. Griffin strips off his shirt and uses it to smother the fire as the other boy looks on. Immobile. Frozen by fear.

When I reach him, Raffe is cradling his injured arm close to his body. His jaw is clenched in pain. Griffin's eyes narrow as I pull a towel and a bottle of water out of my bags and ask him to help me clean and bandage the wound. Despite his suspicion, he takes Raffe's uninjured arm and helps ease him to the ground. Using my pocket-knife, I cut away the singed fabric of Raffe's sleeve and examine the patch of angry flesh that stretches from just above his wrist to below the elbow. The wound must be painful, but it's not as bad as it could have been. The loose fit of the shirt helped keep the flame far enough from his flesh to prevent blisters or worse. Tomas's brother was once burned when a tractor's engine caught fire. Those burns took months to heal. This will cause Raffe discomfort, but shouldn't slow him down too badly. Especially if he keeps the injury clean.

I rip the towel into several pieces and wet the first with water. Raffe clenches his teeth as I clean the burn. I start to bandage it when I hear, "You should use this first."

Enzo holds out a small white tube of anti-infection ointment. He must have packed it in his University bag when they instructed us to be prepared. I'm thankful he did. I spread the cool ointment onto Raffe's arm and see some of the tension leave his shoulders. When I'm done, I hand the tube back to Enzo, wrap the makeshift bandage around Raffe's arm and tie it in place.

Raffe touches his injured arm with his right hand and looks up at me. "Thanks. You didn't have to come back and help."

"Yes." I meet Raffe's eyes and then glance at the others on his team, who are looking at me with various levels of anxiety, anger and distrust. "Yes, I did." To do any less would be against everything my parents taught me. Would dishonour the colony I grew up in. "Keep the burn clean, avoid touching the yellow patches of dirt around here, and you should be fine. We have to get going."

Raffe nods, and I follow my teammates back to the wall. As I throw my leg over, I hear him yell, "Just so you know, we're still going to beat you to the end."

I can't help but laugh and yell back, "You can try," before dropping to the other side.

We decide to wait until we reach the exit of the zoo before we open the next clue. When we reach the bridges, we find three small silver skimmers marked with the numbers 1, 2 and 3 waiting for us. Team four must have already left for the next part of this Induction task.

As Will and Damone check out our skimmer, Enzo and I break the seal on the envelope and read aloud.

"*Go to the place where armed vehicles once left the ground for the sky. Your next clue and task wait there for your team to try.*"

"The old air-force base. Right, Damone?" Enzo asks.

"That'd be my guess," Damone says, opening the front cab of the skimmer. "Let's get going."

"Wait," Will says. "We want to be the first team to finish this team challenge. Right?"

"You just figured that out?" Damone sneers.

Anger flashes across Will's face, but his voice is calm

when he says, "One team is already gone, but the other two haven't reached their skimmers yet. How fast do you think they'd get to the end of this challenge if they had to walk?"

Damone's mouth spreads into an unpleasant smile. "Maybe you're smarter than I gave you credit for. We can start with that one."

"No."

All eyes swing to me. Will's eyes, which normally sparkle with charm, are now filled with calculation.

"No. We don't need to sabotage other teams to succeed."

Will frowns. "But if it helps us win—"

"Anyone who has to cheat to win doesn't deserve to be here. And they don't belong on my team either. There's one team ahead of us. I'd rather spend our time catching them than screwing with teams that are already behind. If you don't agree, you can stay here and do whatever the hell you want." With that, I climb into our skimmer.

Out of the corner of my eye, I can see my teammates looking at me with varying degrees of concern or disbelief. Enzo takes a step towards the skimmer but Damone yells for him to stop. That I'm bluffing and won't leave them behind. He might be right, since leaving my team here on their own will only encourage them to steal a skimmer that belongs to one of the other teams. I just have to hope my threat to leave them behind will make them abandon their thoughts of sabotage.

Ignoring the argument taking place outside, I survey the controls. The skimmer is much like the one my father uses in Five Lakes – old, with frayed seats and barely enough room in the cabin to squeeze in four people. I slide behind the controls and hit the Start button. It takes two tries before the engine catches hold. When it does, I pull the hover switch and feel the skimmer vibrate as it lifts off the ground. It isn't until I pilot the vehicle forward that my teammates race over.

"Wait." Will is the first to reach the skimmer. I stop the skimmer, pilot it back to the ground and open the door to let my teammates inside. Will laughs as he climbs into the seat next to me. "You know how to make a point. We'll do it your way and win without interfering with the other teams, all right? That will make it all the more fun to celebrate when we mop the floor with them. Now, the real question is whether you know how to pilot this thing well enough to race the other team to the next location."

While I think I'm capable of piloting the skimmer, I'm glad when Will asks if he can switch positions with me and takes the controls, since I've only driven one a handful of times.

"See? I knew you wouldn't be able to control this thing," Damone says, sliding into the back seat. "Will and Enzo should have listened to me. Instead, they give in to a girl who doesn't understand what it takes to win and overreacts to an idea that's different than her own. When this is over, I'll have to talk to my father about the lower admittance standards allowed for colony students."

Will's hands tighten on the steering wheel, but he says nothing to defend or condemn my actions. Enzo too keeps silent as Will pulls the lever and makes the skimmer hover above the ground. While I don't believe I was wrong to insist we succeed on our own merits, I can't help wondering if those in charge will judge me as Damone does: weak, histrionic and unable to lead.

Damone watches me with a smirk. He is enjoying the doubt he planted in my mind and the minds of my teammates. Determined to prove his words incorrect, I swallow my concern and discuss the location of our next task.

The instruction sheet from the upper years says site number two involves aircraft. The clue says the vehicles that soared in the sky are armed. The old United States had several military forces that helped defend the country – land, sea and air. While I have never heard of the air-force base Enzo and Damone instruct Will to pilot towards, I have no doubt the destination is the right one.

"How far do we have to go to get there?" Will asks as the skimmer lurches forward.

"I'm not sure exactly where we are now, but the base is located outside the south-east border of Tosu City," Enzo says.

"I can tell you where we are." I dig through my bag, pull out the Transit Communicator and flip the switch. I read off our current co-ordinates. According to Enzo and Damone, we are just past the boundary of Tosu City on the north-east side. After some discussion, I plug in our best guess for the co-ordinates of the base. The readout claims the air-field is eleven miles away. Our skimmer is slow but as long as it doesn't break down and we don't get lost, we should make it there in less than an hour. Hands tight on the control, Will offers none of his usual banter as he concentrates on steering the skimmer east.

"Which way?" Will asks when we reach a wide road. We can either follow the road we are currently travelling, which angles to the south-west, or go down the hill to a smaller road that heads south-east. To the south-west, I see grass, shrivelled trees and greyish soil. An area yet to be revitalised. To the south-east are the outlines of buildings and healthier plant life.

According to the readout of the Transit Communicator, the south-east path is the shortest route, but it might not be the smartest, since it appears to go directly through the city. Navigating the skimmer through streets filled with people and other modes of transportation could take more time than travelling around the outskirts.

"What do you think, Will?" I ask.

"Why are you asking him?" Damone crosses his arms across his chest. "Are you scared to make the decision yourself?"

"Will is the one piloting this thing," I say. "He should get the final say in the direction we take."

Damone looks like he wants to debate the issue, but Will cuts him off. "The controls aren't responsive. We can go faster if I'm not worried about crashing into buildings when I have to turn."

"Okay," I say before Damone can object. "Let's go."

Using the Transit Communicator as a guide, Will steers the skimmer to the south-west. Through the window across from me, I see a river that runs parallel to the road. The water has a green tint but is otherwise clear. To the left of us, far in the distance, I can see the revitalised centre of the city. Closer to the road, perhaps a half-mile away, are collapsed buildings. Broken walls. Empty city streets. I scan the horizon for signs of people but find none.

"Don't people live out here?" I ask. I am surprised to see an area so close to the city uninhabited after a hundred years of revitalisation. In Five Lakes, my father's team is constantly working to push the boundaries of our revitalised community. With so many people living in Tosu City, I'm surprised they haven't worked harder to repair the land and spread out.

"Not many," Enzo says. "Most of the farms and skimmer factories are located to the north, so the Commonwealth encourages those wanting to leave the city to go in that direction. No one wants to move into unrevitalised areas alone. My parents talked about it once, but there are too many dangers outside the current boundaries of the city. It's safer to stay where we are."

I look towards the city and its buildings. Over a hundred thousand people live in that area. They have power, clean water and the comfort of being near one another. Few wild animals venture into the streets. No threat from the chemicals that still corrupt the earth beyond the city's limits. I can understand why people choose that safety for themselves and their families. There are a few citizens in Five Lakes who prefer living near the square, where there is less chance of animal attacks or being isolated during an emergency. But most of us are spread out. If necessary, we can survive on our own. I wonder how many people in Tosu City could say the same.

It is Enzo who first spots the chain-link fence that announces we have reached our destination. The fence stands at least eight feet high and stretches far into the distance on each side. As we get closer, I can read the dirt-streaked signs posted on it.

DANGER.
THIS AREA HAS NOT BEEN REVITALISED.
HAZARDOUS MATERIAL INSIDE.
DO NOT ENTER.

"How are we supposed to find the next task?" Damone asks. "This fence goes on for miles."

"The final years want us to find the task," I reason. "They must have made the location obvious." I hope.

Will steers the skimmer east along the fence line while the rest of us look for signs of the next Induction task. There. In the mid-afternoon sunlight, a red flag flutters from the top of the fence a hundred yards away. When we reach the spot and exit the skimmer, four large steel boxes, about three feet wide and six feet long, are sitting on the ground next to the fence. Each has a keypad embedded into the top. None of the boxes appears to be disturbed. We are the first team to arrive.

While Damone pumps his fist into the air, Will throws open the lid to our box. Inside there is a note that reads:

> The planes of the past used Newton's laws of motion to reach the skies. Now it is your turn. Choose a team member to climb into the box and close the lid. When the box locks, the marker

and clue to the next task will be dispensed. Solve
the problem on the display to release your team
member and be on your way.

"Someone has to get in there?" Enzo asks.

Will reads the note again and nods. "That's what it
says." He closes the lid on the steel box and opens it again.
"There must be a weight mechanism on the bottom that,
when engaged, activates the lock. Maybe we can fill it with
rocks or something heavy enough to simulate a person."

I doubt the final years will let us off the hook that easy,
but I follow Will's lead and pile several heavy rocks into the
box. When the lock still won't engage, Enzo frowns. "They
must have heat sensors set up to ensure that we comply
with the guidelines."

Either that or we're being watched.

"Okay." Will nods. "Who's going to get in?"

"Cia will," Damone says. "She's the captain and the
smallest."

Both good reasons, but the idea of being locked inside
a steel box and reliant on my team to release me makes
me want to run far and fast.

Damone notices my hesitation and says, "You picked this
team, Cia. Don't you have enough faith in your judgement
to rely on us to solve this task on our own?"

I look from Damone's smirking face to Will's, with its lack of expression, to Enzo's concerned one. All three are smart. They wouldn't be attending the University if they weren't. Do I believe they will come up with the correct answer to whatever problem they are given? Yes. Do I trust them with my life? No. But I don't have a choice. Damone has cornered me. Refusal will alienate my team. Even if we pass Induction, I will have made enemies.

"Okay," I say as I set the green team bag on the ground, keeping my own bags with me, and climb into the cold steel box. As small as I am, I have to bend my knees and twist my shoulders to fit myself into the container.

"Why don't you give me your bags?" Will offers, and reaches for the straps. "That'll give you more room."

"No." I pull the bags tight against my chest. While I have been manoeuvered into putting my life in my team's hands, I will not trust them with my secrets. The Transit Communicator will stay locked in this box with me.

"Here." Enzo puts his flashlight in my hand. "We'll get you out of there quick. I promise."

As I watch Will reach for the lid and pull it down, I hope Enzo is right. Metal closes over me. Everything goes black. I hear the snap of a lock that tells me there is no going back. Until my team comes up with the correct solution, I am trapped.

I hit the switch on the flashlight. The small beam reflects off the silver of my prison. Even though I know it is futile, I push against the metal above me. It doesn't budge. I run my fingers along the edge of the lid. The seal on the box appears tight. A click of the flashlight confirms my suspicion. There is no hint of outside light. Unless I am mistaken, this container is airtight. If my team does not release the locking mechanism in a timely manner, I will die.

I need to conserve air, but my breath comes fast and harsh. Knowing my life lies in the hands of someone who in the past tried to kill me fills me with terror. The pounding of blood in my veins rings loud in my ears, drowning out the sounds of the voices outside the steel walls. Or maybe the material of the walls is too thick to hear clearly.

Pushing aside the panic that bubbles in my chest, I focus on my breathing. Measured breath in. Slow breath out. Growing up, my brothers liked to play hide-and-seek. As the smallest of us, I could wriggle into the best hiding spots. And yet my brothers never failed to find me. Until finally Zeen explained that the excited sound of my breathing gave me away. It took practice on my part, but eventually my brothers needed to use more than just their ears to find me.

When my breathing calms, I strain to hear what is happening with my team. The voices are muted. Mumbles tell me they are hard at work, but I cannot tell what the task is or how long it is going to take. Here and there, I make out a word.

"No... second law..."

"... force..."

"... wrong..."

In between the words only silence and the pulsing of my heart mark the passing of the seconds. Minutes. Maybe hours. Time stands still. During that time, I think of Tomas and wonder what trial he is facing in his own Induction. I wish he were here with me now to help keep me safe. A whirring sound followed by a jubilant shout pulls me from my thoughts, but my prison door does not open.

The voices outside are louder. I jump when something bangs against the box, but the lock stays firmly in place as my teammates continue to shout words that, no matter how hard I try, I cannot understand.

The voices go silent. To keep calm, I count the seconds. Ten. Twenty. Sixty. One hundred. Still nothing. Just darkness and silence. Did my team fail at their task and suffer a penalty? Or did they succeed and choose to leave me behind?

I close my eyes tight, clutch my bags to my chest and continue to listen for signs that my team is still there. That I haven't been abandoned. That I will not suffocate in this metal coffin. That I will not die here – alone.

The metal surrounding me vibrates. Over my quickening breath is the roar of a skimmer motor. Once again, I have trusted where trust was not warranted. Once again, I will suffer the consequences.

I should stay calm. I should breathe carefully to conserve my air supply until I find a way out of here. Instead, I bang against the lid of the box and scream. The sound of the motor might drown out my cries, but I keep screaming on the chance that those leaving me behind can hear my voice. I want them to know that I am alive now. That if I die, I do so at their hands.

My throat is raw. My hands ache when I stop my pounding. By now, my team is long gone. If I want to survive, I have to find a way out of here. I shift in the tight space so I can reach the fasteners on my bag. My fingers hunt through my belongings until they settle on the handle of my pocket-knife. A click of the flashlight bathes the small space with light. I struggle to shift positions in the tight space as I run the blade along the top and bottom of the right side of the box, hoping to find a flaw in the design. When I find none, I roll to my left so I can reach the other side.

So intent am I on my mission, it barely registers when I hear something scrape against the outside of the box. I hear the sound again and hold my breath. Voices murmur. I knock three times on the lid, hoping someone will understand I am trapped inside. I almost cry with relief when three knocks sound in return.

"Hang on, Cia," someone yells. "We've almost got it."

The sound of a latch sliding confirms the words. The metal above me shifts upward. I squint into the sunlight and see Will's and Enzo's faces peering down. Will's hand feels warm and strong in mine as he helps me stand and climb out. To my left, I see Jacoby and two other members of their team arguing. Their skimmer sits twenty feet beyond them.

"I heard the engine and thought you'd left." My voice is raspy from the screaming. Evidence of my lack of trust.

"I would have thought the same thing." Will hands me the green team bag and glances over to a grove of trees growing near the fence about fifty feet away. Glaring at us from the centre of the trees is Damone. "If Damone had gotten his way, we'd have hit the road after getting the clue. He wasn't interested in wasting time on the second part, to free you. It took a few minutes, but we helped him see the error of his ways."

The darkening bruise on Will's cheek gives me an idea as to how.

"You got it wrong," Jacoby yells at the girl next to him. "Get out of the way and let me try."

"We should probably cut Damone loose and get out of here before they figure out the solution," Enzo says.

"I think we should leave him." A smile devoid of happiness crosses Will's face. "Give him a taste of his own medicine. It's no less than he deserves."

I look at the steel box where Damone would have left me to die, and my heart hardens. Will is right. Damone should understand what it feels like to be betrayed. Leaders – real leaders – must think of others before themselves. They need to consider the consequences of their actions and only sacrifice lives when the needs of many outweigh the needs of the few.

And I realise, as much as I want to penalise Damone for his cowardly actions, I cannot. Not without performing the same kind of act I am condemning Damone for. I am this team's leader. I will not leave someone I am in charge of behind.

"Damone is coming with us," I say, digging my pocket-knife out of my University bag. "Get the skimmer ready. We'll be back in a minute."

Without waiting for agreement, I walk towards the cluster of trees. The grey cast to the bark speaks of the lack of revitalisation in this area. But the state of the trees and other foliage does not hold my interest. Damone's reddened face and angry eyes do. He goes still as I approach and says nothing as I walk around him to examine the restraints Will and Enzo fashioned. His arms are wrapped around the tree behind him and bound at the wrist with strips of sturdy brown fabric. The same fabric that Damone's shirt is made of. Blood streaks his skin where it has rubbed against the tree in his efforts to get free.

"What do you want?" Damone sneers. "Are you going to pretend to leave me behind again? We both know you can't do it. Can you?"

For a moment, my knife stills. The urge to leave him and his insults behind is overwhelming. To do so would almost certainly keep him from a leadership position. I could prevent him from making decisions that would affect me, my family and my country. I have only to walk away and betray everything that I believe in.

My knife slices through the restraints. Damone offers no thanks or show of gratitude as he stalks towards the skimmer. The anger I pushed aside returns. I take two steps and feel my foot catch. My knees and hands jolt with pain as I hit the unforgiving ground. Tears caused by my stinging palms, my anger with Damone and my disappointment in my own desire to punish him prick the backs of my eyes. I ache for home. For my family. For Tomas. For people who love me. For people I can trust with my life.

But they are not here and I need to get moving. I push to my knees and realise whatever tripped me is still wrapped around my left ankle.

I reach down and find thin, pliable wire where I expected to find a vine or root. Carefully, I unhook the metal from my ankle and examine it more closely. No rust. No wear. Extending from where I sit to somewhere to my right. Sliding my fingers along the length of the wire, I follow it to its end, which is expertly secured around a small but sturdy bush.

A snare. A simple one designed to catch an animal bounding through this grouping of trees. If an animal steps into or puts its head through the loop and keeps walking, the loop will tighten. As it did around my leg. The more the animal struggles, the more tightly it is trapped. Only, instead of dinner, this snare caught me.

"Are you okay?"

I turn and see Enzo standing near a scraggly tree, looking at me.

"I'm fine." I brush off my knees and glance around for signs of other snares. "My foot just caught on something."

There. Sunlight glints off silver metal. Only, this time the snare is located on the other side of the fence. As I take a step towards the fence, Enzo says, "If we don't want the other team to pull ahead of us, we need to get going."

Enzo has a point. Still, I step towards the fence. "I just want to take a closer look at something. It'll only take a minute."

"Cia." Enzo's voice holds authority and a whisper of nerves.

"There's nothing we need inside the air-force base. We need to go back to the skimmer. Damone and Will won't wait around for us much longer."

I look to the skimmer and see Will waving at us. Enzo is right. It is time for us to go. I cast one last look at the wire trap set on the other side of the fence before walking away. As we climb into the skimmer, I don't think I imagine the relief on Enzo's face or the tension that leeches from his shoulders. Being left behind is reason enough for worry, but does his concern indicate something more?

The rise of the skimmer and the roar of the engine pull my thoughts away from what lies behind and refocus me on the task ahead. "What did the last clue say?" I ask.

Enzo pulls a grey piece of paper from his pocket and hands it to me.

> The end is in sight. The next stop is near. In the foundation of our Commonwealth you shall search. Look for the symbol of where you now live and find what you seek upon its perch.

The answer seemed straightforward enough. "The Central Government Building," I say.

"That's what we thought," Will says, his eyes fixed firmly on the road. In the seat next to him, Damone sits with his arms crossed as he stares out the window. Saving him from the snake and choosing to keep our team intact were the right things to do, but by making those choices, it is clear I have also made an enemy. Then again, maybe he was always my enemy and I just didn't know it. Even after spending an entire day with Enzo and Damone, I know little more than I did before about their families or the values they've been raised on. With Damone, I can make a guess. His willingness to get ahead at the cost of others must have been a skill he learned from his government-connected father or the teachers who helped prepare him for the University. But Enzo is a mystery. From the way the others treat him, I can guess his family is not connected to the Tosu government. Who they are and what they believe in, I do not know. But the worry that sprang to his eyes when I made a move to examine the snares makes me determined to find out.

By the confident way he directs Will through the scenery that changes from dirt and plants to roads, walkways and small buildings, it is clear Enzo grew up nearby. Through the smudged skimmer windows, I study the landscape. The buildings and plant life surrounding the houses look well tended. More like the dwellings we create in Five Lakes than the ones I have seen in the heart of the city. Children stop their playing to wave as we drive past. Citizens on bicycles or the occasional motorised scooter steer down the streets as people hurry to whatever tasks await them.

The number of personal skimmers filling the roadway increases as the buildings grow larger and less spread apart. Some stand five or six storeys high. Books tell us taller buildings once graced the city streets – some reaching hundreds of feet into the air – but they were too tall, too exposed to survive against the trembling earth and destructive winds. While the tallest buildings faltered during the final Three Stages of War, most structures in this city, while shaken and sometimes cracked, stood strong. Their smaller stature proved to be an asset. One a country could rebuild upon.

Will's face is a mask of concentration, and his hands tighten on the controls as the streets become more crowded. He speaks only to ask Enzo when he needs clarification about the direction he is going in. Finally, I see in the distance the riverbank that signals our destination is near. The flowing river sparkles. A carpet of green, healthy grass frames the river on either side.

"So we just need to find a picture of a balanced scale," Will says once he safely steers the skimmer into a vehicle zone and turns off the engine. "Sounds easy enough."

"Easy?" Damone shoots Will a withering look. "Have you been inside the Central Government Building? It'll take a miracle to find anything in there."

I hate to think it, but as we walk towards the Central Government Building, I realise Damone's right. The United Commonwealth government was officially created a hundred years ago in a large structure that sits on the east bank of the river. Two storeys tall with circular walls and a low-domed roof, the building has a short but sturdy design that helped it survive the worst of the natural disasters with little more than a few broken windows. The lack of damage and the large rooms that can accommodate thousands of people made it an ideal site for the survivors of the war to lay the foundation for a new country.

It is hard to imagine those first days when the earth quieted and people began to assess the damage. Corrupted rivers that caused illness or worse. Destroyed homes and a ground too contaminated for many plants to grow. A world filled with sorrow and fear. Instead of closing the doors and cowering in the dark, people gathered here to pool their resources and restore hope.

I glance at the large square building on the land just north of the Central Government Building. Now named Tosu City Hospital and Medical Research Centre. I don't know what it was called then, but it was once used as safe living spaces for those without homes or those too old, young or terrified to be alone. An enclosed walkway allowed people to pass safely between the two structures without having to brave the chemical- and radiation-laced elements.

Leaders were elected. Laws made. Crews organised and sent outside to evaluate the city. Canned food was gathered and rationed. The dead found inside were buried in a crevice opened by an earthquake on the west side of the city. A group was formed to scout around the city for signs of still-living plants, animals and people. Water was boiled and filtered. Even then, drinking the water made people sick, which prompted leaders to send the surviving scientists to the University labs. The scientists used the equipment there to run tests on the river, hoping to discover a way to make it pure once again.

One by one, buildings were repaired and deemed safe. Families left the safety of living with the entire community and moved into their own dwellings. Scientists found plants, like clover, that thrived in the damaged soil, and began splicing their genes into less hardy vegetation. With hope, organisation and care, the world came alive again.

And it all started here.

People mill in the courtyard or stand talking in small groups. A hundred feet from our position is a small flight of stairs that leads to the entrance of the beige stone building. On either side of a fountain is a tall silver pole. At the top of each is a flag. The red, white and blue one from the past that will never be forgotten and the other, displaying a stark white background trimmed with purple. In the centre of the field of white is a single crimson rose. White to symbolise hope and purity of purpose. Purple for courage. The red petals of the flower signify the promise of a people determined to make the rose and the rest of the country thrive. I can't help but wonder how The Testing was allowed to grow from that promise. Did those who conceived of it intend for the price of failure to be so high? How many people walking the halls of this building know the true nature of The Testing? How many more have feigned deafness because they don't want to hear and recognise what, by ignorance, they condone?

We walk up the steps, and I glance over my shoulder to look for the other teams. None are in sight as we step into a room buzzing with activity. The antechamber is filled with people. Large white panels hanging from the two-storey ceiling bask the room in light. On the wall to the right is a mural of the colonies and boundaries of the current United Commonwealth. Directly in front of us are two large sets of doors that lead to the Debate Chamber.

"Where do we start looking?" Enzo asks. "The observation gallery? The offices?"

Will frowns. "Cia and I came here for orientation a couple months ago. I don't remember seeing anything with scales on it. Then again, we only went through about half the rooms in the building."

"We should split up," Damone suggests.

I have only to think about Damone's desire to leave me locked in that box to reject his idea. "We should stay together. Otherwise, we'll spend even more time trying to reconnect with one another."

Damone gives me a flat stare. "Fine. You're the captain. You tell us how we're going to search hundreds of rooms and find the scales before the next team does."

"I don't know," I admit, but my desire to outthink Damone has me determined to find out. Our orientation leader said the building contained almost two hundred thousand square feet of offices, meeting rooms and discussion chambers. Searching through them all could take days.

"We're wasting time. Can someone make a decision already? Or is talking all they taught you how to do in the colonies?" Damone scowls at me and Will.

Will glares back. "At least they taught us something. The only reason you're here is because your father is a hotshot Commonwealth official. I bet he knows where the scales symbol is in this place. Too bad he isn't here to ask. Instead, we're stuck with you."

Damone moves fast. Before I realise what's happening, he pushes Will back towards the wall behind us. I see shock register on Will's face a moment before he slams into the hard surface. Will grabs Damone's shoulders and shoves, sending Damone staggering back. I race in between the two, hoping to talk some sense into them before we get thrown out of the building or worse.

"Stop," I snap, trying to mimic the tone my mother uses on my brothers when they are fighting. "Unless you're hoping to impress the government officials with your right hooks, I think we should find what we came here for. After that, the two of you can beat each other senseless for all I care. Okay?"

I wait for Will or Damone to object. Neither does.

"Good." I push hair off my forehead and take a deep breath. "Now, maybe we can get back to solving this task."

"Well, according to Will, we're not smart enough to figure it out on our own," Damone sneers.

"That's not what I said."

This time Enzo steps in to keep the peace, and I let him because Will and Damone have given me an idea. The clue did not say we had to find the scales on our own. While Damone's father isn't here for us to ask, there are dozens if not hundreds of government officials who work in this building every day. Some of them must know where the symbol of the scales of justice is. We just have to ask.

I approach a lady sitting in a nearby room with a glass window. When she sees me looking in her direction, her lips curve into a sympathetic smile. Taking that as a positive sign, I leave the boys behind and walk over.

The woman slides open a panel of glass. "Can I be of assistance?" Her eyes shift behind me; she no doubt wonders if the help I need is with my unkempt, ill-mannered companions.

"I'm hoping you know where I can find a picture or sign or statue with balanced scales depicted on it. There's supposed to be one somewhere inside this building."

With a nod, she says, "If you go through those doors there, I believe you will find a small rendering of that symbol on the back of the moderating justice's chair."

She points to the double doors situated between the two maps. The doors that lead into the Debate Chamber. Next to the door is a sign that lists the discussion and voting schedule for the day. I look down at the watch strapped to my bag. The Debate Chamber session is almost over. Once it ends, the chamber doors will be locked until the debate floor opens again – at nine o'clock in the morning. Unless we can convince someone to unlock the doors for us, we will have to wait to search the chamber during one of the session breaks tomorrow.

Or will we? I think back to the second line of the clue. 'Look for the symbol of the house you now live in and find what you seek upon its perch.' If an image of balanced scales is on a chair, then what we seek isn't going to be waiting for us when the chamber is empty. It's what is at this very moment seated on that chair. The moderating justice – President Anneline L. Collindar.

CHAPTER 9

I thank the woman for her help and walk towards the double doors. In my head, I try to picture what I saw when I was here. Up front is a raised platform. A podium and chair in the centre for the moderating justice, who leads the discourse. A desk and another chair for the assistant moderator, who records the proceedings. Seats and desks on the main floor for representatives of the ten departments of the government. More seats in the balcony for those who want to observe or, in some cases, add their opinions to the discussion. When we were here with our orientation instructor, most of the seats in the balcony were empty. Citizens were too busy with their jobs, homes and children to care what change to the law was being made.

When I pull back the heavy doors and step inside, I hear murmuring somewhere overhead that tells me today at least some of the seats in the balcony are occupied. So is the debate floor. All ten department leaders are required to send two delegates to represent their interests on the debate floor. When I was last here, the requisite twenty were in attendance. Today there are at least twice as many listening to a speaker explain the need for more textile production.

My teammates join me in the open doorway.

"What are you doing?" Damone growls. "You're not allowed on the Debate Chamber floor when the council is in session."

"The next clue is in here," I whisper.

"Where?" Will asks.

Taking a deep breath, I point to where the leader of our country sits with an unreadable expression on her face. "There."

"Are you crazy?" Damone asks. "You can't go up there. You'll get us thrown out of the University and detained, or worse."

He's right. Our orientation instructor reminded us that detainment is the penalty for stepping uninvited onto the Debate Chamber floor. Doing so is construed as a threat against the president and the Commonwealth government. The penalty was instituted during the early days when the fatigue and frustration of non-government citizens boiled over and resulted in injuries and, on one occasion, death.

Enzo nods. "If the next task is up there, we'll find it when the session is over. We just have to wait."

The more I think about it, the more convinced I am that waiting will do us no good. Thus far, each of the tasks set for us by the final years has tested specific skills. Mathematics. History. Mechanical knowledge. But in addition to classroom-learned knowledge, the tests have measured something more. They have judged our ability to work under pressure. To trust one another. To listen to instructions and critically think through problems. Successful government officials do all these things, but the best of them do more. They follow their instincts and figure out a way to do what needs to be done.

I count four men and two women dressed in black and standing near the stairs on either side of the raised platform. The wide white band on each of their right arms identifies them as Safety officials. The weapons at their sides and the respect our country's citizens have for the work done here have ensured that no unauthorised person has set foot on the Debate Chamber floor for decades.

Since I can't walk onto the floor without risking detainment, I have to find another way.

"Cia," Will hisses, "we have to wait outside until the session ends."

Damone, Enzo and Will take a step backwards, but I stay put. This session will last a half-hour more. Then the room will be locked until morning. Damone might be able to convince one of his father's friends to open the doors and let us search, but there is a chance that the president has to be seated on the platform for us to complete the task. Waiting will not help us. There has to be a second option. But what?

Ignoring the stares from officials on the debate floor and the insistent whispers from my teammates, I glance around the room for a solution. My mother always told me the best way to solve a problem is to ask for help. But while that worked the first time, I doubt the woman in the lobby will be able to assist me in this next step even if she knows what it is. The officials on the debate floor might be able to provide an answer, but unless I want to yell across the massive room, I—

Wait.

I close my eyes and think back to my Five Lakes classroom. Sitting in my seat behind Tomas. Listening to our teacher as she discussed the creation of this room. The founding government officials chose this space to house the Debate Chamber because they wanted a room large enough to house not only the governing body but those citizens who wanted to voice their concerns. In the early years of the Commonwealth, the debate floor was filled with people who wanted a voice in the reconstruction of our country. During the last several decades, no ordinary citizen has stepped onto the Debate Chamber floor. They've been too busy with their own lives to take responsibility for the government and the country. But just because no one in recent years has chosen to use that privilege doesn't mean it doesn't still exist. At the end of that lesson, my teacher mentioned an antiquated law that said any citizen may request a hearing on the Debate Chamber floor. We were never tested on that law or the wording required to gain access to the Chamber. At the time I was relieved. Not any more.

It takes me several minutes to locate the thin, dark cord that hangs far to the left of the entryway in a dimly lit alcove. The cord is coated with dust, but when I tug, the gong of the hearing bell echoes through the room. One by one, the people on the floor shift their attention from the speaker to me. The man's words falter. The Safety officials' hands move to the weapons holstered at their sides, but they do not draw. Not yet. I can hear the surprise in the hushed whispers from the gallery above.

Part of me wants to withdraw. To avoid such attention. But the law states any citizen who rings the bell and follows protocol will be invited onto the chamber floor. While I am young and unimportant to the workings of the Commonwealth, I am a citizen. The law gives me this right.

Only those who use the proper phrase are given leave to enter the chamber. One wrong word and the petitioner will be denied for her lack of respect for the process and those she seeks to address. I take three steps forward, swallow my nerves and say the words my classmates and I were taught years ago. "As every citizen has not only the right but the responsibility to participate in the due course of this government, I respectfully ask permission to address the moderating justice and the official currently holding the Debate Chamber floor."

Everything is quiet. The entire chamber is holding its breath. Watching. Wondering if I have spoken correctly. If I will be granted permission to take the floor. Time stands still as the president rises from her seat and studies me from across the hall.

"Permission is granted." She nods. "You may approach."

Relief floods through me. I hold my head high and keep my eyes forward as I walk to the stairs of the raised platform. Four steps up, and I cross the stage and come to a halt four feet from the leader of the United Commonwealth.

Several heartbeats pass as we look at each other. Me with my untidy hair and rumpled, dirt-stained clothes standing on the wooden platform. The president standing in front of a large, black wooden chair, with her short, perfectly styled ebony hair and a ceremonial red robe.

Then she smiles. "What can the United Commonwealth government do for you, citizen?"

The president stands seven inches taller than me. Her face

is long and angular. Not what most would call beautiful. But the almond-shaped brown eyes and strong jaw would draw attention anywhere. Almost all the United Commonwealth presidents have been female. It has been argued that women are less aggressive, more maternal and thus more focused on the well-being of the country's people. Less focused on politics or power. Perhaps this is true, but there is nothing maternal about President Collindar's appearance or voice. Both carry a shimmer of absolute authority.

Taking a deep breath, I shift a few steps to the side so I can clearly see the back of the chair. And I smile. Dangling from a wire on the back of the chair is a picture of the balanced scales of justice. I swallow my nerves, smooth my sweaty palms on my pants and say, "I apologise for the interruption, President Collindar, but I believe you have a message for me."

The president's eyes shift to the balcony and then back to me.

"As a matter of fact, I do." The smile spreads as she reaches into the pocket of her robe and pulls out a familiar-looking grey envelope. "I wish you luck in the rest of your studies, Ms...?"

"Vale. Malencia Vale."

"Where are you from, Ms Vale?"

"Five Lakes Colony, Madam President."

Surprise lights her eyes, but President Collindar's pleasant smile doesn't change as she holds out the envelope. "I'm certain we'll meet again, Malencia. Have a safe journey back to school."

I take the envelope and she sits back down in her chair. I've been dismissed. I turn and glance up at the balcony as I make my way to the stairs. A dozen people are scattered in the gallery seats. Among them are two familiar faces. A tight-lipped Professor Holt, watching my every move, and Dr Barnes, whose gaze is affixed on the only person behind me – President Collindar. I can't help but wonder if Professor Holt and Dr Barnes will judge my actions to be the correct ones. While the envelope in my hand was the goal, I know from The Testing that the right answer doesn't always ensure a passing grade. Coming in first during this Induction doesn't mean we will be assigned the most important internships. It's the skills and leadership we demonstrate during these tasks that will make that determination.

Hoping that I have shown whatever qualities Dr Barnes and Professor Holt are looking for in their top government interns, I walk up the aisle to where my team stands holding open the double doors. Their expressions range from celebratory to sullen as I walk past them into the antechamber. I see the blonde seated behind the glass window smile at the envelope in my hand. I smile back and, when the double doors close with a soft thunk, I let out a relieved sigh.

"I can't believe you got the words to that petition right." Will laughs and shakes his head. "I would have blown it."

"Then the administrators made a mistake letting you into the University," says Damone. "Anyone who truly belongs in Government Studies can recite that request. It's not like she did anything special."

Will gives Damone a tense smile. "I dare you to walk into the Debate Chamber and request your own audience. I bet anything you'll prove you don't belong."

Before the two can start shoving again, I say, "Instead of arguing about the last task, how about we concentrate on the next one? It's getting late. I'd rather not have to finish this Induction in the dark."

When no one objects, I open the envelope given to me by President Collindar and read:

The end is near. You'll soon be done. Now it's time to have some fun. Return to the place where you embarked on this quest. Induction awaits for those who complete one last test.

The place where we embarked on this quest? There are two possibilities. The zoo, with its booby-trapped monkey cages, or the University, where we boarded the skimmers that took us to the initial location. Since the clue implies our Induction adventure will be complete after we finish the final task, and since none of us wants to return to the zoo to face any other deadly inhabitants, we climb into the skimmer and head north-east to the University.

Damone knows this area best, so we let him navigate while Will steers through the well-tended busy streets of downtown Tosu. Being in charge seems to put Damone in a more cheerful mood, which is a relief. With one Induction task remaining, we need his co-operation.

Personal skimmers and a few old-fashioned cars cruise down the smoothly paved roads next to us. Kids play games on small patches of grass. Citizens with bags on their shoulders travel the walkways. I plug the co-ordinates I saved into the Transit Communicator and monitor our progress in case Damone is steering us wrong. We have just over four and a half miles to travel before we are back at the Government Studies residence.

The buildings lining the streets grow smaller. Some of the streets we pass are cracked. The roofs on the houses sag. The children playing outside wear frayed coats and shoes. Their cheeks are hollow. Their eyes resigned. I can see Enzo's jaw tighten as we travel through those areas, which soon give way to larger houses in perfect repair.

"My parents' house is just a few blocks down there." Damone points to a block filled with large structures, green lawns and young but healthy trees. "My school is over there." He indicates a large fenced-in white building in the other direction. The windows sparkle in the sunlight. The paint looks new. Several kids in thick, colourful coats sit on the front steps of the school, laughing. Their faces are round and healthy. The difference between the schoolchildren and the ones we passed just blocks before forms a stark contrast.

"Why aren't all the streets like this one?" I quietly ask Enzo.

After casting a glance at Damone, who is directing Will to go faster, Enzo leans forward and says, "Every sector of the city has a Tosu council member who requests resources and services for the people in that sector. The people on the streets I grew up on weren't as friendly with their council member as people in Damone's neighbourhood."

"What does that have to do with it?" I ask.

"Are you serious?" He gives a shake of his head. "Just because council members are supposed to represent everyone in their sector doesn't mean they do. People look out for themselves and their friends."

Enzo falls silent and stares out the skimmer window as the buildings speed past. I barely register the landmarks that announce our proximity to the University as I consider

Enzo's words. I grew up believing our leaders had learned from past mistakes. That, if nothing else, the Seven Stages of War taught us that life is fragile and precious. That those who survived have an obligation not only to repair the damage but never to repeat the actions that brought us to the brink of disaster. Distrust and anger caused governments to hurl angry words. Angry words led to bombs being dropped. A world destroyed.

Perhaps it is the size of the population that allows leaders to neglect some of those who look to them for assistance. In Five Lakes Colony, Magistrate Owens knows every citizen living within our boundaries. She might not know them well, but she has seen their faces and looked into their eyes. Would she show the same kind of leadership if she were appointed to oversee a city the size of Tosu? Would she be able to in a place where more than one hundred thousand faces look to the government for guidance and resource allocation?

During the early debates about whether to create a post-war government, many were vehemently opposed to the idea of a formal administration. They believed everyone should be allowed to survive in the way he or she thought best. Not forced to answer to the same kind of government that caused the wars in the first place. Some of the fiercest opposition went so far as to threaten the lives of those who were in favour of a new governing body.

Despite their tactics, I have to wonder if they had a point. Maybe it wasn't just the leaders but the size of the governments that caused the world to falter. The bigger the government, the bigger the population it can claim. The larger the population, the less our leaders feel personally accountable to each citizen under their care. It makes it easier to sacrifice a few for the good of others. To make choices that might otherwise be unthinkable – like sending unknown kids from families you never met to The Testing to fight not only for a place at the University but for their very lives. Meanwhile allowing students from families you have known all your life to be held to a different selection standard.

Will's celebratory cheer pulls me from my thoughts. I spot the large arching silver gate and the small plaque next to it that reads UNIVERSITY OF THE UNITED COMMONWEALTH. The sight fills me with a combination of pride, happiness and fear. Pride that I have made it this far. Happiness that Tomas, the one person I love in this city, is close by. Fear at what is to come. Not just with this Induction, but everything that follows. This is not the end of the challenges I will face. There are more. Harder. Maybe deadlier. I must be ready for them all.

"Now that we're here," Will asks, "where do we go?"

"The Government Studies residence," Damone says. "It has to be." I can see Damone's hands ball into fists as Will and Enzo look to me for confirmation. His fists stay clenched in his lap even after I agree. Will steers the skimmer past buildings that were created long ago. Glass. Stone. Brick. All constructed to encourage young minds to reach beyond what has already been done to something more. Something great.

The Government Studies residence comes into view. I see the earthquake-wrought ravine that circles the grounds, and my heart sinks as I realise that getting back to the residence won't be easy. The bridge is missing.

CHAPTER 10

My heart drops into my stomach as I climb out of the skimmer and look at the gaping crack in the earth between us and our final destination. Twenty feet across. Hundreds deep. Near the residence, Ian and Professor Holt are among a group of other people waiting for us to reach them. On this side are four small boxes next to stacks of boards, ropes and tools. The most sophisticated skimmers can hover up to fifteen feet above the ground. The one we've been using has been lucky to rise as high as my knee. However, sophisticated or not, the propulsion mechanism that makes all skimmers operate requires there be ground somewhere underneath. If a skimmer glides over a large hole, like the one in front of us now, the skimmer stops gliding. We cannot travel to the residence in our vehicle. If we are to get across, we will have to find another way.

While I'm surprised to find the bridge missing, I'm more disconcerted that I hadn't previously noticed the bridge was built to retract. Ian never mentioned that when he first led us here. Slats and rails hang against either side of the ravine, waiting to be reconnected, and I wonder why University officials chose to build a bridge that could disappear at a moment's notice. They couldn't have built it specifically for the purpose of testing new University students. Which prompts the question: Did they build it to ensure people had to stay in or to keep unwanted visitors out?

A quick study of the bridge support nearest our position gives me a good idea of how the retractable bridge works. The mechanism on each support is designed to slide each half of the bridge backwards on iron tracks when it is retracted. When it is raised, the system first elevates the bridge ninety degrees. Then a separate machine must slide forward to provide the support necessary to withstand the weight of both the bridge and those who cross it. Once both sides of the bridge are raised, they hook together seamlessly. At least, I never saw the seams. The looks on my teammates' faces say I wasn't the only one who missed that detail. I find that of little consolation when I realise the controls for the bridge are all located on the other side.

Enzo walks to the small black box marked with our number and pulls out the instructions for this task. "Come home." He looks at the hole in the earth, the missing bridge, the supplies and then back at the note. "Are they kidding? They want us to get across that? There's no way."

"If they want us to cross the ravine, there has to be a way to do it without getting ourselves killed," I say with confidence. This isn't The Testing. They won't kill students in full view of other students. But they aren't going to make it easy, either. Will reaches into the pile and fingers a large length of thick rope. "We might be able to hoist this side of the bridge up with this."

Enzo shakes his head. "The bridge is probably locked into place. But even if it isn't, we aren't strong enough to lift that kind of weight."

Will frowns. "My brother and I helped a neighbour of ours build a rope bridge over a stream a couple years ago. We used trees to anchor the bridge on either side. The supports for the bridge that normally spans this are still here. We can use those."

"Brilliant. Of course, the only way to use the anchor on the other side is to be over there to attach the rope to the bridge." Damone rolls his eyes. "Which would eliminate the need for building the bridge in the first place."

He's right. While building a bridge is something I've never done, I understand the basic physics involved. The supports that are already in place will be strong enough to hold up whatever we build if we could attach it properly, but there is no way we can do that. And while I don't think the University officials intend to watch us plunge to our deaths,

I doubt they will lift a finger to prevent it. There has to be another solution.

"Why don't we break into teams of two?" I suggest. "One group can go north. The other south. Maybe we'll find a better place for us to get across." I doubt it, but the possibility needs to be explored.

Will and Damone take the south. Enzo and I go north. We start out at a fast clip, certain we will find a way to cross the twenty-foot chasm of brown and grey rock and dirt that is between us and our destination. The crack begins to narrow, and Enzo and I smile at each other as we hurry ahead. That's when we see it. Another rent in the earth that juts off from this fissure towards the west. Even if the fissure we are standing next to narrows enough for safe passage, we would still be forced to cross another gaping barrier. Crossing here will not be possible. We can only hope Damone and Will have had better luck on their scouting mission and have remembered I hold all the markers. If they have found a way across and have not waited for Enzo and me to go with them, they will still fail.

One look at their dejected faces when we return tells the story. More barriers lie to the south. If we want to get to the finish line, we will have to cross here. And night is falling fast.

My three teammates study the building supplies and

tools as I once again examine the supports and machinery. I shake my head. My skill is with machines. If the bridge's controls were on this side, I'm certain I could make it rise. But they aren't. And even if I could make the gears fire, I'm not sure I should try. Without our fully understanding how the mechanism works or how the two pieces of the bridge lock into place, attempting to cross the ravine could be akin to suicide. I've survived too much to allow University officials to push me into doing something stupid. And crossing on a contraption created with the tools and supplies provided would be even crazier. We could do calculations for days and still not be positive that the forces created by our weight and that of the bridge will balance with the upward force and properly absorb torque. A few more years studying with the professors here, and we might be able to pull this off. But now? How can anyone expect any of us to succeed at this task? They must realise it is impossible. Is that what Professor Holt and the others are waiting for? For us to fail? Why? What purpose would teaching us defeat serve? They want us to be leaders. Leaders are required to find solutions no matter what.

Or are they?

Bombs were dropped. Millions of people killed. A world destroyed because the leaders of our country and those around the globe were not willing to declare failure. They could not admit that the path they had embarked on was doomed. Instead, they forged ahead. More bombs. More destruction. More need to prove that they were right. That others were wrong.

I think about the Induction thus far. It has required us to carefully think through answers before putting them into action. To trust when trust is not only hard, but potentially deadly. To speak as an equal with the head of our government. All skills essential for government leaders. As is learning when to say enough is enough.

Turning my back on those who watch, I walk over to where a tree stands thirty feet away and sit. After leaning back against the tree, I open the green team bag and take out my bottle of water.

"What are you doing?" Damone yells as he notices me seated on the grass. "You should be helping us figure out how we're going to get to the other side."

"He's right, Cia." Enzo frowns. "The only way we're going to beat this task is if we work together."

"We're not going to beat it." I nod at the cluster of observers across the way. "They don't expect us to, so there's no point in giving them the satisfaction of seeing us try and come up short."

"They wouldn't have given us this task if there wasn't a way to pass it." Damone throws a plank to the ground and grabs a hammer. He takes three steps towards me, eyes bright with anger. The hammer wielded like a weapon. "I am not going to fail this test because some girl from the colonies doesn't want to make the effort to win. Get the hell up or you'll be sorry that Will and Enzo were too soft to leave you trapped in that box where you belonged."

Damone lashes out with the hammer, and I scramble back out of its path. "Are you crazy?" I yell.

He starts to swing again and is brought up short by a hand grabbing his wrist and yanking the hammer free.

Will's jaw is clenched and his eyes glitter with violence. This is the Will from The Testing. "Move away from her now, or you're going to be sorry."

"Let go of me." Damone tries to yank his arm free. "My father is going to hear about this. Do you remember who my father is?"

Will holds fast. "I don't care who your father is, but he might care that his son is so weak he had to be saved by a colony girl. She saved your life. She's smarter than you. Than all of us put together. And you can't stand it." He releases his grip on Damone's wrist, but keeps the hammer tight in his fist.

Damone rubs his arm where Will's fingers dug into his flesh and scowls.

"Now, if you're done demonstrating your lack of control

to our viewing audience, Cia will explain why she thinks we can't get across. I know I'm dying to hear it. I mean, while I'd love to impress the professors, I don't plan on risking my life in order to do it." His mouth curves into a half smile. "But I would be happy to risk yours, Damone, if you want."

The smile. The hammer held confidently in Will's hand. Both scare the crap out of me. Damone, however, doesn't look scared. He appears on the verge of rage. But Will, as is typical, has said the right thing. Damone shifts his eyes to the people across the way watching our every move. His jaw clenches. His breathing is fast and uneven as he fights for control. Something he probably hasn't had to do very often. And he wins that battle – for now.

"Okay." He blows out air. "I'm not saying Cia is right, but I'll listen." Damone looks back at the wide stretch of emptiness behind him. "Prove to me that the final years don't intend for us to be able to get across this on our own."

I have lots of reasons, but proof? "I can't."

Damone's nasty grin makes me want to scream. So I turn away from him and focus on reasoning with the rest of my team. "I think this Induction process has been about teaching us lessons. Teamwork. Trust. Government procedure."

"And failure." Enzo completes my thought. "No matter how smart our leaders are, there are problems they cannot solve. This is one of them."

Will walks to the edge of the ravine and studies the drop. After several long moments, he shifts his attention across the divide to the people on the other side. His fists clench. Something intense flickers in his deep-green eyes before he turns back to us and smiles. "So what should we do while we wait for them to realise we've given up?'

Damone whirls. "No one is giving up. We're going to do exactly what the note says and get to the other side. I'm not losing my chance to win this Induction competition and throwing away my future just because some stupid girl from nowhere says she thinks we should give up. I'm not giving up. None of you are giving up."

Will steps away from the edge, shoves his hands in his pockets and saunters over to stand next to me. Enzo flanks me on the other side. Damone's face colours as he realises his words have had no effect. Right or wrong, Enzo and Will have chosen to stand with me.

Damone's eyes meet mine. Glittering in their depths are anger and hate. My muscles clench as I brace for the attack that is sure to come. Damone might have been smart enough to pass the Tosu City application exams, but he has demonstrated all day that he has no control over his emotions. Perhaps he has gotten this far based on people confusing bullying for strength of personality.

Whatever the reason, he is unprepared for others to take charge. I am certain he plans on taking back control by any means necessary.

"Hey, look," Enzo says as a whirring sound fills the air.

Damone stops his advance and turns as the east side of the bridge slowly begins to rise. The support shifts backward. Across the ravine, Ian stands next to the support. He pushes a button, and our side of the bridge begins to move. After several minutes, the beams shift and lock together with a resounding clang.

Ian crosses to the centre of the bridge and smiles. "Welcome back. You are the first team to arrive."

Will and Enzo slap hands and let out celebratory shouts before they race across the bridge. Damone glares at me before crossing behind them. Us finishing our Induction will not make him forget that I was right. That the others sided with me. That he wanted to be a leader and was pushed to the side. Vowing to do my best to stay out of Damone's way in the future, I follow.

As I pass Ian, his lips barely move as he whispers, "Meet me in Lab Two at midnight."

I want to ask why, but I curve my lips into a smile for Professor Holt, who watches from under a tree fifty feet away. The students standing outside the residence converge on me and my team. People slap my back and yell congratulations. Behind me, I hear the whirr of machinery and know the bridge is once again being retracted to challenge the next group who arrives.

"Cia. Enzo. Will. Damone," Ian calls, and the voices around us go quiet. The four of us walk to where Ian stands next to Professor Holt. "Congratulations on returning with your entire team intact. Do you have the markers?"

I dig into the green bag and hand the markers from the first three challenges to Ian. "We don't have a marker for this task."

"There wasn't a marker for the final test. This task was designed to be insurmountable." Professor Holt takes the markers and gives me a small smile. "Ian was told to engage the bridge when we deduced that you had figured out that solution."

My heartbeat measures the silence until Professor Holt says, "It takes a lot of courage to choose to do nothing when you aren't certain of the outcome. We believe this is an important lesson to impart to all University students and one many students find almost impossible to accept. I'm happy to learn that most on this team are more... open-minded."

I see Damone flush.

Professor Holt hands the markers back to Ian with a small nod. Ian turns and gives us a wide smile. "Congratulations

Cia, Enzo, Will and Damone. Since you arrived first with all of your markers, we are happy to declare you the winners. Once the other three teams arrive, we will hold a formal Induction ceremony where you will be officially welcomed into the Government Studies programme. Until then, I suggest you get lots of rest. I've seen your class schedules. Trust me, you're going to need it."

The students standing behind Ian laugh. As my teammates celebrate, I notice that Professor Holt isn't the only one watching me. In the distance, next to the willow tree where just yesterday I stood with Enzo, is Dr Barnes.

"You should all be very proud of yourselves," Professor Holt announces. "These Induction tasks have taught us a great deal about you and the way you approach problem solving. But more importantly, this process not only gave you a glimpse of the revitalisation work that still needs to be done, but also allowed you to learn about your fellow Government Studies students. All of you will be competing for the top grades, but I hope these challenges have taught you also that success comes only if we trust and work well with those around us."

To my left, I see Damone nod, but I know the only thing he learned was to despise me.

After more applause, Professor Holt adds, "I have been told the next team will not arrive until tomorrow at the earliest." The teams must not have gotten to the Central Government Building until after the debates ended for the day. Briefly, I pull my coat tight around me as the wind kicks up and wonder if those teams will be forced to spend the night outside or if they will seek shelter with their families. An option none of us had during The Testing.

Professor Holt continues, "Our official Induction will not begin until all teams have arrived and their performances have been evaluated. Until that time, I recommend you take Ian's suggestion and get some rest. And you might want to know that dinner will be served in an hour."

Perhaps I am paranoid, but I search my rooms for signs of cameras or microphones that might have been added since the scavenger Induction challenge began. I examine every piece of furniture, every inch of wall and each light fixture. Tension drains from my body when I finish. For the moment, there are no signs of my being watched. I am alone and safe.

Stripping off my clothes, I step into the shower. The sweat, grime and anxiety of the day wash away. My legs tremble as fatigue sets in. While I am hungry, I am not interested in facing Damone again so soon. Instead, I stretch out on the bed and close my eyes. I picture Tomas and feel a tug of loneliness as I wonder how he is doing. Is he facing his own Induction now? Praying Tomas is safe, I allow myself to slip into sleep.

The room is dark when I wake. I find myself starting to panic before I realise the darkness is not part of another Induction. The sky outside my window is black. I have slept longer than intended and night has fallen. Eleven o'clock. I haven't missed the meeting with Ian.

My stomach growls even as it fills with dread. I have no idea what Ian has to tell me, but the way he requested the private meeting makes me believe it can't be good. Repacking my University bag, I head out of the room and carefully lock the door behind me. While I doubt the lock will keep out those in authority, it might discourage people like Damone from going inside.

Despite the late hour, lights blaze in the common spaces of the residence. Most, if not all, of the students are still awake. The hangout room is filled with people laughing and talking with friends. I spot Will flirting with a girl I don't recognise. Damone and Enzo are nowhere to be seen.

Before anyone can notice me, I head to the dining room, where I find an array of breads, fruit, cheese, sweets and milk chilling in a large bowl of ice. The rest of the room is empty. I cut off a hunk of white cheese and make a sandwich with two thick slices of some kind of bread with tomatoes baked into the top. I keep an eye on the watch on my bag as I make myself eat the sandwich and drink a glass of milk. The sounds of laughter and conversation grow fainter as the minutes tick by. My fellow students must be starting to seek out their beds. I clean the crumbs off the table, put away my glass and sling my bag over my shoulder.

I hurry past the doorway to the hangout room without stopping to see who is still awake and walk to the other end of the building. The lights on this side are set to low for power conservation, and this part of the residence is silent. I see a bright glow under the door to the lab. A creak of the floorboard makes me jump, and I glance back down the hall. When no one appears out of the shadows, I take a deep breath and turn the doorknob.

Ian pushes the door closed behind me. There's a loud click as the lock bolts into place. "You're in trouble."

Unease churns my meal. "Did I do something wrong?"

"You did everything right."

I don't understand. "Then why am I in trouble?"

"Because you did too well." Ian takes a seat on a high metal stool. "Every year the Induction is different to ensure students don't have advance knowledge of how best to approach the problems that are given. You figured out the purpose of the final test faster than anyone expected. It makes Professor Holt and Dr Barnes wonder whether you received help."

"They think I cheated?" Anger punches through me.

I would never cheat in order to make a better grade. Just the thought of doing so is offensive. I was taught to respect myself and those around me more than that. But the flash of anger burns out fast and is followed by an icy streak of fear. Do they penalise students for cheating? If so, what could the punishment be?

"They don't know what to think." Ian sighs. He nods for me to take the stool next to him. "Look, I only caught part of the conversation. Professor Holt and Dr Barnes were disturbed by how quickly you recognised the insolvability of the task. Dr Barnes said The Testing demonstrated that one of your greatest strengths is your willingness to trust your intuition. You trusting your instinct now is to be expected, but there were things about your Testing that were never explained. Things that, in light of these most recent tests, concern him now."

"Like what?"

"He didn't say, but Professor Holt seemed to know. She agreed that there have been irregularities and your past results should be re-examined. If necessary, she said, the University should take action."

"What kind of action?" Redirection or something else?

"I didn't hear anything more, but Professor Holt pulled me aside after your team went inside the residence." Ian frowns. "She wants me to use my influence as your guide to get close to you. I'm also supposed to tell her the minute I see you struggling to keep up with your studies."

"If you're going to spy on me, why are you telling me this?"

"Because I'm not going to be spying on you." Ian smiles. "I'm going to help you. When Professor Holt asks, I'm going to tell her you're a hard-working student who's dedicated to her studies and the University."

"Why?" The word is barely a whisper. "You're graduating this year. Why risk your future to help me?" Michal said he would find someone to assist me. Is Ian that person? Is he one of the upper-year rebels? If so, which faction does he support? And what does he remember about his own Testing?

I can't ask. And he doesn't say. So I can only wonder and worry as his smile fades and he says, "You've done everything they've asked. You left your friends, your family and your colony behind to come here. You not only made it through The Testing, orientation and your Early Studies exams, but you excelled. If you were from Tosu City, Dr Barnes and Professor Holt would be praising your deductive reasoning. Instead, they are looking for a reason to eliminate you from the programme, because they're worried you're too smart. That you could be too strong a leader."

I can barely breathe. "Has Professor Holt asked Will's

guide to spy on him?"

"I talked to Sam a couple of hours ago. Professor Holt never spoke to him."

Will, who proved his inability to trust and be trusted, who killed and betrayed during The Testing, is not being watched. Only me.

Did someone besides Michal see me running from the TU Administration building after Obidiah was Redirected? Do they suspect I now know what Redirection means and that Dr Barnes's precious Testing process disposes of those who are not deemed smart enough but are too smart to let go? Did Michal say something that made them wonder?

"So now what?" I ask.

"Classes start on Monday. You go to class. You do the work. Your class schedule is going to be tough. Professor Holt wants you to fail. We're not going to let that happen." Ian takes a piece of paper off the metal lab table. My class schedule. One by one, he tells me what to expect from the classes. What kinds of tests the teachers will give. Which professors favour students who speak up in class and which ones like those who stay silent and prove themselves through papers and exams. And though I listen carefully and am grateful for the assistance, I can't help wondering why Ian is giving it. Yes, he is a colony student like me, but I know that doesn't tell the entire story. There is something more at work here. Something I believe directly relates to Michal and the rebellion. But without Ian's confirmation, I can't know whether my suspicions are right.

"The homework and tests are going to be hard to keep up with when you add in the internship. Officially, your internship responsibilities will only fall on Fridays, when no classes are in session, but that's rarely the case. When the internships get assigned, we'll know exactly what you're dealing with in terms of extra workload."

"What was your internship like?" I ask.

My father once mentioned he worked with soil scientists during his time at the University. They were perfecting a method of removing radiation from samples collected during a research tour made of the East Coast. I always assumed his work was part of a class, but now that I am here at the University, I understand that it was something more. He wasn't working with professors. My father was working side by side with the people who were in charge of the biological revitalisation plan for the entire country. The idea that we get to in some small way begin to help alter the path of the country is thrilling, but the fact that my father said so little about the experience makes me nervous about what surprises the internships themselves might hold.

Ian describes his job working as an aide for the department head of Resource Management, which sounds less exciting than I might have imagined. "Mostly, I ran errands and wished I was back here studying for whatever test I was worried I'd fail. At one point, I was given the job of summarising colony reports about resource production. I spent hours detailing crop yields and livestock births, thinking I was finally doing something important. Then I learned the reports were several months old. They just wanted to see whether I understood which parts of the reports were important."

Another test. Ian passed. I hope I can do the same.

Sleep doesn't come easy. When it does, my dreams are filled with images of events that may or may not be real. My father telling me to study hard. Malachi's hand in mine as life drains out of his eyes. A dim hallway, at the end of which are brightly lit doors marked by numbers. Blood being washed down rain-soaked streets. A yellow dress. The sound of gunfire. Broken streets.

I bite back a scream as I wake. The sky is still dark. The clock says only an hour has gone by since I climbed into bed. I push away the dreams, force myself to breathe in and out until my muscles relax. In three days, classes will begin. Professor Holt has set me up to fail. Why? Do the administrators believe I have regained my memory of The Testing and because of that understand better how they think? Is there a chance Dr Barnes and Professor Holt know there is an underground movement to remove them from power, and are they looking for people who may be in contact with it?

Whatever the reason, Dr Barnes and Professor Holt have a problem with me. They have set things up in a way they believe will lead to my downfall. Or, at the very least, my being ranked below the other first-year students. They mentioned irregularities in my Testing as the cause of their concern, but I can't remember enough to know what I did to gain their attention.

The Transit Communicator recording tells me I figured out how to remove the bracelet and the listening device it contained. I must have removed it to make the recording. Could they be aware of my ability to keep some things hidden from them? Is whatever I kept from their watchful eyes now the source of their concern? I don't know. And while the only way to beat them at this new game is to do as Ian says and excel at my classes, I cannot help but worry. If they expect me to fail, how will they react when I do not? Will scoring top marks keep me safe, or will it prompt anger and punishment?

All my life, I have believed that hard work and effort will be rewarded. Not just with grades but with results. Healthy plants. Abundant food sources. Clean water. Energy to light our homes. Machines that make it possible to communicate and share information to further our country's growth and help us all not only survive but thrive. For the first time, I am forced to contemplate the possibility that the harder I work, the less I will achieve. That I should work to be average instead of endeavouring to excel. But I'm not convinced that doing so would not draw even more attention, since I have spent the last few months striving for the top marks in my class. Anything less might make my professors question my dedication to the University or make them wonder if I'm aware of their scrutiny. The only real hope I have for success is Michal and Symon's rebels.

Tension makes my head throb. Closing my eyes, I pull the blankets tight around my shoulders and will the nightmares away. But the dreams still come. A grey-haired man smiling through a fence. Zandri asking me to explain how she died. I open my mouth to tell her, but nothing comes out. Because I don't know. I need to know.

Zandri fades away, and I see Tomas smiling at me. Holding me in the dark. Speaking of love. Whispering that he might have found a way to keep our memories. He holds up a pill and smiles, and I yank myself out of sleep. Pushing aside the sweaty, tangled sheets, I sit up and work to hold on to the dream. Or is it a memory?

There is only one way to find out. Tomas.

The idea that Tomas has retained his Testing memories is hard to believe. That would mean he not only betrayed me by not telling me what happened to Zandri in The Testing but has deceived me ever since by keeping silent. The Tomas I grew up with in Five Lakes Colony was always honest. He would never have kept his memories of The Testing to himself.

But Tomas is changed. Just as I am. Memories or no, all of us who went into The Testing emerged different. Despite the alterations of our memory, somewhere in each of us resides the truth. Whether I like it or not, it is time for me to discover what that is.

Unfortunately, until the other three teams arrive and the bridge is replaced, I have no choice but to wait. With Professor Holt monitoring my behaviour, the enforced inactivity is probably a good thing. All morning, I find myself pacing the floor of my room or walking around the grounds outside.

It is early afternoon when Griffin's team arrives at the ravine and climbs out of the skimmer. After several minutes, I see them doing what we did – exploring the length of the divide for a better spot to cross. An hour later, they are joined by the four members of Jacoby's team. From my place under the willow, I squint into the late afternoon sunlight and try to make out what both teams are doing. Jacoby's team has begun to tinker with their skimmer – perhaps thinking they can use the parts to activate the motor on the bridge. Most of Griffin's team is working to knot ropes together. All but Raffe. From here, I can see him rubbing the bandage on his arm as he stares into the void. Griffin yells at him to help with the work, but Raffe ignores him. When Raffe does finally turn back to talk to his team, it is obvious he has figured out the solution. They all drop their ropes. Then Jacoby's group stops work as well. Ten minutes later, they are all standing in front of the residence.

The bridge has barely retracted when the last skimmer comes into view. Olive, Rawson and Vance climb out. I wait for the fourth, and realise it is only these three. The fourth of their team, a girl with long brown hair whose name I can't recall, is missing. Stranded at the zoo? Locked in a metal box, screaming for those who abandoned her to return? Or has her voice or air run out? I look towards the residence entrance, where Dr Barnes and Professor Holt stand. Neither looks surprised by the missing team member. Do they know if she is alive or dead? Do they care?

I turn back and watch Olive and her remaining team members pick up the knotted rope Griffin's team constructed. An hour passes. The rope bridge grows longer. Vance hammers pieces of wood together and attaches them to the ends of the rope. The sun begins to sink. The wind picks up, and several of the older Government Studies students disappear inside. After fifteen more minutes, Rawson throws down a section of rope and stalks away. Olive screams at him. He turns and yells something back. Vance stops his work and watches as his two teammates argue.

I see Rawson walk to the edge of the ravine and point across. Has he figured out the solution? Whatever he yells is too muddled for me to tell. Olive storms towards him, screaming something I can't make out. I see Olive's arms extend, make contact with Rawson's torso, and shove. Deliberate? Out of anger? It doesn't matter, because whatever the intent, the momentum pushes Rawson backwards and he disappears over the edge.

Screams fill the air. I race with everyone on this side towards the ravine. Ian pushes a sequence of buttons that engages the bridge's mechanisms. Several students peer over the edge. I pray that Rawson somehow landed on a ledge or grabbed on to a piece of protruding rock and choke back a sob as those who are closest shake their heads. The bridge locks into place, and I can't help it – I run onto the platform and look down into the hole that goes on for hundreds if not thousands of feet. And see nothing. Rawson, a boy who left his colony and survived The Testing, is gone.

CHAPTER 11

Mine is not the only face streaked with tears. As I look around, I see students huddled in groups, their eyes wide with shock and sorrow. Across the bridge, the final-year guide Sam has his arm tight around Olive, who is kneeling at the edge of the ravine, shrieking Rawson's name. Horror is etched into every inch of her face. The shrieks turn to sobs as Sam gets Olive onto her feet and steers her to the bridge.

Olive takes one step onto the metal walkway, breaks free of Sam's hold and runs. Not over the bridge towards the residence, but away. Sam turns and races after her, but Olive is fast and soon disappears. Whether the push was deliberate or an accident born of anger and stress, it's clear from her reaction that Olive never intended for Rawson to go over the edge. I can't imagine how she will live with the guilt that action will bring. Quiet murmurs and sniffles fill the air as we all watch the horizon, waiting for Olive and Sam to return. They do not.

Once a dry-eyed Vance stands on this side of the bridge,

Professor Holt steps from under the tree into the dwindling sunshine and asks us to gather near. "Normally, we would hold the Induction ceremony tonight. However, in light of this tragedy, it will be postponed until tomorrow so together we can mourn the loss of Rawson Fisk. Dr Barnes and I will be available to talk to those who need help dealing with this terrible event. All leaders are forced to confront tragedy, but we are sorry that you have to face it so early in your careers. Please let an official know if you are struggling to cope with this horrible loss. We are here to help."

Dr Barnes puts his arm around a sniffling girl and leads her into the residence. His posture speaks of caring and concern, but I see the cold calculation in his eyes as they sweep across the mourning crowd. Is he making note of the students who cry or the ones whose eyes are dry? Does he believe tears make a better leader? Will the students who come to him in search of comfort find themselves suddenly placed behind the rest of the pack, or will they be considered worthier of a high leadership position? It is impossible to know, and I am not interested in staying here and finding out.

When Dr Barnes and Professor Holt disappear inside the residence, I head in the opposite direction. Away from whatever new test Rawson's death has spawned. When I cross the bridge, my throat tightens. I know I will see Rawson in my dreams and wonder for the rest of my life if making a different choice when selecting my team could have saved his life. Would he be safe inside, preparing to start classes on Monday, if I had picked him first instead of the person I thought would help my team come out on top? While I know Rawson's death is not my fault, I cannot help the guilt I feel. My team won this Induction task, but that victory wasn't worth the cost. No victory is.

One more tear slides down my cheek and into the darkness below as I stop at the end of the bridge and whisper my farewell to Rawson. I wouldn't have counted him among my friends, but he deserved so much better. Then, taking a deep breath, I turn in search of Tomas and the answers only he can give.

The Biological Engineering residence is easy to find. Unlike Government Studies, Biological Engineering houses its students just steps away from the classrooms and labs they'll be studying in. But while it is easy to find the red-brick two-storey structure, I'm not sure what to do now that I'm here. In the short time I've been assigned to my residence, I have yet to see anyone other than Government Studies students inside or around our building. If there are rules that govern how students of different designated studies interact, I'm unaware of them. Still, there's a chance my appearance at the Biological Engineering residence could cause trouble. Tomas might not appreciate the unwanted attention, and I'm held in enough suspicion as it is.

I find a spot on the grass next to the building across the street from Tomas's residence and pretend to stare off in the distance, all the while keeping the front door in my periphery. Several older-looking students come out laughing. A few students go in. I wonder whether the Biological Engineering first years are still undergoing their own Induction. Maybe that's why I see so few students come and go. A metallic taste fills my mouth at the idea of Tomas and the others facing the same kinds of challenges we did. The same dangers. But then I see a familiar tall brunette strut out the front door, and I spring to my feet. I'd almost forgotten that Kit was assigned to Biological Engineering. If she is here, Tomas could be nearby. She might be able to tell me where to find him or pass along a message.

I follow Kit as she heads down the walkway and turns a corner. Once we are both out of sight of her residence, I pick up the pace. "Kit. Wait up."

She stops and turns, and her eyes narrow. "What are you doing here? I thought people in Government Studies were going through orientation this week."

"Who told you that?"

"Tomas. He asked his final-year guide if he could visit some of his friends in other designated fields of study and was told both the Medicine and Government Studies students were unavailable until classes on Monday." She tosses her waist-length hair and smiles. "What happened? Did you get Redirected like Obidiah?"

The mention of Obidiah's name and the amused expression on Kit's face, combined with the fresh horror of Rawson's death, makes my hands ball into fists. I want to lash out the way I used to do when I was younger and my brothers picked on me.

Swallowing the bitterness bubbling inside, I say, "There was an accident. Rawson is dead."

The smug expression vanishes. "Rawson? Our Rawson?"

The tears that glisten in her eyes make the ones I've been holding at bay surface. Wiping the wetness from my cheeks, I nod. "They postponed our Induction ceremony so people could get counselling. I needed to get away." It's the truth, even if it isn't the entire reason for my being here. "Do you know where Tomas is? I want to tell him about Rawson before he hears it from someone else."

"I think he said he was going to the library. A few of our final years were talking about a new gene-splicing technique we've never heard of. He wanted to see if he could find out more about it."

Before she finishes the sentence, I'm turning and yelling my thanks. Then I run as though I can outdistance the sorrow that threatens to spill over.

The library is large. Made of concrete, glass and faded brick, the building somehow survived the worst of the wars with its contents intact. Most of the damage it suffered was caused after the wars were over by people using the books and furniture for kindling. No one knows how much of the history once contained inside is now missing because of the cold, sometimes chemical-laden winds that whipped through the Midwest during the Sixth Stage. When the United Commonwealth was officially established, one of its first laws banished the practice of book burning. Though our leaders agreed that warmth was important, they believed preserving the written documentation of our history and culture was even more vital. All citizens who had books were directed to bring them to this library, where an official exchanged the valuable pages for blankets, clothing or other resources. The exchange allowed the country to retain memories from the past that could help rebuild the future.

The result of that law is housed inside this building. Row upon row of books. Some filled with mathematics and history. Others with stories meant for entertainment. Books deemed too faded or damaged to be of use are sent to Omaha Colony for recycling. As revitalisation expands the borders of Tosu City and the colonies, new books are found and added. Each colony has its own library. Our collection in Five Lakes is housed in a small waterproofed shed next to the school. But none can rival the pages of our past that can be found here.

I catch sight of a figure bounding down the library's concrete steps. My heart swells as Tomas's handsome face turns in my direction. I can tell the minute he spots me standing in the shadow of a tree, and I wait for happiness to light his face.

But it doesn't.

Love doesn't leap to his eyes. The dimple that makes me sigh stays hidden from view. His expression and the defensive way his arms are crossing his chest tell me loud and clear that my appearance is unwelcome. After the death of Rawson and learning that Professor Holt is monitoring my life, I should be incapable of surprise or of feeling more hurt. I'm not. Despair builds inside me, making it hard to breathe. A cold chill of panic follows closely behind.

"Hey, Tomas, wait up." A small, wiry-haired boy with a pointed nose hurries down the stairs. Tomas turns so I can see only his profile, but it is enough to spot the dimple appear as he waves his hand in greeting. The other boy reaches Tomas and says, "I'll walk back to the residence with you."

"I'm not going back to the residence yet. There's a plant I spotted yesterday by the chicken coop. Because of the Induction, I didn't have time to look..." Tomas's words trail off as he glances at the pointy-nosed boy, who is sagging under the weight in his arms. "I could find the plant after I help you take your books back to our residence. They look a little heavy for you to carry on your own."

The boy frowns. "They're not that heavy. I've carried far more than this back to the residence. Go ahead and track down your plant. I can take care of myself." The boy shifts his grip on the books and trudges down the walkway as if to prove his point.

Tomas immediately walks in the opposite direction. Not once does he glance at me or encourage me to follow. But I do. Because, despite his earlier expression, I know Tomas. He will be waiting for me.

With classes out of session until Monday, few people walk the campus. Still, I am careful not to walk behind Tomas in case someone is watching. I leave the walkway and cross the grass, taking a more direct route.

The chicken coop doesn't contain chickens. At least, it doesn't now. Though a great number of animal species were killed off by the wars, for some reason chickens survived mostly unscathed. Scientists speculate that the genetic enhancements and antibiotics given to the female chickens to help protect such an important food source helped keep them immune from the worst of the post-war afflictions. Male chickens, however, were not as lucky. In the years leading up to the Seven Stages of War, roosters were given fewer drugs since they weren't as vital a source of sustenance. Fewer of them survived the onslaught of chemicals released by biological warfare. Those that did survive suffered a variety of physical ailments, including partial paralysis, nerve damage or cancerous growths. With so few living roosters, the chicken population began to die off, so this coop was created.

Through a great deal of trial and error, Commonwealth scientists boosted the roosters' immune systems, filtered out the genetic changes caused by the wartime chemicals, and created a new breed that could thrive in this new environment. This old brick building was too small for most of the University's needs, so it was chosen to house the new generation of roosters as they were studied and refined. During orientation, we learned that the building was last used to house animals over sixty years ago. Since then, the building had been cleaned of chicken feathers, but no other official use for it had been found. Instead it has become a destination for the occasional student looking for a quiet indoor place to study when the tension of the residence and the library gets too high. Of course, this is only when the weather is nice. The roof is known to leak.

The red brick of the building is faded. The bright sunshine highlights every crack in the mortar. I stand on the walkway in front of the door and look around the area to see if anyone is watching before I turn the handle and step inside.

The interior of the building is filled with bits of grass and dried leaves. My nose wrinkles as it catches the scent of a mouse or small animal who must have died somewhere nearby. Though it would be more pleasant to go back outside and wait, I do a thorough search of both the main room and the smaller one to the right for hidden cameras, all the while pretending to examine the electrical systems. If someone is watching, I don't want that person to know I'm aware of it. When I find no signs of observation, I walk to a corner of the main room, where I will be out of view from anyone who might glance through a window, and slide to the dusty floor. Slipping the bag off my shoulder, I pull my legs up to my chest, rest my head on my knees and wait. I shiver as the cold of the concrete seeps into my body.

More than once, I stop myself from moving around to keep warm or glancing out the window to see if Tomas is coming. Instead, I close my eyes and think about the happiness I felt when I first arrived at the University and saw this building. It was a week after The Testing. The sun was hot on my skin and I couldn't stop smiling. I had made it through the Testing. I was living my dream of following in my father's footsteps. Everything was possible, especially with Tomas holding my hand firmly in his. I hadn't known then how precious that happiness was. How free I felt or how quickly I would realise that nothing about my life was as I thought. That I was trapped.

Did Tomas know that then? I try to picture his face as we walked around the campus, discussing our futures. Were there signs that he retained his Testing memories? Did he understand then what our future really held? And if so, can I live with not only the betrayal of his silence but whatever actions his silence is hiding?

All thoughts of betrayal and secrets disappear as the door swings open and Tomas walks inside. When he opens his arms, I don't hesitate for a second before rising and stepping into them. No matter what has happened, Tomas is part of my past. He is part of my home. In the warmth and safety of Tomas's arms, the tears fall unchecked. As I bury my face in Tomas's chest, the picture of Rawson stumbling into nothingness replays in my mind. I was too far away to see the look on his face, but I can imagine how the frustration over the task jolted into terror as he slid into the abyss. He left his colony to come here and provide aid to the country. So much hope. Gone in an instant.

Tomas says nothing as I soak his shirt in tears. His arms hold me tight, offering comfort and protection. When my emotions are wrung dry, he doesn't ask for an explanation. He just places a soft kiss on my lips, tells me he loves me and says, "I'm sorry it took so long to get here. I was worried you'd think I wasn't coming."

"I knew you'd be here." It might be the only thing I really was certain of. "Were you worried someone was following you?" I know I backtracked once on my way here just in case Dr Barnes had someone trailing me.

Tomas shakes his head. "I ran into Professor Kenzie, the head of our residence. He wanted to talk about whether I'd be interested in adding another class to my schedule."

"How many have you been assigned?"

"Six. Agreeing to take the new class was the fastest way to get here to you, so I guess I'm now taking seven."

That's a lot, but still two less than me.

The tension I feel must show on my face, because Tomas's eyes narrow with concern. "How many classes do you have?"

"Nine." By the way Tomas's eyes widen, I can tell none of the first years in his field of study have been assigned as many. I doubt anyone in any discipline has. Dr Barnes has singled me out. Already, I feel the pressure. Pushing that aside, I ask, "What is your residence like?"

"At first it was great. There are ten labs in the basement for us and a greenhouse out back so we don't have to walk to the controlled environment dome in the stadium. We were excited to get our class schedules and start work. Then our Induction started."

Dread grips me as he talks about walking with his fellow

first-year students into the large stadium at the edge of the University campus. Our Early Studies orientation instructor told us the stadium contained a greenhouse. Inside that greenhouse, the final-year Biological Engineering students had constructed an obstacle course designed to test the knowledge and resourcefulness of the incoming class. I try to picture what Tomas describes – seven stations where students were required to identify plants or animals by touch or smell or by reading lines of their genetic code. A correct answer meant passing to the next station. An incorrect one required the first-year student to face a physical challenge. Failure to pass the physical challenge resulted in elimination from the obstacle course and Redirection out of the Biological Engineering programme and the University.

Redirection.

Bile rises in my throat. The word rings loud in my head, so I barely hear Tomas talk about the one question he answered incorrectly and the hundred-foot-long, fifteen-foot-wide path filled with hazardous plant life he had to navigate before being allowed to proceed to the next station.

"Most of the ground and shrubs were covered with poison ivy. Not the kind with the pink veins, although I saw a few of those near the edges of the path. Mostly, it was the typical variety we have growing at the edges of my father's farm."

Tomas is healthy and whole and seated beside me, but I still let out a sigh of relief. The garden-variety poison ivy isn't fun. I walked through a patch of it when my father let me tag along on a scouting mission when I was six. If it weren't for the salve Dr Flint put on my ankles, I would have scratched them raw. The red, itchy skin was unpleasant, but it didn't kill me. Had I run into the other kind of poison ivy, I wouldn't have lived. My father says radiation interacted with the oily allergen contained in the leaves, transforming that strain into something incredibly deadly. While brushing the skin with the allergen will only cause blister-laden rashes, a touch of the oil on the tongue or an open wound as small as a pinprick will allow the poison to penetrate. Once the poison is inside the body, it attacks the cardiovascular system and typically results in pulmonary failure. Burning the plant and breathing in the fumes causes an even speedier death.

My father and brothers have carefully destroyed several small patches of pink ivy around our colony, using gloves to pull the roots from the soil and a special chemical to kill the plant and counteract the effects of the poisonous oils. I shouldn't be surprised that someone would think it appropriate to use such a dangerous plant as part of a residence initiation, but I am. Perhaps because I know from my father's work that pink ivy has been spotted in only six colonies. Never once has it been reported in the area surrounding Tosu City. Students who grew up in the city might never have come across or even heard of the deadly plant. Unless they got lucky, they wouldn't stand a chance.

Tomas continues. "Your dad would have been able to identify all the plants there, but I couldn't. I spotted poison sumac, prickly poppy and the red-flowered jessamine that killed off Scotty Rollison's goats when we were kids."

The red flowers are another wartime mutation; they're filled with pollen that attacks the immune system.

"Since I didn't know all the plants, I tucked the bottom of my pant legs into my boots and stuck with the path I knew wasn't going to kill me. I walked across the poison ivy, reached the other side and moved on to the next station."

Smart. Although, by the way he scratches at his left calf, I'm guessing he might need some salve.

Tomas doesn't seem to realise he is scratching. His eyes are far away. Lost in a memory. "There were fifteen of us first years when we started Initiation. Only eight made it through. Five of us from the colonies and three from Tosu City. The rest..." His voice trails off, but I know the ending to the sentence.

The unsuccessful students were Redirected out of the programme. Removed from the University? I picture Obidiah being loaded into the skimmer and feel tears threaten again as I grieve for students whose names I don't know and wonder about those I care about. What has become of Stacia? Did she survive the Medical Induction? And what has become of the others? Will I see their faces on campus, or will they join the ones in my dreams?

I take Tomas's hand and entwine my fingers with his and then tell him about my experience. The scavenger hunt. Picking teams. The snake. The air-field. The trek around the city that showed how much work still needs to be done to rewind the clock to the days before the wars. I don't tell him about the conversation I had with Michal before moving to the residence or about the rebels. Not yet.

Tomas's hand tightens around mine when I mention teaming up with Will. Ever since listening to the recording, I've wondered if Tomas's subconscious remembers the events I outlined on the Transit Communicator. But now I'm forced to consider whether my dream was right. If this dislike of Will is proof that Tomas's memories of The Testing are intact.

Ignoring the gnawing anxiety, I tell the rest. Being manoeuvered into climbing into the steel box. My certainty that I had been abandoned. Choosing to free Damone despite his horrific behaviour. Reaching the final task. Learning that Dr Barnes and Professor Holt are watching my every move. Waiting for me to do something that will result in my elimination from the University. My Redirection.

I hug my arms to my chest as I tell of Rawson's final moments. The hands that pushed him and sent him stumbling to his death. The shattered reaction of the girl who killed without understanding what effect her act of frustration would bring. Finally, the guilt I feel over my part in the loss of Rawson's life.

"It's not your fault, Cia." Tomas shifts so he is sitting across from me. His eyes meet mine with fierce intensity as he reaches for my hands.

"I know." I do, but part of me still believes my choice in teammates would have made a difference.

I glance down at my hands held tight in Tomas's and notice he no longer wears the bracelet of the Early Studies colony students. Circling his wrist is a heavy gold and silver band. Etched on the centre disk is a stylised tree underscored by three wavy lines. The tree is an obvious symbol for a field of study dedicated to revitalising the earth. The tangible proof that Tomas has become a part of something I am not tugs at my heart. For the first time since we left Five Lakes, we are not part of the same team. Separated by symbols. Maybe more.

Removing my hands from his, I know it is time to find out how great the divide between us is.

CHAPTER 12

"I've started having dreams," I say. "Like my father."

Before I left for The Testing, my father told me about his dreams. Dreams filled with a decaying city and explosions that ripped apart flesh and bone. Whether the dreams were real or imagined my father couldn't say, but he shared them with me in the hope they might prepare me for what was to come. He used the dreams to demonstrate a lesson he needed me to learn. Not to trust anyone. But I did.

The way Tomas stills and the wary look in his eyes makes my nerves jump. "How long have you been having them?"

"A while." The scars on my arm tingle, and I swallow hard. "I don't recall everything yet, but I remember some things."

His eyes search mine. "What do you remember?"

"Not much. Mostly flashes. Malachi dying. Will smiling over the barrel of a gun. You and me plotting to prevent the memory loss." My heart slams against my chest as I wait for him to say something. Anything. The silence lasts a minute. Two. Each second that passes stretches my nerves. Pulls at my heart until I can't take it any longer. "You remember."

Sorrow, horror and an emotion I can't identify flicker across his face before his features go blank. "Remember what?"

"Everything. You took the pills. You kept your memory of The Testing. All this time. You remember." I scramble to my feet even as my conscience is pricked by the fact that I too have some memories. That the Transit Communicator gave me a glimpse into the past. Something I never shared with Tomas.

But that self-reproach burns away as I hear guilt and fear snake through Tomas's words. "I didn't know how to tell you." He climbs to his feet and holds out a hand I refuse to take. Pacing the small area between the windows, he says, "We were each supposed to take one of the pills, but I didn't have time to get you one before they gave out the results. I thought there would be time. I'm still not sure why I took one of the pills before getting my results. Maybe I was hoping the medication would wear off before they performed the memory erasure. You wouldn't think I went back on our agreement, and I wouldn't have to remember. But I do."

Pain blooms deep at the confirmation of Tomas's betrayal. Hot anger. Icy terror. How could he not have told me? I force myself to stay strong and not give in to the rush of emotion. There are things I have to know if I want to survive. Answers that only Tomas and his memory can give.

I take a deep breath, swallow down the suffocating hurt, and will my voice to stay steady. "Dr Barnes is watching me. Something I did during The Testing made him think I'm some kind of threat. What did I do?"

"I don't know." The words and concern on his face ring true. "You figured out how to remove the identification bracelets, which allowed us to talk without being overheard. Maybe Dr Barnes is wondering about the silences that occurred when we left them behind."

A possibility I'd already considered.

"When you realised the bracelets contained microphones, you were worried that Testing officials recorded our conversations before we reached The Testing centre. I didn't think they would bother since they had cameras watching us, but maybe they did. Dr Barnes could have heard you mention spotting the cameras or you telling me about your father's dreams."

The idea that Dr Barnes might know about my father's flashes of Testing memory makes me shiver. But while that would give Dr Barnes cause to strike out at my family, I can't imagine why my pre-Testing conversation with Tomas would draw his attention now. Surely, if that discussion was recorded, Dr Barnes and the other Testing officials would have listened to it before finalising their decisions about who would attend the University.

If Dr Barnes were concerned about those things, he would be targeting Tomas, too. But Tomas hasn't been assigned nine classes, and he has not had a sense of being watched more closely than anyone else. Which means something else has prompted Dr Barnes's interest. Something Tomas doesn't remember or refuses to say. I will have to figure out Dr Barnes's motivation on my own.

Now there is only one last thing to ask. I look into Tomas's handsome face. His grey eyes are filled with worry, guilt and love for me. I yearn to touch him, but keep my hands firmly at my sides. I open my mouth to speak the words that have the potential to shatter everything between us.

But I can't do it.

I would rather live with speculation and uncertainty than lose the one piece of my life that connects me to my home and family. The alternative is too painful to think about. If that brands me a coward, so be it. I do not want to face being here at the University alone.

Tomas takes my hand, and I let him web his fingers through mine and pull me back to the ground. I lean my head on his shoulder and try to ignore the hollow ache

I feel. We talk of inconsequential things – the size of the rooms at our residences, our guides, the attitudes of the first-year Tosu City students.

"The ones in my house didn't have any interest in talking to those of us from the colonies until after the Induction. Maybe that was part of the reason for those tests. To make us realise that, no matter where we grew up, we all have the same problems to solve. We're not that different," Tomas says.

I wonder if he's right. Are the Tosu City students more likely to think of us as equals now?

Tomas pulls me close. I lay my head against his heart. Its beat is steady and strong. Quietly, he says, "I meant to tell you that I kept my Testing memories, but I didn't know how. You were so happy when The Testing was over. So much like the girl I graduated with back home. I wanted to give you time to just be happy. I promised myself I'd tell you after your birthday, but I could never find the right moment. The subject would change, or you'd smile and kiss me and I'd put it off. I kept telling myself that I'd do it tomorrow."

He's not wrong about the subject changing. I knew Tomas had something to tell me, and I didn't want to learn what it was. I was a coward. Terrified that whatever secrets Tomas harboured would shatter my fragile hope that the stories on the Transit Communicator weren't real. I didn't want to face the truth, so I ran from it then. Now I have to face my fears.

"What happened to Zandri?" The words are barely a whisper.

Tomas stiffens beside me. The hand that was stroking my hair stills. He knows the answer, but says nothing. Part of me wants to pretend he didn't hear the question. Everything inside me screams to walk away now before I lose everything. But I don't, because I don't want to be like Damone. Because Zandri deserves better. Because if Tomas was behind her death, then I have already lost everything. I just don't know it. Pretending otherwise is a lie. I have had enough of lies.

I turn my head to face Tomas, and my words are stronger this time. "During the last test, what happened to Zandri?"

Tomas's eyes shift away from mine. "I don't know."

Something inside me shuts down, and I pull away from him. "That's not true. You had her bracelet in your bag."

Silence. This time I refuse to be the one who breaks it. Tomas finally does. "What do you remember?"

Nothing. Just my whispered, sometimes unintelligible words asking Dr Barnes about Zandri's fate. His laughing response that I should already know. Finding the bracelet among my possessions. Not knowing what it meant. Only that I had found it in Tomas's bag while trying to keep him alive after Will's final betrayal. In the darkness, I assumed the bracelet was from another Testing candidate who was killed during the test, but I was mistaken. Tomas met Zandri on the unrevitalised plains of the fourth test, and he never told me.

But my secrets aren't the ones in question now, so I say, "It doesn't matter what I recall. I want to know what happened. You saw Zandri. I know you did because you took her identification bracelet off her bag and put it in your own. Why? What happened to her? What did you do?"

Tomas clenches and unclenches his hands, and suddenly I am not here. I am standing on the cracked earth. Back in the Testing area. My left arm aches under white bandages. My skin itches and is coated with sweat and dirt. Tomas stands in front of me, looking travel-stained and tense as his hands clench at his side. Next to his hands, hanging from a sheath strapped to his pants, is a knife. A knife streaked with blood. There are hundreds of ways the blood could have gotten on Tomas's blade, but only one that explains his silence now.

"You killed Zandri."

"It was a mistake."

"A mistake?" Part of me has desperately held out hope that Tomas was not responsible. That's the part that begins to scream. "How do you kill someone by mistake? Zandri was our friend." More Tomas's friend than mine. She flirted with him. She might have even been in love with him. And he ended her life.

I can't stay here. I'm on my feet and bolting for the exit, but Tomas is fast and gets there before me. Not just fast. Years of working side by side with his father on the farm have made him strong. I kick and push, but no matter how I fight, I can't move him out of the path of the door.

"You have to listen to me." Tomas clamps his hands on my shoulders, and I jerk back. I can't bear to have him touch me. I want to lean into the warmth and security he has always provided, but I won't let myself. Not any more. The safety I feel with him is a lie.

Tomas removes his hands and runs one through his dark, wavy hair. "You have to listen. I never intended to hurt Zandri. You left to find water. Will and I fought. I was so angry. Mad that I was injured. Angry that you wouldn't leave Will behind and that you stormed off and left me there with him. And I was furious that we were out in the middle of nowhere because Dr Barnes and his people wanted to see who would kill in order to succeed. Will walked off carrying the canteen with the last of our water. He probably thought taking it would keep me from leaving, but I didn't care. I picked my bicycle off the ground and climbed on, thinking I'd come find you. That's when I saw her."

Blood pounds through my ears. My stomach heaves. I don't want to hear about the death of the blonde artist who was always so beautiful and confident. But I wrap my arms around myself as though they will provide a barrier against the chill seeping through my body, and I wait for the rest.

"At first I didn't recognise her. Her arms and face were stained with dirt. It wasn't until the sunlight caught the gold in her hair that I realised who was staggering down the road towards me."

Closing my eyes, I picture Zandri outside of the Five Lakes school – her eyes laughing, the gauzy dresses she favoured smudged with paint, and her golden hair shining bright in the sun. It's almost impossible to imagine her as Tomas describes. Dirty and dishevelled and dead.

"She screamed when she spotted me and ran from me. I should have let her go. She might have lived if I hadn't given chase." Pain shadows Tomas's face. Guilt weaves through his halting words. "But I had to see if she was all right. I knew you'd want me to."

The words slap my heart.

"She wasn't steady on her feet, so it wasn't hard to catch up. When I did, she snarled and bit until I finally made her understand who I was and that I wasn't going to hurt her. I never meant to hurt her."

Tomas's face is pale. His eyes filled with grief. "She was so relieved finally to find someone she could trust. Then Will appeared, and Zandri went crazy. She lunged at Will, and he pushed her back and yelled at her to stop. But she didn't. She accused him of sabotaging their team in the third test and then started shouting at me. Seeing me with Will must have scared her. She said that I couldn't be trusted – that no one could – and attacked. She had a stick that was sharpened to a point.

"She caught Will in the side, and he punched her hard across the mouth. Suddenly, I had my knife in my hand. She must have thought I was going to use it on her. Or maybe she wasn't thinking at all. I don't know, because I didn't pay attention to her. I was too busy yelling at Will. Watching him pull out his gun. I threatened him with my knife. He laughed, which made me even angrier. I was glad I had an excuse to hurt him. I didn't know I could be happy at the thought of causing someone pain. I don't know why I listened to him when he yelled for me to watch out. But I did, and I turned."

Tomas looks down at his hands. "The knife punched through her stomach. I can still feel her blood as it drained her life across my hands. The next thing I knew, Will was helping me lay her on the ground and she was gone."

There are tears on Tomas's cheeks. My arms ache to reach for him, to soothe the pain and grieve with him for the loss of our friend. But I don't know how to cross the divide our secrets have built between us.

"Will grabbed Zandri's canteen. I took the bracelet off her bag. We buried her in a dry riverbed." He wipes the tears from his face and shakes his head. "I've replayed it a hundred times in my mind. If only one thing had gone differently. If I hadn't taken out my knife. If Will hadn't appeared when he did or yelled for me to turn. If you hadn't left Will and me alone—"

Disbelief steals my breath. "This is my fault?"

"I don't know." Anger and guilt simmer in every word.

Tomas might say he doesn't know, but I do. I can see the accusation. The bitterness. The hurt. Tomas is angry. Angry he took a life. Angry he was put in the position to do so.

Because of me.

But while my choice to trust Will was wrong, I was not to blame. Dr Barnes and The Testing officials put us on that patch of cracked earth. Tomas allowed his frustration with Will to boil over. He let his emotions get the best of him and drew his weapon. He will have to live with that.

Some of what I'm thinking must show on my face because Tomas reaches out his hand and steps towards me. "I don't blame you."

"Yes, you do." My words are quiet. Calm. The truth.

My voice is as hollow as my heart when I say, "It's getting late. We both need to get back. People are watching."

Tomas doesn't stop me as I walk around him and open the door, but his voice chases over my shoulder as I start to step outside. "You aren't to blame, Cia. I am. But so is The Testing and every official who works for it. They deserve to pay for what they've done."

The words make me stop and look back at the boy I have known and cared for almost all my life. He looks years older and wiser than when we first climbed into the skimmer that delivered us to The Testing. We've changed. The Testing did that to us.

"You're right," I say. "They deserve to pay."

I want to be angry with Tomas. For his deception. For the terrible part he played in Zandri's death. I want to hate Will. His willingness to trade others' lives for his own success makes my stomach turn and my soul ache. Anger and hate are powerful, hot, energised. So different from the icy cold despair that fills me now.

I take a winding path through the University campus as I return to my residence. I tell myself that I am doing it to make sure anyone who sees me assumes I am out for a casual walk, but deep inside, I know different. Part of me wants Tomas to look for and find me. To convince me that we can still be partners. That our love is stronger than the terrible choices we have been forced to make. That I am not alone.

But I am.

By the time I arrive at the bridge to the Government Studies residence, all evidence of the final Induction task has been cleared away. No boxes or planks or tools. Nothing that speaks of the tragedy that occurred just hours earlier.

I step onto the bridge and peer down. This time I am not looking for Rawson; instead, I feel like I am looking for myself. Staring into the rocky void is like peering into a reflector of my emotions.

Shadows.

Emptiness.

A hole where once grass and flowers grew that has been transformed into a place where nothing thrives.

I close my eyes and see Rawson. Zandri. Malachi. My Testing roommate, Ryme. Other faces I have no names for, but whose empty eyes haunt me in my sleep. Lurking somewhere in the residence is Will. One who has been rewarded for murder and betrayal. How many others inside that building have killed without hesitation? How many have been rewarded for their treachery with the future leadership of our country? How can I face my fellow students each day wondering what horrors they are capable of?

The five scars on my left arm burn. The darkness of the void beckons, and for the briefest moment, I consider answering its call. I grip the steel railing and let the chill of the metal fill me. How easy it would be to let the emptiness swallow me. To find release from sadness at the bottom. To be welcomed by those I have lost and turn away from the problems I face now.

But I don't. I take my hand from the rail and step back. This is one choice I will never make.

There was a time immediately after the end of the wars when the hopelessness of the scarred world led many to seek the peace of death. I understand better now the despair that can lead to that choice, as well as the courage it takes to fight. The vision it takes for scientists like my father to create hope in his lab and watch it die over and over again until finally it flourishes in the blighted soil. The strength it requires to turn from the easy path and face the hard.

I look at the University campus – a place built on hope and a promise that those who study here will make this world better. A promise I believe in and will find the strength and courage to fight for. Starting Monday, I will do what it takes to get the information Michal and those working in secret need to bring down Dr Barnes and The Testing – no matter what the cost to me might be.

CHAPTER 13

Four of us are missing.

"Induction Day is a day filled with hope. Today you, our new students, will officially be accepted into the Government field of study." Professor Holt stands behind a small podium that has been placed under the willow tree near the Government Studies residence. Her hair is slicked off her face. Her scarlet-painted lips curl into an expression of geniality as she addresses those of us assembled here who are in her charge. First years stand in front. The rest of our fellow Government Studies students are behind us, ready to celebrate the entrance of our class into their ranks.

Or most of our class. Rawson is dead. Olive never returned to campus after her flight. Neither did the girl named Izzy who failed to finish Induction with her team. Those losses I knew about. But one student I expected to see is also unaccounted for. Vance – the blonde boy and fourth member of Olive's team – is missing. An entire team from Induction is gone. There are whispers that Olive,

Izzy and Vance left the University and returned home. For their sakes, I hope that is true.

"The Induction process was designed by the final years to show that not only will you rely on your own resourcefulness, but you will also need to trust and work effectively with others in order to succeed in the careers you have ahead of you. Those who cannot be trusted to consider the effects of their actions on others cannot be trusted to lead." Professor Holt sighs.

"Sadly, not all students who demonstrate the intellect required of Government Studies students also work well with others. We work hard to identify those students early in their careers so they can be Redirected into more appropriate fields. Because of this, only twelve of the sixteen initially directed into this field will embark upon studying it. It is our hope we will not need to re-evaluate the twelve of you remaining in the future."

First-year students shift beside me. The threat is unmistakable. Professor Holt's serious expression is replaced by a wide smile. "Your guides have collected and turned in the bracelets that identified you as members of the University's Early Studies programme. It is my honour to replace them now with the symbol you will serve for the rest of your lives."

She calls our names one by one and asks us to come

forward. Griffin struts. Damone preens. Others show various forms of pride as they hold out their arm and allow Professor Holt to fasten a thick bracelet onto their wrist. When my turn comes, I am careful to keep a pleased expression on my face despite the way my nerves jump as Professor Holt reaches out for my hand. The silver and gold coiled bracelet is cold as it slides over my skin. There is an audible click as Professor Holt fastens the band around my wrist.

Will's name is called as I take my place in line and study the bracelet. Gold and silver. The joining of the materials used for the colony and Tosu City Early Studies bracelets. Now the two types of metal are combined in a pattern that, like The Testing versions of the bracelets, makes it impossible to see where the band comes together. Fused to the centre is a disc made of silver, outlined in gold. Etched across the disc is a picture of scales suspended from a bar, hanging in perfect balance. Streaking through the middle of the disc from the top of the bar to below the scales is a lightning bolt. My personal symbol combined with the symbol for justice.

After Enzo receives his bracelet, Professor Holt congratulates us all again before her expression turns solemn. "Though today is a day of happiness, I would be remiss not to remember the life of Rawson Fisk. He was a student of keen intellect with a love of history and a passionate desire to do whatever it took to improve the lives of his family and colony.

He will be missed. But though his death is terrible, it is not without purpose." Professor Holt's tone changes from one of kindness to fervent conviction. "This tragedy demonstrates better than any classroom lesson that leaders can never let their emotions get the better of them. Cool heads and calm logic must always prevail if we are to succeed in restoring our country to what it was before the Seven Stages of War."

I hear murmurs of assent behind me.

"We will hang a plaque commemorating that sentiment in the residence to make sure Rawson Fisk's lesson is never forgotten."

As Professor Holt invites us inside the residence for a small celebration, I look towards the ravine and the bridge that was once missing.

"Hey, the party is inside."

Slowly, I turn to see Ian watching me. "I know. I wanted a few minutes to remember Rawson before I go in." The truth, but only a shade of it. "Professor Holt never mentioned what happened to the others. Were they Redirected?"

Ian looks over his shoulder at the residence. "I don't know." But I can see by the sorrow in his eyes that he does.

I finger the band on my wrist. "Are we ever allowed to take these off?"

"Dr Barnes insists on students wearing their identification at all times." A fierce intensity shines in Ian's eyes.

"Dr Barnes believes that the bracelet allows people you come in contact with to understand you are a future Commonwealth leader. More importantly, wearing your symbol demonstrates that you have accepted the future it represents."

A compelling reason, but I doubt it is more than a shadow of the real one. Horror streaks through me. The Testing bracelet contained a listening device. I was not wearing one of these Inducted-student bracelets in the chicken coop, but Tomas was. Did officials hear our conversation? Does Dr Barnes know Tomas remembers his Testing? Does he know that even though the two of us are separated by guilt and anger, we are unified in our desire to end the process that brought us here?

"Do you mind if I take a look at your bracelet?" Ian takes my arm and probes it with his fingers. "I thought the design looked a little different this year. See..." He uses his index fingers and thumbs to squeeze two spots on the band, and it clicks apart. "This one is thicker and looks a little heavier." He refastens the bracelet with a nod. "They talked about replacing the recorder with a tracking device last year. One of the first years got turned around while returning to campus from his internship. He was lucky safety officials found him in an unrevitalised part of the city before a wild animal did."

A tracking device. That is what is contained inside this

metal band. Since Ian freely shared this information, can I assume no one is recording or listening to our conversation?

"Hey, we should get inside so you don't miss the entire party. Trust me when I say you won't have a lot of time for parties when classes start in two days." As Ian turns towards the residence with a grin, I do the same.

I eat. I laugh at jokes. All the while, I feel the weight of the bracelet and the tracking device it contains on my arm. The party lasts long into the night. It is only when the upper years seek their beds that I feel I can return to my room without arousing comment. It takes me a dozen tries before I can replicate Ian's removal of the bracelet. I place it on the table and rub my wrist before examining the woven metal. I fish my pocket-knife out of my bag, hold the bracelet to the light and probe the back of the disc with the thinnest blade. The blade slides off the metal and nicks me twice before I find the almost imperceptible groove on the edge of the disc and pry off the back panel. Inside are a battery and an even smaller copper pulse radio transmitter.

Professor Holt spoke of the need for trust. Yet in front of me is the evidence to the contrary. I study the device. My father has never used homing devices, but Hamin and Zeen experimented with them as a method for tracking farm animals. The design of this one seems simple. A pulse signal is sent from this transmitter to a separate receiver, which communicates the location of the device. The size and simplistic design of the battery and transmitter suggest it is not that powerful and probably can only transfer data to the receiver if the receiver is somewhere close by. After several tries, my brothers were able to boost the power of their transmitter to reach a receiver up to a mile away. I doubt this one's capabilities are much stronger, but I can't be certain. I just have to assume the device is more powerful than I think and find a way to limit its ability to report my movements.

Since I have no idea how I'm going to do that, I climb into bed. Dreams of Tomas stabbing Zandri, or Dr Barnes yanking me out of a hiding place and pushing me into the ravine, chase me from darkness until dawn. By the time I wake, I have still not come up with an idea of how to limit the tracking of my movements without alerting Dr Barnes that I am aware of the device. I could remove the transmitter and leave it in my room, but people might start to wonder why the transmitter never moved. The best idea I have is to enclose the transmitter with a thin layer of metal to block the signal and hope those who monitor our movements believe my device to be faulty. But that too might raise more questions than I want asked.

Putting the bracelet back together, I snap it on my wrist and head downstairs for breakfast. With no classes to study for yet, the first years are still in a celebratory mood. Although, as the day progresses, I see faces turn serious. For good reason. We have all been Inducted into the Government Studies programme, but that acceptance is not a guarantee of our success. Only our performances in our classes can do that. I still haven't figured out a good way to counteract the transmitter in my bracelet by the next morning. But, today, if they monitor my movements, they will see what they expect to see. A University student going about her first day of classes. The pull of new ideas and learning is strong, but so is my fear that I might not measure up to the standards Professor Holt has set for me. As I finger the Government bracelet around my wrist, I can't help but wonder how many other first-year students from the colonies have made it through their Inductions. Will Stacia be seated in one of my classes, or will she be remembered by future Medical students for the lesson she provided?

Breakfast conversation in the dining hall is subdued, and I notice I am not the only one who barely eats the food on the tables in front of us. Ian catches my eye as I push back my chair and hoist my bag onto my shoulder. He nods. I nod back, grateful for the support though uncertain as to the motive. It is time for my first class. Global History.

Fourteen of us are seated in the classroom when

Professor Lee arrives carrying an armload of papers. He drops them on a large black table in the front that is already stacked with worn books. The only students I recognise in the room are Enzo and a broad-shouldered boy named Brick, who is a colony student like me. The rest are Tosu City students I know nothing about. Enzo does not look at any of them as they talk among themselves. He looks up only when Professor Lee finishes organising his materials and addresses the class.

"Welcome to Global History. To make sure we don't repeat the mistakes that led to the Seven Stages of War, we must understand past mistakes. In this class, we will learn what the landscape of the world looked like before the wars and study the countries and governments that dominated that landscape. Each week, we will focus on a different time period. You will be required to learn the names of the leaders, identify countries based on maps, and explain the pros and cons of the government structures of the most influential countries during that time. I will then select the most advanced students in the class for a special study of what is known about the current global structure and what it means for our future."

The prospect of learning how the world is recovering beyond the United Commonwealth borders has me sitting up straighter. And I'm not the only one. The room crackles with excitement and something more. Under the exhilaration is an underlying tension. Only the select few chosen by Professor Lee will be allowed to participate in that portion of the class. Another competition. Another test.

He gives us a big smile and pushes a button on the wall. "So, let's get to work, shall we?"

A large screen descends, and depicted on it is a world from the past. The next hour is filled with names of countries and people long dead. Governments destroyed by war or corruption. New regimes that rose to take their places. My pencil races across the page in front of me as I try to capture every word, knowing that any detail missed might be the difference between success and failure. Almost two hours later, my hand aches as I scribble down the homework instructions before heading to the next class. Enzo walks with me across the campus to Science Building Four.

Advanced Calculus.

Vic smiles at me from a corner desk. A boy named Xander nods from his seat in the front. Then class begins. Ordinary differential equations. Partial differential equations. Bessel and Legendre functions. Several pages of homework are assigned. A test will be given on Wednesday to assess our understanding of the material.

When class is over, I hurry out to avoid the familiar faces in the room. While I am grateful to see them, I am not sure I'm prepared to hear what they have to say. Will they tell me Stacia, whom I have yet to see, or other members of our Testing candidate class have failed their Inductions? That they have been Redirected? Instead, I find a spot outside that is mostly hidden from view to eat the apple and roll I slipped into my bag this morning. I have an hour to start on my homework before the next class begins.

United Commonwealth History and Law are followed by World Languages. Then my last class of the day: Chemistry. States of matter, properties of solutions, kinetics and atomic and molecular structure are discussed. A project assigned. And finally, classes are done, but my day is far from over. There are chemical equations to balance, a paper on the Commonwealth Government's founding debates to write, and maps to memorise. All must be complete by Wednesday, with more to be assigned by my other professors tomorrow. I know Dr Barnes will be watching to see which students fall behind. I will not be one of them.

The dining hall is filled with laughter and conversation. Students compare notes on their homework and teachers, and buzz about the news that internships will not be assigned for at least another week. I say nothing as I fill a plate with greens, some kind of spicy pork and sliced potatoes cooked with onions and walnuts. Part of me is relieved to have one less thing to worry about for the next seven days. The other part is anxious to learn whether or not I will be assigned an internship that will allow me to collect information for Michal and the rebels. Pushing thoughts of the internship aside, I ignore Ian's and Will's beckoning waves and head upstairs to study while I eat. When I finally sleep that night, Malachi and Zandri join me in my dreams. They quiz me on the names of country capitals, help balance chemistry equations and insist the ending to my paper could be stronger.

They're right. When I wake, I rewrite the final page before getting dressed for the second day of class.

More professors. More assignments.

Electrical and Magnetic Physics. The Rise and Fall of Technology. Art, Music and Literature. Bioengineering.

Here and there, I see familiar faces. Brick and Kit in Physics. Will, a girl named Jul and a Boulder kid named Quincy in Art and Music. And finally I see Stacia – along with Vic and a girl from Grand Forks named Naomy – in Technology. All are here. All wear bracelets that report their movements back to Dr Barnes and his officials.

News of Rawson's death has spread. In the minutes before and after class, we band together and talk about the loss of our classmate. I had almost forgotten Naomy and Rawson were from the same colony, but Naomy's puffy red eyes speak loudly of her sorrow and the love she has felt for him since she was ten years old. While I have never been close friends with Naomy, I find myself feeling sorry for her. During class, I notice some of the Tosu City students passing scraps of paper. Notes. With paper so precious, our Five Lakes instructors punished this practice with extra work. Here, where paper seems to be less of a concern, the instructors don't seem to mind. Biting my lip, I tear a small corner off the page in front of me, write a couple of words asking to meet after dinner and work on homework, and pass the note to Naomy. The smile she gives me when she reads it makes me feel happier than I have in days. When Stacia shoots me a questioning look, I tear off another corner and pass her a note too. When she grins, I feel better, more in control, knowing I will spend part of tonight with friends.

All through the day, I find myself looking for signs of Tomas. When I finally see his familiar grey eyes watching me from the back of the Bioengineering classroom, I realise I am unprepared to deal with the emotions storming inside me. Love. Guilt. Need. Uncertainty.

My heart pounds loudly in my chest as I slide into the seat next to him. I can't help but notice the pallor of his skin and the smudges of fatigue under the eyes that meet mine. Class begins. The teacher drones on about viscoelasticity, and though my pencil is clutched tight in my hand, my writing is barely legible as I try to ignore the ache in my heart. The same ache I know is in his at the possibility that we will never be able to look at each other without death and guilt between us.

The two of us stay seated when class ends. We say nothing as we watch everyone shove papers into their bags and head for the door. A few glance in our direction as they file out, but none linger. I wait for Tomas to speak. The quiet grows more uncomfortable with each passing second. In his eyes, I see self-condemnation and a weariness that scares me. Now that Tomas has admitted his actions to me, he is drowning in guilt. And though I still feel the sting of his betrayal, the anger I have held since hearing his confession fades, and fear takes hold. Unless Tomas finds a way to forgive himself for Zandri's death, the weight of guilt could drown him. I see a flash of my roommate Ryme swinging from a yellow rope. I want to convince Tomas that Zandri's death was an accident. He, unlike so many, did not make the choice to kill. But I have known Tomas too long to think words will help. Until his confession, Tomas pushed aside the guilt in order to protect me. He had a purpose. Now he needs another.

Leaning forward, I ask, "Did you work with my brothers on the livestock accountability project?"

Curiosity crosses Tomas's face. "My brother did most of the work, but I had some input. Why?"

I look around the room. Not sure if someone could be

listening, I grab my bag and stand. "I should get going if I want to make it back for dinner. Do you want to walk with me?"

We exit the building side by side. When we are far away from anyone who could hear us, I explain about the transmitter locked inside my bracelet and my desire to outwit it. Tomas asks questions as we walk towards his residence. By the time we reach his destination, his eyes have lost some of the shadows.

"A few of us are meeting together at the library to study tonight." I brush my fingers against his hand. "You could join us."

Tomas looks down at our hands. His fingers tighten against mine for a brief moment before they drop away. "There are some things I have to do." As he holds up the wrist circled by his Biological Engineering symbol, I once again see the mix of determination and hopelessness.

His lips brush my cheek. Then Tomas turns and walks away before I can think of anything else to say.

Dinner at the residence is filled with undercurrents of tension. At least half a dozen first years are bent over books while they eat. The upper-year students look less tense, which leads me to believe the first-year course work is designed to test not only our knowledge, but our ability to cope with stress and adversity. To keep from failing that test, I once again fill a plate with food and take it to my room. Naomy and I agreed to meet at seven. I will work on other homework until then.

When I was too young to attend school, I used to watch my brothers do their homework at the scarred kitchen table. I longed for the day when I too would sit beside them with my mother close at hand to lend guidance. However, when my turn finally came, I found it almost impossible to concentrate surrounded by my brothers' antics. So, each day, I would abandon the table and spread out on the floor in front of the living-room fireplace. Which is why, when I enter my rooms, I ignore the desk in my bedroom and dump my bag on the floor. Sitting cross-legged, I eat bites of chicken and carrots while working on potential difference equations.

I jump as someone pounds on my door. Ian barely waits for me to get out of the way before coming into the room and shutting the door behind him.

"Did you think I was joking when I said Dr Barnes is watching you? What do you think you're doing up here?"

"I'm studying. You told me not to fall behind in my classes."

"And I meant it." Ian looks at the papers and books strewn across the floor and rubs the back of his neck. "But you can't segregate yourself from the rest of us. Especially after Rawson's death. Everyone in the residence is going to think your behaviour shows you can't handle loss or you don't want to be a part of the University."

His words make my nerves jump. "Tell them I have nine classes to study for."

"No, because then they'll report to Dr Barnes that your class assignments are too much for you. Luckily, Raffe said you weren't feeling well during class today. Enzo backed him up, which defused most of the grumbles." He frowns. "Cia, it's not enough to get passing grades. You also have to look like everyone else while doing it. That means eating meals in the dining hall, spending some time in the common areas and making it look like you're having fun."

"I'm supposed to make handling nine classes look easy?"

Ian nods. "That's what leaders do."

I look down at the pages scattered across the floor. Pressure builds behind my eyes and in my chest. It's only day two of class, and already I'm feeling the effects of the stress. But I only have to think of the leaders from Five Lakes Colony to know that Ian is right. Though she has the weight of our colony on her shoulders, Magistrate Owens never looks flustered. Even when voicing a serious problem, she has a way of making it feel like a puzzle rather than a life-and-death concern. My father is the same. No matter how worried he might be about a contagion corrupting crops or the way an unrevitalised piece of land is responding to his team's ministrations, he never shows it. Not to the public. He keeps his frustrations and concerns at home. The minute he walks outside our door, he knows people will be watching his actions. The success of his team means the difference between starvation and survival.

"All right," I say. "I'll be at breakfast and dinner tomorrow."

"Good." Ian smiles, moves some papers off a chair and takes a seat. "Once internships start, you won't be expected at every meal. Unexpected tasks come up all the time. You'll be able to blame them for the time you take alone to study. Now, since I'm here, do you want me to look at the assignments you have to turn in tomorrow?"

"Why?" I ask. Suspicion wars with gratitude. Is Ian's offer of assistance due to his own experiences or something more? "Did someone suggest I need help?"

I search Ian's face for the truth behind his actions. Is he rendering me aid because I am a fellow colonist? Is he the friend Michal spoke of when he said he was being reassigned? Ian sharing information about my Government Studies bracelet tells me he is on my side. But I still don't know why.

"A friend did tell me that helping a pretty girl with her homework would be a great way to gain her trust. It can be hard to know whom to trust." Ian pauses. My heart pounds in my chest as I try to hear the message communicated between the words. "That friend trusts me, Cia. You can too."

Wordlessly, I hand over the pages. Then I try to work while Ian pores over them. He points out a mistake on my calculus assignment and is making suggestions about how to strengthen the ending of a paper when I notice the time. Stacia and Naomy are waiting.

"I have to go."

"Where are you going?"

"I'm going to the library before it closes."

Ian's eyes narrow. "As long as you're not meeting with your friend Tomas."

Tomas's name on Ian's lips renders me speechless. As far as I know, the two of them have never met.

Ian sighs. "If you're planning to meet him, don't. You won't be doing him any favours. Until we know why Dr Barnes has singled you out, the only way to keep your boyfriend safe from Dr Barnes is by staying away."

Since Tomas turned down my invitation tonight, that won't be a problem. But if we are going to work together to outwit the tracking device, we will have to meet in the future. We could meet in secret, but until we find a way to work around the transmitters in our bracelets, people in charge will know we are together – which, according to Ian, will put Tomas in more danger.

I know what Zeen would do. My brother wouldn't put a

stop to his plans. He would simply find a way to achieve his objective without alerting those watching to his actions. The Transit Communicator in my bag is a perfect example of his ability to follow his own agenda in plain view, and in such a way that no one notices he is doing anything at all. Perhaps I can use that same trick to cover any discussions I have with Tomas.

I shove the papers I need into my bag, shrug on my coat and go down the stairs. I hear voices coming from the hangout room. Standing in the doorway, I look for familiar faces. Most of the students are upper years. But I spot Raffe and Damone with a couple of other first years in the back corner.

"I'm going to the library to work on my history of technology assignment," I say as startled eyes swing towards me. "Do any of you want to come with?"

Most say no, which I expect. But Raffe surprises me when he gets up, hoists his University bag onto his shoulder and says, "I was just about to head over there. Let's go."

We walk down to the bridge in silence. Raffe's steps slow as we cross the bridge. So do mine. Out of the corner of my eye, I notice Raffe glance over the rail.

Once the bridge is behind us, he asks, "Are we really going to the library?"

"Where else would we be going?"

He shrugs. "I'm just glad to get out of there for a while. Griffin and Damone are starting to get on my nerves."

"I thought they were your friends."

Raffe stops walking. "Just because we're all from Tosu City doesn't make us friends. I don't know about you, but friendship is a luxury I've never had time for. I was too busy beating the competition to get here."

I can't help but wonder about Raffe's words as we walk across campus. Friendship is something I've always taken for granted. In Five Lakes, we competed to be the best in the class, but we all worked hard to get along. It's impossible for me to imagine growing up without Daileen's whispered confidences or Tomas's kind understanding. Are the people here in Tosu City so different that they don't place value on that kind of connection? Or maybe Raffe is just using this opportunity to gain my sympathy in hopes of using it later.

Naomy and Stacia are waiting outside the library when we arrive. I introduce them to Raffe. If either of them is surprised that I brought a non-colony student with me, they don't show it. The four of us go into the well-lit library, pick a table in the back corner of the main study room and get to work.

Several upper-year students and professors take notice of us, but none seem to be surprised or unhappy with the group study session. Nothing could be more natural than students working together to succeed. When I convince Tomas to join us, no one will think twice about his addition. At least, that's what I hope.

In between discussing how much history was lost when computer networks were destroyed, we talk about ourselves. Raffe mentions he is the youngest son of the director of education for the United Commonwealth. Of the seven children in his family, six were accepted to the University. Naomy says she's envious of large families. While her parents were proud of her being selected for The Testing, they couldn't quite hide their sadness at the prospect of saying goodbye to their only child.

"At least you got to sleep in your own bed growing up," I say. "I shared a room with my four brothers. All of them snore."

As we fetch books and look up information, we do something more important. We laugh. It feels good. Normal. Happy. How long has it been since I felt either of those things? Even Stacia, who is usually so reserved, unbends enough to talk about her little brother, Nate, who was born too early and as a result learns slower than his classmates. She wonders how he is doing now that she isn't there to help him with his schoolwork and keep the other kids from teasing him. "Dad and Mom don't always have enough time to spend with him."

Stacia shrugs off the hand Raffe places on her shoulder and changes the subject, asking me to help her find a book. The two of us climb the stairs to the second floor. Several heads turn our way. Stacia studies them before leading me down a row of medical texts. Under her breath, she quickly tells me about the Medical Induction, where first years were asked to select the correct treatments for a dozen common diseases with the help of a medical textbook. Once answers were given, each student was taken to a treatment room. On the table inside, twelve sets of medications sat waiting to be dispensed to patients who, one by one, walked through the door. The medication inside the cup representing the correct answer was a placebo. Wrong answers contained poison.

"The final years made us watch each patient take their medication. They wanted to test our confidence in diagnosis and our ability to cope with losing a patient. I guess some people have trouble living with a mistake that causes someone else to die. Anyone who demonstrated psychological unfitness or gave more than two incorrect answers was Redirected."

Bile rises in my throat. "The patients didn't actually die, right?" It would be almost impossible for Dr Barnes to explain that kind of loss of life or get officials to volunteer for that kind of job.

Stacia shrugs. "The one I lost looked dead, but I was

instructed not to touch a patient after treatment had been dispensed. So anything is possible."

Stacia is driven and sometimes aloof. Of all of the colony students, she has always accepted the challenges we face with calm resolve. But the fisted hands and tightening of her jaw when she speaks of death and the three students who her head of residence said were Redirected to work in the colonies indicate worry she has never mentioned. For some reason, seeing Stacia unnerved is more disturbing than if she had maintained her stoic resolve.

The overhead light catches the bracelet on her wrist. In the centre of it is a symbol I remember seeing in Dr Flint's house. A snake coiled around a staff. Dr Flint had it displayed in the room he used to treat patients. When I asked him about the design, he said it was the ancient symbol for medicine. However, unlike Dr Flint's version, this one has what looks to be a second snake coiled underneath it, ready to strike. After hearing Stacia talk about the Induction, I can see why this symbol was chosen to represent her.

I quickly answer Stacia's questions about my Induction experience before grabbing a book and heading back down the stairs to join the others.

The next day's classes get harder. Professors collect our homework. Several give quizzes to assess our level of understanding of the basic material. Others announce that tests on more advanced concepts will be given the following week.

I pass more notes during class on Wednesday. Tomas's note instructs him to wait to join the group until the following week. By then I am hoping people will be so used to seeing the group they won't be surprised by the addition of one more. In the evening Stacia, Naomy, Raffe and Vic meet me at the same library table we occupied the night before. We don't all have the same assignments to complete, but we still work together. We help each other out when one of us needs someone to double-check a chemistry formula or proofread a sentence – like I used to do with Tomas during our Early Studies classes.

Thursday's classes are more of the same. Assignments collected. Lectures on important literature, basic cell engineering and the equilibrium properties of alloy systems. We are told the classroom buildings will be open over the next few days so we can use the labs and the resources in the rooms to complete our projects. I do, never forgetting my other projects. The one I vowed to help Michal with and the one that circles my wrist. As I work on a pulse radio assignment, I think I might know a way to address the second.

By Monday, the strain of the workload shows on almost every first year's face. Too much reading. Too little sleep.

Worry about the cost of failure shows in red-rimmed eyes and tense smiles. The exercises I have started doing alone in my rooms to improve my muscle strength have helped me fare better than some. Still, I find myself soaking a cloth in cold water and putting it across my eyes to hide the fatigue brought about by late work nights and dreams filled with disturbing images.

I pull myself out of sleep after every dream and sit in the dark, trying to decide if the smell of the blood and the sound of the bullet leaving the gun are simple nightmares or Testing memories lurking in my subconscious. If only I can find the key to unlock them.

I pass more notes, and our study group grows in number. Enzo joins us. As do Brick and a Tosu City Biological Engineering student named Aram. Internship assignments are postponed for another week. The tension builds.

Enzo starts walking with me to class. He is the one who spots Damone trailing behind us. When I look back, Damone stares at me. The next day, Enzo and I leave the building earlier, but still Damone is there. Watching. I notice the lock on my door is scuffed and scraped. Nothing inside the room is missing. No cameras have been added, but I can't help feeling that someone has been inside. I sleep with a chair propped under the door handle and jump at every sound in the night as I lie awake – wondering if Symon's faction of rebels has found a way to end The Testing without bloodshed or if war is coming while the rest of my classmates sleep, unknowing, in their beds.

I pass another note to Tomas, asking him to join us and sharing the idea that I have. When he walks up to the library table where we are gathered, the shadows in his eyes have faded, replaced by a hint of excitement.

For a while, he works next to me in silence. When some of our study companions begin to work together on assignments, Tomas turns to me and asks, "Did you finish the transmitter assignment yet?"

No one at the table is in our class. They have no idea what assignments we are working on. So I dig through my bag, pull out a piece of paper and say, "I have a couple of ideas written down."

While conversations about physics and literature swirl around us, I show Tomas my idea for an external transmitter that would be set to the same frequency as the ones in our bracelets. In theory, the external transmitter would create enough interference that the signal from the device in the bracelet would be drowned out. Whoever was monitoring on the other end would read the problem as natural signal obstruction instead of tampering.

Tomas grins, helps perfect my design and suggests we make extra transmitters to scatter around campus so other students' signals experience the same technical difficulties. By the time we pack up our books for the night, we have a workable plan in place. When I get back to the residence, I head for the labs and get to work. I find a variety of resistors, batteries, capacitors, wire, coils and transistors in the lab's supply cabinet. My eyes are tired and my fingers cramped by the time I have assembled and tested five two-inch-long, one-inch-wide transmitters. I have also created a small receiver set on a different frequency that will light up when I flip a small switch. Now I will be able to signal to Tomas if I need his help. I hide one blocking transmitter behind a portrait in the currently empty hangout room before going upstairs to bed.

During classes the next day, I hide three of the transmitters on campus. When Tomas and I cross paths, I give him the receiver and an update on where I've hidden my transmitters. Tomorrow he will hide his. At dinner, an announcement is made. The internships will be assigned on Friday.

When Friday dawns, the first years and our guides are asked to assemble in the gathering room after breakfast. Most are dressed in their finest clothes. Boys wearing jackets. Girls in gauzy dresses. I did not bring fancy clothes with me for The Testing, so I am dressed in brown pants, a turquoise shirt and my scuffed boots. Instead of pulling back my hair, I brush it until it gleams, like my mother did when I was little. Since I am more than happy to let officials track my movements today, I leave my transmitter hidden under my mattress when I go downstairs to learn what my assignment will be.

Dressed in deep crimson, Professor Holt stands near the fireplace. Lips that match the colour of her jumpsuit are curved into a smile. "Today begins one of the most important parts of your education. It's not enough to answer test questions correctly. You must be able to work well with others and apply the knowledge you have received to real-world situations. Your internships give you important experience that will help you be effective leaders after you graduate from the University."

Her eyes pan the room. "Unfortunately, after meeting with your final-year guides and talking to your professors, we have concerns that some of you are not up to the challenges thus far presented. We have taken your academic achievements up to now into consideration when assigning internships. Some of you might be disappointed with the choices we have made, but we do so in the best interests of your future and the future of the United Commonwealth. Remember, while we consider these internships essential to your education, your classwork is just as important. Alternate arrangements will be made for students whose work falls below acceptable standards."

Alternate arrangements.

Redirected.

Dead.

"When your name is called, your final-year guide will escort you to meet with a representative from the government department in which you will be working. Regardless of what internship you are assigned today, you should be proud of how far you have come and all that you have accomplished. We'll start with Juliet Janisson."

The dark-haired girl rises from a seat in the corner, joins her guide, Lazar, and disappears out the door. I wipe my palms on my pants as we wait for the next name. No one speaks as the seconds tick by. Several times I catch Griffin watching me. He whispers something to Damone that makes them both smile.

One by one, students are called. Guides walk with their charges out of the room and then return to act as escort to the next first year. Finally, only Ian, Professor Holt and I remain.

The fire crackles.

The ceiling above us creaks.

I fight not to squirm under Professor Holt's penetrating gaze. Finally, she breaks the silence. "I'm sorry you had to wait until the end, Malencia."

"Someone has to be last," I say, glad to hear my voice

doesn't betray the nerves I feel.

Professor Holt nods. "That's true, but in your case, it was a deliberate decision. Certain events during your Induction raised questions about the kind of future you should have within this institution."

My heart swoops into my stomach and my knees go weak. I'm thankful Professor Holt doesn't expect me to reply, because I doubt I could squeeze the words through my clenched throat.

"Because of your unique circumstances, we had to wait until a time when the officials interested in your case could be available for this discussion." She looks at her wrist and smiles. "That time would be now. Please follow me."

Professor Holt sweeps out the door without a backward glance, and I follow. I look to Ian, who's keeping pace beside me. When he takes my hand and holds tight, I know I am in serious trouble.

We are led across the bridge, where a sleek silver skimmer gleams in the sunlight. I want to run fast and far, because the only reason for a skimmer to be here is to transport me away from the University. To what or where, I don't know, but it can't be good. Despite my desire to flee, I hold fast to Ian's hand and wait for whatever surprise Professor Holt has in store.

The passenger compartment door opens, and Professor Holt gestures for me to enter. Ian drops my hand. My legs are uncertain as I approach the skimmer. After one last look at Ian, I take a deep breath, climb inside the cabin and see Dr Barnes seated on one of the soft grey seats that line the wall. He gives me a familiar smile.

"Sit. Please."

Despite the pleasant tone, I understand the words for what they are. A command. One I obey.

"I apologise for the unusual location of this meeting. As you know, at this juncture in your University career, Professor Holt and I normally assign you the internship we believe best suited to your skills. In this instance, however, we have been asked to pass along that responsibility to someone else."

Hope blooms as I realise Dr Barnes is in fact talking about an internship. I am not being Redirected.

"Who's assigning my internship?" I ask.

"I am."

I turn, and a shiver travels down my spine. Standing in the doorway, wearing a severely cut blood-red dress, is the United Commonwealth president Anneline Collindar.

CHAPTER 14

"I apologise for making you wait, Malencia." President Collindar takes a seat opposite me and crosses one leg over the other. "Being a United Commonwealth leader means your time is never your own."

"I'm sure your father would agree with that," Dr Barnes says. "Don't you think, Cia?"

Hearing Dr Barnes mention my father steals my breath.

President Collindar speaks before I can wonder what the reference means. "I know that Jedidiah has other things he needs to attend to, as do I, so I'll make this quick. I was intrigued when we met during your Induction. Of all the students who came into the Debate Chamber, you were the only one who recited the request without error and the only female who made the attempt for her team. Taking that kind of risk in public is often more difficult for women than men. I'm not sure why." Her smile says she has never found it to be a problem. "My interest was further piqued when you mentioned your home colony.

Debate Chamber etiquette is not as well known as it used to be, especially outside the Tosu City boundaries. After discussing your Testing results and academic achievements with Dr Barnes and Professor Holt, I asked that you be assigned to intern in my office. As president, my loyalties are to all United Commonwealth citizens, but it is rare that I get the opportunity to pass beyond the borders of Tosu City and talk to colony citizens. The times that I do meet with colony residents, they are too nervous or intimidated by my office to speak frankly. But a girl like you, Malencia—" She uncrosses her legs and leans forward. "Cia. A girl who is willing to risk embarrassment and possible failure by taking control of the Debate Chamber floor will be more likely to tell me what I need to know. Don't you agree?"

"You want me to tell you about Five Lakes Colony?"

"If you think I need to know about it, yes." She smiles.

"I hope you'll have her do more than tell you about Five Lakes Colony," Dr Barnes says smoothly.

The president's smile widens. "My office has never been included in the University internship programme. Dr Barnes and Professor Holt expressed some concern about the lack of a set curriculum, but I persuaded them of the educational value that comes with working alongside the staff of the president of the United Commonwealth."

Dr Barnes stiffens. "Remember, Cia, that like your fellow first years, you will have to keep up with the classwork assigned by your University professors. Just because you work in the president's office doesn't mean you will get special consideration."

President Collindar lets out a light laugh. "Don't worry. I'll make sure Cia has plenty of time to complete all her assignments. How would it look if the president's intern flunked out of school?"

Suddenly I realise that the tension I feel in the skimmer isn't just coming from me. No. The angry flush under Dr Barnes's grey beard and the challenging gleam in President Collindar's eyes speak of something greater than an internship assignment.

A power struggle that I don't understand, but one in which I have become unwittingly involved.

President Collindar looks at her watch. "It's getting late. We'd better get going if Cia is going to have time to tour the presidential offices. I'd offer to let you ride with us, Jedidiah, but I'm sure you have business you need to attend to here on campus."

The dismissal is cutting, despite the cordial tone. It's clear from Dr Barnes's stiff movements as he exits the skimmer that he has felt the slight. The passenger door swings closed, and a loud hum fills the compartment as the skimmer's engine is engaged. I look around the cabin and spot a small round lens in the back-right corner. Whoever is operating the skimmer must have a screen in the front that displays what is happening back here.

The president sees the direction of my gaze and nods at the camera. "Sometimes, if you aren't certain of the outcome of a meeting, it is best to have another pair of eyes watching. You never know when you might need a hand."

The skimmer lifts off the ground and moves forward. From the window, I watch the campus fade into the distance and feel a sense of relief even as I brace myself for whatever challenge comes next.

President Collindar leans back against the grey cushions. I try my best to sit still as my mind whirls. I have been assigned to intern with President Collindar. The most influential person in the United Commonwealth government – who, from the looks of things, does not get along with Dr Barnes. Michal implied Symon's plan to end The Testing peacefully requires the support of President Collindar. I will be keeping my eyes and ears open.

After several minutes of silence, the president turns and looks at me. Not sure what to say, I ask, "Are we going to the Central Government Building?"

"Not today. When I was elected president, I moved my

private offices to a building a few blocks away. I find it is easier to think in a space that isn't quite so chaotic."

"I didn't know that." In fact, I remember our guide showing us the entrance to the president's offices when we toured the Central Government Building during orientation.

President Collindar smiles. "We don't advertise. You'd be amazed how many people can't make a decision without asking my opinion if they think I'm right down the hall. Now that they have to walk a few blocks, they can handle the little problems. The big ones..." She sighs. "Well, those are the ones the citizens of the United Commonwealth expect me to deal with. Today, you'll meet some of the people you'll be working with. But before we arrive, I'd like to stress that I am dedicated to the entire country. I believe in the mission the survivors of the Seven Stages of War embarked on when they founded the United Commonwealth government. Not everyone does. And those who do often have different visions as to how that mission should be carried out. As you might have guessed, Dr Barnes and I don't see eye to eye on a great many things. Because of that, I often find that I am not as well informed about the University programmes as I would like. I'm hoping you can remedy that situation."

"I don't understand."

President Collindar leans back. "Don't you?" Her eyes

search my face. "The students who attend the University are the next great hope of this country. It disturbs me when I hear that many of those students fail to make it to graduation."

She waits for me to speak. Words bubble inside me. I want to explain what I know of The Testing. Expose the brutality Dr Barnes and his team have advocated. Condemn the process that has been allowed to flourish in the centre of a city that was created to represent hope. This is the moment I have been waiting for. That the rebels have been waiting for. Yet, instinct stills my tongue. President Collindar is the most powerful person in this country. If she wants information about The Testing and the University, why hasn't she received it before now? I shift in my seat. Surely, if the president demanded answers, someone would be compelled to give them. Too many people are involved in The Testing for them all to remain silent. If it is answers she seeks, why is she posing her questions to a first-year University girl instead of to those who have not had their memories removed by The Testing? There is something more at work here. Something I need to understand better before I risk my future and the future of the rebellion.

When I don't answer, President Collindar sighs. "I don't expect you to trust me. Not yet. But I hope that by working with my staff, you will realise that I have the best interests of this country at heart. If there is something more about the University programme that I should know, I hope you'll feel comfortable enough to share that information." She glances out the window as the skimmer begins to slow. "We're here."

The door opens. President Collindar walks to the doorway, takes someone's hand, and gracefully exits. I follow behind and take the hand held out to help me. When my feet hit the ground and I start to thank the person, the words lodge in my throat. Standing in a purple United Commonwealth uniform with a pleasant but impersonal smile on his face is Michal Gallen.

Michal is here. I try to feign interest in the building in front of me as he releases my hand, but I cannot stop the pounding of my heart. Michal said he was being reassigned. If he is here, the rebellion must know what I know about the president's dislike of Dr Barnes. Symon's faction should be in a position to end The Testing. But if the president is asking questions of me, she either doesn't believe what she has been told or they have yet to approach her. Why?

I try to catch his eye, but Michal keeps his attention straight ahead as we approach the offices, which the president informs me are housed in one of the oldest buildings in Tosu City. Constructed several hundred years ago out of grey stone, with rounded turrets and a functioning clock tower, the structure resembles the castles in some of the fairy-tale books my mother read to me and my brothers when we were little.

Michal opens the large wooden front door and President Collindar sweeps past him. Two men and two women in Commonwealth uniforms greet us in the white tiled entryway. A muscular man in a black jumpsuit stands behind a desk near the front door. The president nods and he takes a seat, but not before I see the glint of a metal handle at his belt.

"Cia." The president turns to me. "Several pressing matters have come up and need my attention. This is our newest team member, Michal Gallen. He'll give you a tour and introduce you to the staff. When you've finished, we'll go over the first assignment I've set aside for you."

The four Commonwealth officials flank her as she disappears through a door down the hall to the right. When the sound of footsteps fades, I turn to Michal and smile. He doesn't smile back. He just glances at his watch and nods. "The president's main offices are on this floor. To save time, we'll start the tour on the top floor and work our way down."

He walks quickly towards the black iron-railed staircase and starts to climb. I hurry to catch up and am breathing hard when we step onto the narrow fifth-floor hallway.

"The clock tower stairs are through that door." He points. "The clock and this entire building do not run off city power, but instead run off three-dimensional monocrystalline solar panels. The power we don't use is then fed into the Tosu City power bank to ensure nothing is wasted. As President Collindar mentioned in the skimmer, she doesn't like waste." He turns and shrugs. "I probably shouldn't have listened to your conversation with the president, but the inside of the skimmer isn't designed for privacy. Kind of like this building. Everyone here tends to know everyone's business. You'll get used to it."

I understand the words for what they are: a warning.

The top three floors house cramped offices and larger spaces filled with historical objects and pictures. As I walk by the pieces of my country's past, I can't help but run my fingers across them. Framed photographs of soldiers. Women in long dresses holding what I think are called tennis racquets. An old-fashioned car from the early twentieth century. A display of hand-held weapons. An ornate organ. A phonograph. Wooden desks in a room designed to look like a late-nineteenth-century classroom, which makes me smile. The classroom is smaller, but it doesn't look much different from the one I studied in back in Five Lakes.

As we continue the tour, Michal introduces me to

several of the younger officials walking the halls or sitting in uncomfortable-looking chairs. Most look tired but excited to be working here. He points to one of the four desks in the corner of a room on the third floor and says, "That's where I sit. So far, in the week I've been here, I haven't done much of that."

We walk down to the second floor. To our right are two purple-clad officials standing on either side of a massive wooden door. Michal nods at them and steers me to the left, explaining, "The president's private rooms are through those doors. There are a few more offices on this side and some sleeping quarters for anyone who wants to catch a nap after a late night."

"Does that happen often?"

"I've already used one of the rooms. The president likes to have as much information about the upcoming debate topics as possible. It's our job to do the research and provide her with all sides of the argument. Talking to experts from the various departments and sifting through opinions is rewarding, but it takes time."

On the first floor, there are more offices, a meeting space with a board displaying the debates scheduled for the upcoming week, and a technology room equipped with several powerful pulse radios, six televisions and a number of visual and audio recorders. Pictures flicker across the television screens. I want to take a closer look, but Michal hurries me through. While I've seen photographs of televisions and studied the history of their use, I have never seen one in operation. My father once mentioned that the magistrate of Five Lakes was in possession of a television in order to receive certain types of communication from Tosu City. I can't help but wonder if the pictures flashing on the screen now are part of that communication network and, if so, what the transmitted information might be.

Finally, Michal leads me to a large wooden door. A purple-clad official at a desk to the right nods, and Michal ushers me inside. The room is large. Larger than my family's entire house. Deep blue carpet covers the floor. A fire crackles in the hearth to my right. Decorating the walls is a map of the United Commonwealth and the country's flag. The officials I saw when I first arrived are seated on chairs facing the president, who is behind a massive wooden desk.

President Collindar looks up. "Perfect timing. We were just discussing your first project, Cia." The president looks at one of the officials, who rises and turns to address me.

The man has flecks of grey in his brown hair that reminds me of my father's. "We are currently working out resource distribution for a railway project. One of the colonies that the new train will connect to is Five Lakes. Since none of us have been to your colony or many of the other colonies this plan affects, we would like you to look at the plans and give us a colony citizen's perspective. We've been told you also have skills in mechanical engineering that should give you an informed point of view when preparing a report for the president."

President Collindar nods. "Too many of the colonies do not have easy access to Tosu City. For us to feel united in our mission to revitalise our land, we must actually be unified. The railway system has connected the nearest colonies, but the outlying ones are still isolated from our help and protection."

Ryme's face flashes in front of me. Flushed cheeks. Sightless eyes. She was from Dixon Colony. I think about Will and his brother, Gill. Twins from Madison Colony. One led to murder. Another gone. Redirected by The Testing. Both of those colonies, like Five Lakes, do not have access to the United Commonwealth train system. While easy communication with Tosu City might appear to provide protection for the colonies, the Testing candidates who have been for ever altered by the protection they received would no doubt argue the point.

Still, I feel a spark of excitement at the prospect of working on a project that affects my family and friends. While I may not ever be allowed to return to Five Lakes to live, I will always consider it my home. Being able to help Five Lakes and contribute to a system that could allow my family and me to visit makes me feel as though I still belong to them.

I am given an overview of the project, including the departments involved, and told that today I must pick up reports prepared by each department. The Debate Chamber will be discussing this project at the end of next week. My report to the president is due on Monday.

"You can pick up the reports from the departments' main offices in the Central Government Building. Feel free to work here or on campus, wherever you feel most comfortable. If you need transportation, let one of my staff know. They'll make sure you have what you need. I look forward to seeing your thoughts on the matter."

The president starts a conversation about the waste management system, effectively dismissing me. Putting a hand on my arm, Michal leads me out of the room. The door closes behind us.

"I'll take you over to the Central Government Building in a few minutes. First we should see about getting you some kind of transportation. You won't want to waste time walking."

Michal leads me to a small building behind the president's offices, unlocks the door and turns on the light. Inside the space are several single-passenger skimmers, two solar-powered motor scooters and a handful of bicycles. I walk to the row of bicycles. Some have sturdy frames and thick, heavily treaded rubber tyres. Others are made of lighter materials, with a design that speaks of speed. I run my finger along a tear in one of the seats and think of another bicycle. One that, according to my recording, helped Tomas and me survive The Testing. Gears, pedals and wheels helped keep me alive then. I will trust them now to do the same.

I choose the bicycle with the heaviest frame and thickest tyres. It is constructed to withstand the stress of travelling over rough terrain and reminds me of the one I rode back home. The lighter, sleeker ones I see on the streets of Tosu City are speedier, but they are also more fragile.

If Michal is surprised by my choice, he doesn't show it. He just logs my selection on a chalkboard hanging near the door and escorts me and my new bicycle into the sunshine. We walk in silence for the next block, me wheeling the black-framed bike in between us. The streets are bustling with activity as citizens hurry about their business. Here and there, I spot officials in their United Commonwealth uniforms chatting in groups or jogging down the street on what must be pressing business. Though the Central Government Building is straight ahead, Michal glances around and turns us down a northbound walkway. Halfway down the block, Michal escorts me and my new bicycle into a building constructed of black metal and dark grey stone.

Inside it is dim and quiet as a tomb. Putting a finger to his lips, Michal motions for me to leave my bicycle before leading me through a maze of doors and hallways. Finally, he pulls out a key and slides it into the lock of a large steel door. The click of the lock disengaging rings in the stillness. Michal flips a switch on the wall, illuminating a grey, windowless room decorated with only a rectangular metal table and six folding chairs.

He closes the door behind us. "We don't have much time," he says, pulling me against him in a tight hug. "Someone will notice if we take too long to arrive at the Central Government Building." He steps back. "I heard about the colony student who died. I'm sorry."

The kindness and sympathy make me want to cry.

But Michal doesn't dwell on the sadness. "Symon says there are signs that President Collindar is ready to challenge Dr Barnes and remove him from his position as head of The Testing."

My heart jumps as the hope I felt in the skimmer is confirmed. "That's wonderful news."

"Only if she has the power to eliminate Dr Barnes and The Testing."

I shake my head. "She's the president of the United Commonwealth. Of course she has the power."

Michal sits on one of the metal chairs. "President Collindar is technically in charge of the government, but as the man who selects the country's future leaders, Dr Barnes has as much power, if not more. Not only do current officials feel a sense of loyalty to him for having selected them for their jobs, they also seek his favour to ensure that their children are accepted into the programme and given preferential treatment. In the past several years, the University has been allocated larger resources. More autonomy to act as Dr Barnes and his team see fit. In the week I've been assigned to the president's office, three Debate Chamber votes have swung in favour of whatever side of the issue Dr Barnes supports. While the president is the head of the government, Dr Barnes and his team actually now control it."

The idea of Dr Barnes running this country makes me want to scream.

"The president is working to regain the power her office has lost. She's scheduled a Debate Chamber vote that would reorganise the administrative structure of The Testing and University so the head of the programme reports directly to her. But unless something changes, she doesn't have enough votes from the department heads for the measure to pass. The Education Department manager is a close personal friend of Dr Barnes. He's been working against the president's measure by saying he has seen reports of The Testing and believes it is being run appropriately. Over the last two years, some officials have claimed that the president is an ineffective leader and should be replaced. Losing a vote of this import could confirm those claims and weaken her further. There's a rumour going around the office that losing the vote will lead to a call for a vote of confidence."

When the Commonwealth Government was created, our founders agreed that leaders should be allowed to govern as long as they were effective. They believed limiting the time a strong leader served was detrimental to the well-being of the country. However, to ensure a weak leader could be removed before he or she did too much harm, the founders instituted the vote of confidence, which requires members of the Debate Chamber to reavow their support of the president. A president who fails to get over fifty per cent of the vote is immediately removed from power and a new president voted upon.

"If the president is replaced, it will be by someone Dr Barnes and his supporters select. Maybe even Dr Barnes himself. The president is not willing to let that happen. So, she and her team have been searching for another way to remove Dr Barnes from power. They believe they've found that method in the other rebel faction."

The faction that believes in taking down Dr Barnes and The Testing by force. With weapons, bloodshed and death.

"President Collindar would prefer a peaceful solution over action that could lead to a civil war, but she believes there is too much at stake for the country to wait. Dr Barnes will find a way to remove her if she doesn't act soon. The rebel faction has begun to recruit citizens from the less revitalised areas of Tosu. These recruits don't care about Dr Barnes or The Testing, but the rebels have convinced them they will have more say and more resources if they join the cause. If the president loses the Debate Chamber vote, the rebels will act. And the president and her people will throw support behind them. Tosu City could be ripped apart, and Symon fears there is a chance that with so many colony-born people living here, unrest could spring up in the colonies. Especially when the citizens there understand what The Testing did to their children."

And war could follow. History shows that it takes only a spark to start a fire that cannot be easily checked. The Seven Stages of War started with the outrage of one leader.

"There has to be something we can do." Violence can't be inevitable.

"The president plans to announce the vote about the restructuring of The Testing in three weeks. Top members of her team are reviewing her key arguments and meeting with department representatives in order to sway votes. So far, they haven't had any luck. Symon believes the only way the Debate Chamber will vote against Dr Barnes is if proof of the true nature of The Testing is revealed in open session. The only way most officials can justify turning a blind eye to Dr Barnes's methods is by discounting the negative things they hear as rumours. No one wants to believe that students who give wrong answers can be killed. Tosu City children are never required to sit for The Testing. Officials can ignore Testing speculation without worrying their own children will suffer as a result. Indisputable proof will change that."

"What about the University Induction tests? Students die during those." I remember Rawson's feet slipping off the edge. Olive's horror-filled face as she realised the consequences of her actions. "The officials can't possibly agree with those methods."

"No, but most Tosu City officials survived some kind of Induction. They feel it's only fair the new students have to suffer through a similar process. And while Dr Barnes and the head residence professors are involved, the final years of each designated study are technically responsible for the Induction process. If someone dies, Dr Barnes calls it an accident." Michal's eyes light with anger. "Government officials are happy to find any excuse to look the other way. But if they are forced to see the truth, they'll have to fix the problem. That's why we need tangible evidence of wrongdoing. Once it is presented in open session, officials will have no choice but to strip Dr Barnes of his authority and put an end to The Testing."

Tangible proof. "Can't you testify on the debate floor?" I ask. "You still have your Testing memories."

"I volunteered to speak out, but Symon and his advisers said my words won't be enough. People could argue I'm making up stories because I wasn't assigned the job I wanted or because I'm jealous. They would say the same about anyone who testifies if we are allowed to get that far. Symon is convinced Dr Barnes is monitoring the president's office and would learn the names of those scheduled to testify before they take the floor. How long do you think I and anyone else who volunteers to speak would live if that happened?"

Hours? Unless they ran. And who knows even then if they would survive.

"We need more than just our testimony to sway public opinion and convince the Debate Chamber to vote against Dr Barnes."

What other kind of proof could they find? I look down at the symbol on my wrist with the tracking device it contains and remember the one I wore before. "The Testing bracelets contained recording devices. We should find the recordings Dr Barnes made." Weeks of conversations recorded. Betrayals made. Gunshots and crossbow bolts that spilled blood. Ended lives.

"Symon has lower-level officials within The Testing and the Education Department searching for both audio and video recordings, but they haven't been able to gain access to them. There is a chance Dr Barnes destroys them after The Testing is complete and University candidates are selected."

"I don't think so." I explain about the conversation Ian overheard in which Professor Holt talked to Dr Barnes about re-examining my actions during The Testing. "They wouldn't be able to re-examine my performance if they destroyed the recordings."

"I'll let Symon know. If you're right, we still might have a chance to end The Testing without plunging the country into war." Michal looks at his watch and stands. "But if we don't want to make anyone suspicious, we have to get going." He opens the door, steps into the hall and looks around before telling me to follow.

"What can I do?" I ask, walking the dim corridors back to where I stashed my bicycle.

"Keep your ears open for any information that can point to the location of the recordings. Talk to whoever is assigned to intern in the Department of Education. Our contacts have heard rumours that the top-level officials have access to The Testing facilities. They might know something about the recordings. If you learn anything, let me know. I'll pass the information to Symon."

"Why not pass it directly to the president?"

Michal's expression is grim. "She doesn't know I'm a member of the rebellion, and we'd prefer to keep it that way for now. Symon orchestrated my transfer so I could report if the president is moving up the timeline for the rebel faction and her allies to attack. So far, she is sticking to her original schedule. She will make her case before the Debate Chamber floor three weeks from now. With luck, we'll find the information she needs to win the vote before then."

In three weeks The Testing will hopefully come to an end and Daileen and others like her will be safe.

Michal asks me to wait as he looks up and down the street. When he is satisfied our presence won't be questioned, he has me follow him. Together we hurry down the walkway to the Central Government Building. Dozens of questions spring to mind. Has Michal told Symon that I remember some of my Testing? Did Michal know about the choices Tomas made during his?

As we approach our destination, Michal asks for my impressions of the residence and my classes. His impersonal tone tells me the conversation is for the benefit of those around us, so I keep my answers upbeat. I stow my bicycle in a waiting area near the front door and enter the building as Michal says, "Don't be surprised if a few people recognise you. You made quite an impression during your Induction."

His words make me conscious of the eyes that follow us as we walk through the lobby to a long hallway. Two older officials stop Michal to ask about his new job with the president's office. At the end of Michal's vague reply, he introduces me to them. An official from Housing. Another from Biological Revitalisation. The latter mentions he has a son who is in his first year of University training as a Biological Engineering student. His pride is obvious, so I smile and say I hope to have a class with his son in the future. Inside my head, though, I hear Tomas describing his Induction. Fifteen students began the process. Only eight completed it. Was this man's son one of those eight, or was he Redirected?

Forcing myself to pay attention, I try to remember the hallways that lead to the four departments I will be working with. At each, Michal helps me locate the person in charge of their piece of the Colony Railway Project. I receive several sets of bound papers and am told to come back if I have any questions; then we move on to the next department. Here and there, I spot other first-year students. Some look excited. Others are working hard to appear relaxed, but the worry in their eyes reveals the truth. I can understand their concern, because when Michal escorts me back to the front entrance, my bag barely holds all the documents I am supposed to review.

But despite the workload, I cannot get the thought of the possible Redirection of an official's son out of my mind. If the Tosu City students were killed or disappeared, wouldn't their parents object? If this official's son did not make it through the acceptance process, wouldn't he wonder what happened to him? Maybe some parents wouldn't, but this one, whose love for his son is so apparent, would. I've heard people say that Tosu City students who did not reach Dr Barnes's expectations were assigned to jobs in the colonies. Yet not one of the colony students I've talked to has ever noticed or heard of younger Tosu City adults coming to work in their area. While I know Five Lakes is smaller than the other colonies, I can't imagine the arrival of new residents from Tosu City wouldn't draw notice, even in the larger settlements. Something else is going on here. Which makes me wonder what Redirection really means. If it doesn't mean assignment to the colonies or certain death, what happens to the students who do not pass Dr Barnes's tests?

CHAPTER 15

I want to ask Michal if he has ever asked these questions, but this isn't the time or place. There are too many people listening. Too much at stake.

As I grab my bicycle, Michal says, "I have to go inside for a meeting. Are you okay getting back to the University on your own? If not, I can ask someone to help you get these papers to your residence."

I shift the strap on the bag so the weight will be easier to manage while riding and tell him I'm fine.

"Good." Michal holds the bicycle while I throw my leg over the seat. "If you need any assistance with the reports, I'll be working late for the next couple days. You'll be able to find me at the president's offices."

His eyes hold mine to make sure I understand. And I do. If I stumble across any important information or get into trouble, I am to find Michal. He will help.

Michal turns and I start pedalling. Despite the weight on my back and the worry of whether The Testing will end before inflicting more death, I smile. My legs pump and the bicycle picks up speed. My hair whips across my face, but I don't stop to fasten it back as I normally would. The freedom I feel is too wonderful to stop for even a moment.

I push the pedals and zip around pedestrians. After several blocks, there are fewer people on the streets, and I ignore caution and push myself to go even faster. The buildings and trees speed by. The sun shines warm on my face. If I close my eyes, I can almost imagine that I am back in Five Lakes, headed home to where my family waits.

Instead of taking a direct route to the University, I zigzag through the city streets, trying to prolong the happiness. Soon my legs begin to tire. Despite the exercises I have done to improve my muscle tone, my body is not used to this kind of exertion. But it will be. Dad always said the best way to keep the mind healthy is to make sure the body is strong. I know my father was right. While my legs and back are tired, my mind is more focused. More like the girl I was before I was chosen for The Testing. The one who believed that the government wanted the best for us all and that her fellow students could be trusted. This girl would never have believed that friends could betray or that a fellow student would happily abandon her to die in a metal box.

Despite the nightmares that have plagued me, I have tried to avoid remembering the time I spent locked inside a case of steel or the revenge I wanted to exact when I was released. The only thing revenge brings is more destruction. More death. That I was willing to embrace that emotion, even for a brief time, scares me more than being locked inside that box. Though I do not like Professor Holt, her message to us during Induction was correct. Leaders must be able to control their emotions. It is a skill I vow to master. If it hadn't been for my tripping on that wire, I might have done something...

The wire. The other wire I spotted on the other side of the fence. After Induction ended, I put them out of my mind. Ignored the questions I'd had when I saw them. Now that I've recalled the snares, the questions and all they imply return. Snares are set by people. People who need food. The signs on the air base fence are clear. They say the area beyond is too dangerous for anyone to venture into. The snares suggest different. If the area isn't as deadly as the warnings suggest, it would be an ideal location for anyone looking to act in secret while remaining close to the United Commonwealth's capital.

Could the rebels be using the air-field? Michal said Symon and his people are nearby, near enough for Michal and the other government rebels to pass information back and forth.

If the rebels aren't at the air-field, who else could be living in the unrevitalised area? Could Redirected students be living among the devastation?

I slow and put my feet down on the ground before crossing the bridge to the residence. Once I cross, my brief escape from the pressure and worry will end. University work will begin once again. The weight of the bag pulls on my shoulder, reminding me of the daunting task in front of me.

Walking my bicycle across the bridge, I consider how to discover what Redirection means for colony and Tosu City students. Symon's faction of rebels is working to find The Testing recordings in order to convince Dr Barnes's supporters to remove him. If the rebels don't find that proof, they'll need other evidence to convince the Debate Chamber to vote with the president. Proof of what happens to the Redirected students might be enough.

Now that I have transportation and an internship with the president, I will have a method and an excuse to leave this campus. Professor Holt and my fellow students will believe I'm working at the president's offices, while the president and her staff will assume I'm doing my work here. As long as I get everything done, no one will have reason to question my whereabouts. Learning the identities of those living on the air-field might not give me the answers I seek, but it's a place to start.

I look in the direction of Tomas's residence and wish I could talk to him about what I plan to do. The fears I have.

The conflict that might be coming.

I am about to turn my bicycle in that direction when a second-year student with pale-yellow hair offers to show me the outbuilding where I can store my bicycle. Vowing to find an opportunity to talk to Tomas later, I follow her directions and take my bulging bag inside. Since it's long past lunch, I grab an apple and some crackers from the dining hall before climbing the stairs to my rooms. The residence is mostly quiet. Students are in class, still at their internships, or locked in their rooms studying.

Sitting on the floor of my room, I pull stacks of papers out of my bag and put them into four different piles based on the departments that created them. I tie my hair back into a knot, pick a pile at random and start reading.

After an hour, I'm sure this project will take years, if not decades, to complete. Once the government decides on the path the tracks should take – and there are seven differing opinions on the best route to each of the currently inaccessible colonies – the ground needs to be cleared of trees and debris. Then bridges must be built to cross chasms in the earth. Those gaps are the reason why Five Lakes and the other colonies were not part of the original rail plan. They are also the reason none of the departments can agree on how to proceed. Those who are involved with land revitalisation don't want the railway to disrupt newly planted crops and trees, which means directing the track over some of the widest fissures. The Department of Resource Management is concerned by the amount of steel required to create bridges over those areas and wants the train directed to the areas where the gaps in the earth are smallest. Both sides have fair points.

For the next three hours, I consult maps, read long-winded documents and scribble notes. When dinnertime comes, I'm grateful for the excuse to get up and leave the papers behind – even though I know I will see faces missing from the dining room. It is time to learn who has been cut from our ranks.

The dining hall is half full when I arrive. I can feel eyes following me as I cross to the back table where Ian is seated. Most of the first years are still missing, but I spot a few. Griffin. Kaleigh. Enzo. I let out a sigh of relief at the latter. Though he has not been forthcoming about himself, I count Enzo among my friends.

When I reach my table, those seated at it stop talking.

"I guess everyone knows about my internship," I say.

Ian grins as the rest of our table suddenly fills with people. One of them is Griffin. Moments later, Enzo follows.

"The president's skimmer on campus was a tip-off that something big was happening," says Ian. "It didn't take long for people to put the pieces together. I've been fielding questions about you and the internship all day." While his tone is light, I can see tension behind his eyes as they slide down the table to Griffin and back to me.

I take a piece of bread and pretend that hunger, not worry, is churning my insides. Will and Raffe slide into the last two seats at the table, and I force a smile. While I'm glad they are not faced with Dr Barnes's Redirection, I still do not understand or trust either of them.

Turning back to Ian, I ask, "Who's been asking questions?"

"My professors. Students. Everyone is talking about the president taking a deeper interest in the University. Some think her involvement means great things for the future."

Some.

Forcing a laugh, I say, "That's because they haven't seen the work I've been assigned. I doubt I'll ever come out of my rooms. People are going to have to start bringing meals to me. I'm glad the president said I can work out of her offices if I need to, because carrying that much paper might kill me."

Everyone at my table chuckles, but Griffin's laughter has something ugly lurking behind it.

Plates of food are placed on the table. Long noodles mixed with tomatoes and greens. Flaky white fish that I've been told is plentiful in the river that runs through the centre of Tosu. A bowl of fresh berries. As we pass platters around the table, I'm asked questions about my first assignment from the president. I answer each as vaguely as possible. After a few more attempts to learn more, my classmates give up and talk of other things.

Will answers a question about his internship in the Health Department as I glance around the room, looking for other first years. I count the faces as I locate them and then count again to make certain I am right. Two are missing. Their names were Geraldine and Drake. Redirected. Perhaps soon I'll learn to where.

My plate is still full when dinner ends, so I put the fruit, bread and cheese in my bag before going back to my rooms. Ian stops me on the stairs and asks if I have any questions about my internship. I know he's offering me a chance to ask for help with my work. Part of me wants to accept. I believe we are on the same side, but without being certain I cannot take the chance.

Back in my rooms, I read the reports on the colonies that are to be joined by the railway. Five Lakes, with 1,023 citizens, is the smallest by far. Picking up the report on my home colony, I immediately realise that the person who sketched the maps and provided the details has never been to Five Lakes. The lakes that the colony is named after are in the right positions, as is the town square. But the apple orchard my father and his team cultivated is on the southwestern side of the colony. Whoever drew the map switched the location of the orchard with the windmills and solar panels that line the south-eastern border.

I dig up a blank piece of grey paper and sketch my own map. Unlike Zandri, who could capture anything in a few strokes of a paintbrush, I have limited artistic talents. But I keep drawing, telling myself that accuracy is more important than perfection. I rearrange the incorrect locations and redraw the boundaries of the colony based on my father's team's most recent revitalisation efforts, which expanded the northern border by two miles – results the officials in Tosu City might not have in their records. When I left, Zeen was scouting the area just west of our colony for the best areas to start the revitalisation process there. I can't help wondering if those plans were finalised or if they have already been embarked upon.

I dig the Transit Communicator out of my bag, turn it over and run my finger along the almost imperceptible button on the bottom. The metal is cold beneath my fingers, but touching something my brother worked on makes me feel less alone. I know Zeen dreamed of being chosen for The Testing. What would he say about it if I told him what I have learned? I wish there were a way to tell him and to hear what he would do next. Because Zeen always has a plan.

I stiffen. Something scrapes against my door. I reach

into my pocket for my knife as I scramble to my feet. When I fling open the door, I'm surprised to see Raffe standing on the other side. "What are you doing lurking out there?"

He jams his hands into his pockets and looks up and down the hall. "Can I come in?"

I study his face, finger the knife in my hand and nod. I'm not sure what he wants, but I figure it's better to find out inside my living room rather than where someone could be listening. I close the door as Raffe says, "Wow, you weren't kidding about the amount of work you were given."

Raffe moves some papers off a chair and sits at the small table. I don't bother to sit. Instead, I ask, "Why are you here?"

"To see if you need help."

I move the reports on Madison Colony and sit across from him. "Don't you have enough work of your own?"

"Not as much as you'd think." His shoulders stiffen. "I'm interning for one of the officials who work for my father. Since my father doesn't want anything to interfere with my grades, I'm going to be using my time at the Education offices to catch up on my homework."

The Education Department. Adrenaline zips through my blood. Sitting across from me is a person who might have access to the information Michal and the rebels are looking for. No one would think to question his desire to look through files. Not with his father in charge.

If only I could trust him...

Pushing away my thoughts, I glance at the papers around the room and say, "Must be nice not to have the stress of extra work."

"Not really." He puts his arms on the table and leans forward. "I didn't study late every night while growing up in order to sit around doing nothing. There are things that are broken that need to be fixed. I want to help fix them."

His gaze holds mine. In his eyes I see passion. For what, I do not know. I am about to ask when a knock sounds. Will. He gives a jaunty wave when I open the door.

"What are you doing here?" Since moving into these rooms, I've had only two visitors – Ian and Will on the first night. Suddenly, I'm popular. It's not hard to imagine why. "Do you want to help work on my assignments for the president too?"

"I saw Raffe leave his rooms and come upstairs." Before I can close the door, Will saunters inside and gives Raffe a wide smile. "I decided to see what he was up to and wasn't surprised when he came here."

Raffe leans back in the chair. "I came to offer Cia my help."

"So you can report back to your father and Dr Barnes that she can't handle her assignments?" Will asks.

"Why would I do that?" Raffe's eyes glitter with anger.

"Maybe because you don't like the idea that a colony student was picked to work in the president's office instead of you? You wouldn't be the first one around here I've heard sounding bitter about that. Griffin won't shut up about it."

"I'm not Griffin."

"No." Will nods. "But you aren't a colony student, either. So why are you here, offering to help Cia?"

"Just because someone is from the colonies doesn't mean he can be trusted, Will." Despite the aid he rendered me during Induction, distrust fills my voice.

Will looks at me. I see surprise, sorrow and regret flicker in his eyes. "Maybe not," he says. Then the cockiness I have always known returns. "But some of us are worth keeping around because of our sparkling personalities and handsome faces."

His words make Raffe laugh, and while I want nothing more than for Will to leave, even I am forced to smile. Will has that effect.

"As much as I appreciate that," I say, "your sparkling personality is keeping me from getting this work done. If the two of you both leave, I can get back to it."

"I'm not leaving until he goes." Will picks up some papers and takes a seat on the small couch.

I look at Raffe, who raises his eyebrows at me. The

expression is almost identical to one Zeen gives when I try to convince him to do something he has no intention of doing. It makes me want to stick out my tongue like I used to do when I was little.

"Hey, this report is about Madison Colony."

I turn to reach for the papers Will's holding, but the naked longing on his face makes me stop. Reading about my colony made me feel closer to those I love. As much as I want to hurt Will for all that he has done, I can't deny him this glimpse of home.

"These plans are about the railway expansion," I explain. "Four departments involved drafted opinions on how best to build a train system to the colonies that aren't part of the current system. I'm supposed to review them and report to President Collindar on which ideas have the most merit."

"Well, whoever drew this map should be pitched off the project." Will holds up the diagram of Madison Colony. "The paper mills are over here." He points to the outskirts of the city, where the report shows only unrevitalised buildings. The perfect site to build the train station. "And this area is all farmland. And why do they think we have corn and soy farms in the middle of the city?"

Raffe laughs. I sigh. "The Five Lakes Colony maps are wrong too. If both the Madison and Five Lakes maps are inaccurate, the others must be as well. I can't give the president a recommendation if the information I'm basing my judgement on is wrong."

Less than a day into my internship and I have already failed. So much for thinking I would get this assignment done quickly enough to strike out on my own.

"I can help," Will says.

"Me too."

Will rolls his eyes at Raffe. "Have you ever been outside Tosu City?"

"No." Raffe shrugs. "But that doesn't mean I can't find people who have. Give me the maps for the other colonies. I'll find students from those colonies who can look them over and tell us the things that are wrong." When I hesitate, I see that glint of passion fire up again in his eyes. "Trust me. I can do this."

Perhaps it's because I see my brother in Raffe that I consider his request. This is my assignment, but it's sheer folly to rely only on yourself when you don't have the knowledge required. My father and Magistrate Owens delegate work all the time. If anyone questions Raffe's assistance, I can say I was only doing the same.

But then I realise I don't need to.

The mistakes in the reports about Five Lakes bothered me, but I could reason them away. Five Lakes is the smallest colony. The most distant. The least communicated with by the leaders here in Tosu. But Will's observations about the flaws in the Madison Colony reports are not so easily explained. Every day the departments that created these reports make decisions that affect citizens across this country. I find it impossible to believe that a project so important would be treated with so little care. Or that the president would put so vital a task in the hands of an untried first-year University student.

I think back to the night Ian asked me to meet with him. He said his own internship was filled with writing summaries of old reports. As an intern, he was being tested on his ability to identify which facts and ideas were most important. The work wasn't real. It was a test.

Just as this must be.

I look at the papers scattered across the room. While paper is utilised more frequently at the University and within the United Commonwealth government buildings, it's still precious. Ian's internship tests were based on documents that already existed and were being recycled for his task. These reports, with their incorrect facts and mislabelled maps, could not possibly have been used before. They were created just for me.

Why? What purpose does this test serve? Did the president want to see if I would rely solely on my own knowledge or search for assistance on the colonies that

I have never seen with my own eyes?

No, my gut tells me this test is not about teamwork or being confident enough to ask for assistance when it is warranted. There are ways to determine those skills that don't involve wasting what at my school in Five Lakes would be a year's allotment of paper.

I close my eyes to block out Raffe's stare so I can think. The volume of papers and the short amount of time to read and report on them ensured I would have to work almost every moment until the deadline in order to complete the task. There would be little time to confirm the information I was reporting on.

And why would I? The documents were created by government departments. By people we depend on to make decisions for the good of our country. They are supposed to be the best at what they do. But if I used these reports to make recommendations and my recommendations were followed, then time, energy and resources would be wasted. All because I trusted something created by people who are supposed to be experts.

And I understand. This wasn't a test I was supposed to pass. Just like the final task during the Induction, this was an assignment designed for failure. The president wants me to learn that just because something is created by people in power doesn't mean it is to be trusted. A lesson I learned in The Testing. And I will not forget it now that I have learned it again.

Opening my eyes, I thank Raffe for his offer but say I don't need his assistance. I have enough information to write my report. I see annoyance colour Raffe's face before he gives a shrug. When I close the door behind Raffe and Will, I wonder about Raffe's irritation. Did my refusing his aid injure his ego, or is he frustrated that he lost the opportunity to report that I could not complete this task on my own?

I'll probably never know.

Sitting on the floor, I write a short list of recommendations for the president, including that she ask the colonies to provide accurate maps of their areas. I also suggest that when building the railway, engineers avoid laying tracks in the middle of already revitalised areas where healthy crops and trees could be affected. There's no point in negating the important and successful work that has already been done. Something I'm sure the officials in charge already know.

Once I'm done, I pick up the papers strewn across the room, pile them neatly on the table and head for my bedroom. President Collindar's lesson has made me realise something important. The signs the government posted on the fence at the air-field imply that it is dangerous to venture into that area, but this doesn't mean the government believes that to be true. Something lies behind those fences. It is time to find out what that something is.

CHAPTER 16

I allow myself two hours of sleep. The sky is still dark when I slide the external transmitter into my coat pocket, sling my bag over my shoulder and quietly descend the stairs. The dining hall and kitchen are empty. Not a surprise, since breakfast won't be served for another three hours. With only the light of the moon through the window to see by, it takes more time than I'd like to grab supplies. I slide two bottles of water, several apples and pears, some dried beef and a few small loaves of bread into my bag. If this trip works as I plan, I won't be gone very long, but it never hurts to be prepared.

Tiptoeing through the dimly lit hallways, I get to the entrance and breathe a sigh of relief as I slip out the front door. The damp, cold air makes me shiver as I walk to the small outbuilding to collect my bicycle. I keep close to the residence in case anyone from the rooms above looks out.

The vehicle shed is unlocked. I grope through darkness to where I remember storing my new bike while casting glances over my shoulder for signs I have been discovered. When I find my bike, I pull it from the shed and begin to pedal – across the bridge, down several walkways, past the library. I slow in front of Tomas's residence and use the transmitter to signal him to join me. If he sees the signal, he will turn on his light. But the residence stays dark. So, though I want nothing more than to have Tomas beside me now, I turn my bicycle and pedal past darkened buildings – all the while fighting the urge to glance behind me. If someone is watching, I want to look confident. Like I have permission to be leaving campus in the blackness of night.

But wait... not everything is dark. In the distance, I see a light on the far side of the campus. While the University is given more power allotment than the rest of the city, the residences are the only buildings allowed electricity past midnight. The light appears to be coming from a building to the north – in the same direction as the building where Obidiah was Redirected.

I swing my bicycle towards the light, not sure what I think I will learn. But anything happening at this time of night is clearly supposed to be secret. If Dr Barnes or his team are doing something they want to keep hidden, I'm betting the president and the rebels need to know about it.

The light is coming from the same building that Obidiah

walked into. Stashing my bicycle in a small group of bushes about a hundred yards away, I watch the illuminated windows for signs of movement. When I see nothing, I creep closer.

I glance through the window and see no one in the hallway. But someone must be inside for the lights to be on. Remembering Obidiah's Redirection, I stay near the brick wall and hurry to the back of the building. I'm hoping to see something to give me an idea of what is happening inside. Four skimmers sit on the ground behind the structure. Whoever piloted the vehicles must be inside. If I hide in the same place I did the last time, I will see them when they emerge. But then I will know nothing about why they are here. The only way to find out is to go inside. If I dare.

Careful to keep to the shadows, I hurry back to the front entrance. The lobby is deserted. Adrenaline, fear and doubt pulse in my veins as I wrap my fingers around the door handle. I should go back to my bike and get out of here.

I tug on the handle. The door opens an inch and I lean close, listening for the sound of anyone who could spot me. The building is silent as stone. Before I can lose my nerve, I slide through the entrance, careful to guide the door closed behind me so it doesn't make a sound. I hold my breath and walk further into the lobby, looking for a clue as to which of the three hallways I should begin my search in.

The creak of a hinge makes me jump, and the sound of

voices stills my heart. People are coming.

"Speaking of projects, did you hear about the new breed of rabbit Professor Richmard's bioengineering students have created?" The nasal male voice sounds as if its owner is just down the hall. I need to get out or hide. I duck behind a tall black reception counter as the nasal voice grows closer. "The rabbits have a genetically modified immune system that will withstand eating the plants growing in the soil out east. The students released a bunch of the new species not far from here last week. They want to see if the genetic improvements have altered survival instincts."

I wedge myself between the receptionist's stool and the counter. Blood roars in my ears as I go still.

"Let's hope this breed does better than the geese Dr Richmard was so proud of two years ago." Professor Holt's voice makes me stifle a gasp. "Not only did they lose all their feathers, the animals were overly aggressive and attacked anyone they came in contact with."

"Both of those traits turned out to be useful. Without any feathers to pluck, the birds were easier to cook, and the aggressive nature meant no one had to go searching for them to see how they were doing. That made it easier for Dr Richmard's team to track them. And it should be noted that both problems were fixed in the next genetic generation." This voice is warm. Amused. Familiar. And right on the other side of the counter I'm hiding behind.

"I can't imagine aggressive rabbits," a deep voice says. "How will Dr Richmard's team know if this new breed is thriving?"

"They're injected with a new chip that transmits their heartbeat and location to a receiver installed on top of the Biological Engineering residence. Once the data is received, it's transferred to a processor in the lab. As long as the rabbits stay within a couple miles of campus, the students can track them." The nasal voice laughs. "So far those chips are working better than the ones in the new identification bracelets. Maybe we should put the bioengineering students in charge of that project next time. We could even put them in charge of monitoring The Testing bracelets, since you had such trouble with that last year."

There are murmurs of agreement. I hold my breath and listen as they are cut off by the familiar voice. "The current issue with the University bracelets will be worked out. As for The Testing, worrying about the past is pointless. I have no doubt that Jedidiah will be happy with the alternative my team has come up with. The new data recorder in the bracelets will tell us if the locking mechanism on the clasp has been disturbed, and we'll know whether the user has removed the bracelet. We will not allow the mistakes of last year's Testing to happen again. Next time we might not get so lucky."

Several voices offer their agreement before the speakers all bid one another good night. Footsteps echo in the lobby and fade as several people go down the hallway that leads to the back of the building. But the rustle of fabric tells me at least someone is still here.

I swallow hard and wonder what he or she is waiting for. Do they suspect that someone entered the building while they were meeting? That an unauthorised person might still be here?

When the sound of walking can no longer be heard, Professor Holt breaks the silence. "Is everything else under control? Jedidiah is concerned there is dissention in your ranks."

"When dealing with the brightest minds, you have to expect some will question the direction we are taking." Despite the reasonable tone, something about the voice sends a shiver up my spine. I know I've heard the voice before. I just can't recall where. But as much as I want to see who it belongs to, I keep perfectly still as the man says, "Those pushing the hardest for change have been given tasks to distract them. They've been given a new goal that they foolishly believe I disapprove of. They think their plan will change the course of our country's history, when in actuality, it will serve to destroy what they think they are building. Once their plans are put into action, we won't have to worry about them any more."

"How can you be so sure?" Professor Holt demands.

"Because, my dear professor, they're all going to die."

Calm. Rational. The same tone my father employs to tell my brothers and me to help our mother with dinner. People killed. For believing something should change. Is this man talking about members of Symon's rebellion? He must be. Their efforts have not gone unnoticed, and now some of them are in mortal danger. As I will be if this man or Professor Holt discovers me listening to their conversation. Michal needs to be warned so he can pass the news along to Symon.

I swallow hard and wrap my arms around myself as the male voice lets out a low chuckle and says, "Trust me, professor. They'll be taken care of. Your precious University programme will continue exactly as Jedidiah and you planned."

"You'd better be right. The president—"

"The president will not be in power much longer. She just doesn't know it. You don't have to worry. Now, let me escort you to your vehicle. The next time we speak, I promise you will see the results we have all been working for."

I let out a sigh as the footsteps fade. The lights blink out. A door slams shut. I force myself to sit quietly and count to one hundred, in case either of them comes back. When no one does, I grab the counter and use it to support my shaking legs as I stand. Part of me wants to search the building to see if it contains something the rebellion could use, but I doubt that they would leave anything incriminating out in the open, and the nearness of dawn makes me head for the exit.

I look through the window to make sure no one is in sight, yank open the door and run. When I reach my bike, I jerk it from its hiding place, throw the bag over my shoulder and ride. Pushing the pedals. Using the terror in my veins to go faster.

When my bicycle is returned to the shed, I hurry to my rooms before the rest of the residence stirs. I turn the lock behind me, lean against the door and start to shake. On trembling legs, I walk to the bathroom with the hope that a hot shower will ease the chill running through my body. I sit on the floor of the shower and let the hot water run until my skin is pink and the room filled with steam. When I'm dry, I pull on my sleeping garments, climb under the covers and close my eyes tight, hoping to leave the cold fear in my veins behind.

When I wake, the room is bright with light. I glance at the clock. Lunch was long ago. I should get up. I need to find Tomas to formulate a plan. But my eyes are grainy and my muscles ache. So instead, I eat an apple from my bag, curl up on the bed and doze until dinner. Even after sleeping all day, I have to force myself to climb out from under the covers and get dressed. At dinner, I do my best to laugh, talk and eat just like everyone else. When Ian teases me about being so overworked I don't have time to come to meals, I laugh and admit I was up so late working that I slept most of the day. The words are easy to say since they are true.

More than once, I catch Griffin and Damone looking in my direction, but I pretend not to notice. When the meal is over, I use work as an excuse to go back to my rooms. I ache for the comfort of Tomas's arms, but I remember Griffin and Damone's watchful eyes. If I go find him, someone will report that to Professor Holt and Dr Barnes. Tomas would end up in danger. Instead, I stay where I am, stare out the window and watch the sky go from light to dark.

I make excuses as to why it is best for me to stay in my rooms instead of pedalling into Tosu City or to the air-field tonight. I don't want to go alone. I don't have a flashlight. My muscles aren't conditioned enough to make the journey quickly. I don't know if Michal will be in the president's office, and I don't have the exact co-ordinates of the air-field. All are true, but deep down, I recognise the real reason I cannot make the trip.

I am scared.

The Testing put my life in danger. Though I still don't have complete memories of that time, I know I faced the fear. I survived. I should be able to do the same now. But this fear is different.

During The Testing, I had no choice but to face the terror Dr Barnes's challenges evoked. Last night, for the first time, it was my choice and my choice alone that put me in the path of danger.

Part of me thought I had accepted the possibility that I might be given the ultimate punishment by Dr Barnes and his team of officials.

I was wrong.

I want to live.

As important as it is to put an end to The Testing and Dr Barnes's current University programme, there's a group already working towards that goal. People like Michal, who are older, more experienced, smarter. They know this city and the people who inhabit it better than I. They don't need help from a first-year University student. Any information I might find can also be found by Symon and his team. And even if I wanted to try, it's too late for me to make a difference. As much as I'd like to think I'm important, I'm not. I'm too inexperienced. Too untried. Too young.

Technically, my school graduation in Five Lakes marked me as an adult. But huddled on the bed with my arms wrapped tight around my body, I have never felt less worthy of the distinction. As much as I always wanted to believe my father when he said I was capable of doing anything, I know I am not. I cannot deliberately make a choice that could end my life.

I am not a leader.

I am a coward.

My sleep is filled with strange dreams. My muscles feel heavy when I wake. My appetite is gone, though I force myself to eat before biking to the president's offices. Since it is Sunday, the office hallways are mostly empty. I drop my report onto the president's desk and immediately return to campus. No detours. No notes warning Michal and the rebels of possible danger; no stopping at Tomas's residence to tell him what I know. No opportunity for Dr Barnes to accuse me of behaviour that marks me for Redirection.

When the next week starts, I go to classes, turn in assignments and take tests. My teachers praise my work. I receive high marks, as do the other members of our study group. Everyone asks questions about my internship, especially those who have been assigned to internships within the Central Government Building. Despite the weight of my fear, my answers are upbeat. Yes, I met the president. Yes, I already turned in my first assignment. No, I have not heard the rumour about the change in law the president will propose on the Debate Chamber floor.

I feel Tomas stiffen next to me as I answer the last question, and when I go upstairs into the stacks to find a book about the former European Union, he follows.

"What change in law is the president going to propose?"

"I don't know."

Tomas put his hands on my shoulders. "The others might believe that, but they don't understand you the way I do." His fingers trace the outline of my jaw. "I know when you're angry or scared. Right now you're both. I can't help you unless you tell me why." When I still don't answer, he drops his hand and asks, "Is it me?"

"No. It's..." The words die in my throat as I stare into the eyes of the boy I have trusted with so many of my secrets and my heart. Do I trust him now? Yes. Despite all that has happened, I believe in him. I love him.

Quickly, I tell him about the rebellion. About the president's upcoming challenge to Dr Barnes, the threatened vote of confidence, and the president's willingness to embrace violence to end The Testing and prevent her loss of power.

"According to Michal, people around the city as well as students here at the University are being armed for this conflict. Unless Symon's rebel faction finds something to convince the Debate Chamber to vote out Dr Barnes, people will die."

"So will Dr Barnes." The cold acceptance in Tomas's voice makes me shiver. "He deserves to pay."

"Yes." I slip my hand into his and squeeze tight to remind him that I am here. That despite what we have been through, we are still the people who came from Five Lakes Colony. People who believe in doing what is best for everyone. "But not like that."

Tomas's grey eyes look into mine. In their depths I see anger and pain, but I also see the warmth and kindness of the boy I have known since childhood. A boy who has turned into a man.

"You're right," he says. "As much as I want Dr Barnes to pay for what he has done, the country can't afford another war. I don't think that my internship in the genetics lab will give me access to the information the president needs, but I'll keep my ears open. You'll do the same. If we're lucky, Dr Barnes will be voted out of power and The Testing will end without the rebels raising their weapons."

"And if we aren't lucky?" I ask.

Tomas's hand tightens on mine. "Then we run. We can take off our bracelets on our way out of Tosu. The city will be too busy with a civil war to worry about missing University students. They'll never bother to ask if we fled and returned home."

Home. My parents. My brothers. A place far away from Tosu City, filled with people I know and trust. Tomas could be right. There is a chance no one will search for us. Not with a rebellion going on. We might be able to go home and use our skills to help the people we grew up with survive.

Five Lakes has so little contact with Tosu City, they may not even realise a war is happening. When we tell them, they will not only understand why we returned, they will welcome us with open arms. Perhaps we can leave the past behind us and build a future without fear. Together. And when Tomas's lips find mine, the kiss is filled with passion and the hope that even if war comes, we will survive.

The days pass. I stash extra food in my bag during meals in preparation for the journey Tomas and I may make. During the study sessions, I try to ignore the faces around the table. Stacia. Enzo. Will. Raffe. Naomy. Holt. Brick. People I am planning to leave behind if violence comes. But the hope Tomas's plan gave me fades as guilt takes hold.

On Friday, I am assigned to work with one of the president's officials on reading through plans for a new communication system. Here and there, I catch snatches of conversation as the president's office prepares for the debate motion on The Testing she will soon be putting forward. Throughout the day, I watch for Michal, hoping for news that evidence to condemn Dr Barnes has been found. I spot him as I'm leaving for the day. He looks tired as he climbs out of a skimmer behind the president and several older officials. His steps slow when he sees me. His eyes watch as the president and her team disappear inside the building, and then he signals for me to follow him around the corner.

Once we are out of sight, he dispels my hope. Tangible proof has yet to be located, and Symon is working hard to persuade the president and the other faction that patience is required to avoid perpetuating the cycle of violence.

The words I heard while hiding in the dark echo in my head. A promise of more violence.

Quickly, I tell Michal about overhearing Professor Holt and the voice that spoke of murder. When I am done, Michal tells me not to worry. Symon would know if Dr Barnes was aware of the rebels. But he promises to pass the information along.

During a whispered study session conversation that evening, Tomas assures me that I have done my part. I have passed along the warning. Other than preparing for flight, there is nothing more either of us can do. I don't tell him about the air-field and the answers I think could be found there, because I'm scared. I want to go home. I don't want either of us to die.

That night, I toss and turn as I wait for sleep to come. When it does, it brings with it faces of people I don't know. Some wear bracelets of silver. Others wear ones woven of silver and gold. Extending from each bracelet is a chain bolted to the brick wall behind them. Some hurl themselves forward, trying to get free. Others seem resigned to their fates, oblivious to the metal links binding them to the wall.

One by one, they turn and notice me. Their eyes look at my wrist. Envy, anger, desire and despair light their faces. When I glance down, I see that I am not wearing a bracelet. I am standing in a field of rich green grass that my father helped create, far away from Tosu City. I am free.

Or am I?

I look around and my heart begins to pound. Something is wrong. I take several steps forward and run smack into a barrier. A wall. I turn and race in the other direction. Five steps. Ten. Another wall. One wall meets another. Then another.

A cage that cannot be seen is no less there than if the walls were made of steel.

The Testing candidates chained to the wall stand still as stone. In their eyes I see terror combined with a hunger that can only be sated by freedom. It's a look I know. The same one I have seen in my own reflector. A look I must wear now.

I stumble backwards, yelling that I can't help them. But I can try.

The walls of my prison are cold to the touch. The chill seeps through my fingers. I shiver, pull my hand away and the cold recedes. I step closer to the centre of the confined space and feel warmer. Less frightened. Safe. A step closer to the wall, and panic gnaws my stomach.

And I realise – the walls are constructed of my terror. To escape, I will have to not only face, but defeat, my fear.

Nausea rolls through me as I push my hand against the wall. A drop of water hits the floor. Then another, until it becomes a steady stream. Water pools at my feet. The wall weakens beneath my hands. I push against the barrier and feel it tremble, but it does not break. I take several steps towards the centre of the space and prepare to run as a voice inside tells me to stop. That what I'm doing is dangerous. That breaking this wall of ice could result in my death.

I know.

I accept.

I run.

The ice shatters on impact – as do the Testing candidates' chains. I feel shards of ice slice my flesh. The pain I feel makes it hard to see whether the others have survived. But when I put my head on the blood-streaked earth, I know it doesn't matter. Whether we are dead or alive, we are better off because we are free.

I jolt awake and run my fingers along the five Testing scars. They burn just like the shards in my dream. I slide out of bed, turn on the light and pace the length of my bedroom. When the dream doesn't fade, I run my hand along the wall. I feel the same chill I did in my nightmare.

But these walls are real.

Hours ago, hiding behind the walls of this room made me feel safe. I now see it for what it is. A prison. The safety is just an illusion. No matter how careful I am or how good my grades are, I will never be free of the threat Dr Barnes and his system present. None of us will be until Dr Barnes and his officials are removed from power.

Unlike in many of my nightmares, none of the faces in my dream were familiar. But I know who they are. Future candidates. Current University students. People who, like my friend Daileen, are at this moment seated at their families' kitchen tables or in their residence rooms, studying late into the night, hoping to ace the next test. To get closer to their dream. They don't know that the people who safeguard that dream are making choices that could lead to their deaths. But I do. No matter the excuses I make or the fear I feel, I cannot turn away from that knowledge. The president must win her vote. Dr Barnes must be removed from power. The Testing must end.

So far the rebels have not found the evidence the president needs to win the vote and defeat Dr Barnes. If the vote fails, the other rebel faction will attack, and – if the man I overheard is correct – Dr Barnes's team will be ready for them. They will do whatever it takes to crush those who wish to end The Testing, and they will sentence the rebels, generations of candidates, and perhaps even the president and her staff to death. I may not be able to find the information that can keep this from happening, but I have to try.

I glance at the clock. It is just past midnight. There's plenty of time to prepare and search the abandoned air-field for information the rebels can use. I strip off my nightwear and pull on my clothes. Lacing my boots, I come up with a plan. First stop, the residence library. Last week, I left without learning the exact boundaries of the air-field. During the Induction, I logged the co-ordinates into the Transit Communicator, but the air-field is large. It would be best to have a more complete picture of the area I will be searching.

The hour is early enough that students are still in the hangout room when I walk by. After looking through the library rooms, I find a tattered atlas of the former fifty United States shelved near the floor. The old air-field base is marked on a detailed map of Kansas, along with its longitude and latitude. Step one complete.

An empty lab completes step two. I find several boxes of matches and a small penlight. I also unearth a narrow, razor-sharp folding knife used to cut up plants. It isn't much, but between this knife and the one in my pocket, I will have protection if I run into trouble.

Back in my rooms, I slide the signalling receiver I built into my pocket. While I do not want to put Tomas in danger, I know he will want to be by my side. Studying the map, I plug the co-ordinates for the centre of the air-field into the Transit Communicator. The machine calculates and tells me it is just shy of ten miles away. If Tomas and I leave within the hour, we should be able to reach it, look around and get back to our residences before our absence is noticed. I place the map book in the bottom of my bag and then add the change of clothes, food, water and matches on top. I hold the penlight in my hand. The knives go in the side pocket. Just in case.

When the clock strikes one, I open my door, step into the hall and listen for sounds from my fellow students. There is silence.

The moon isn't as bright as last week, which makes it easier to cross the residence property without notice. A crack of a stick makes me jump, but when I squint into the darkness, I see nothing. Thanks to the penlight, I find my bicycle quickly. As I start to wheel it away, I hear a shuffling noise.

My heart leaps to my throat as a figure fills the doorway and says, "I knew you were up to something. Wait until I tell Professor Holt about this."

CHAPTER 17

Damone.

I hit the signal button in my pocket and then lift my penlight to his smirking face.

"You scared me to death." I force a quiet laugh. "What are you doing out here?"

He leans against the doorway. "I think you're the one who should be answering that question."

Tension floods me, but I shrug as though I haven't any concern. "I woke up and couldn't go back to sleep. So I thought I'd take a ride."

"That's a good lie." He laughs. "I wonder if Dr Barnes and Professor Holt will believe it. They might, unless you have something in that bag that clues them in to what you're really doing."

I clutch the strap of the bag and pull it tight against me. If Dr Barnes gets ahold of the Transit Communicator...

"What's in the bag, Cia?" Damone pushes off the wall and saunters forward. "Griffin thinks whatever's in there must be pretty important, since you never let the thing out of your sight."

"Why do either of you care what I have in my bag?" I shift the bag on my shoulder so I can reach the side pocket. Sliding my hand inside, I say, "Are you failing your classes and need to borrow my homework?"

My fingers close around the handle of the lab knife as Damone's eyes narrow. "We don't need a colony brat's help to pass. We're the ones who deserve to be here. We should be the ones working with the president. Griffin figures whoever turns you in will be able to request that assignment. He thought you'd never have the guts to venture out after dark, so he went to bed." Damone smiles. "But I know you better."

"I saved your life," I whisper, hoping Tomas has received my signal. That he is at this moment looking for me.

"I saved myself." Anger crackles in his voice. "The snake only attacked because of you. And I was only in danger of being left behind at the second challenge because Will and Enzo were too weak to do what was necessary to ensure we'd win. Your lack of leadership made them weak. You don't belong here, and I'm going to be the one who removes you for good."

I grab my bicycle and throw it forward as Damone lunges for me. He lets out a shout of anger. The clatter of metal and a yelp of pain give me a burst of satisfaction as I flick off my light and dart to the left side of the shed. I slide the knife free of my bag and swing it towards the shadows in front of me as I try to think my way out of this.

But there is no way out. Even if I fight my way past Damone and flee, he will report me to Professor Holt. Dr Barnes will send officials to look for me. Tomas and I only planned to escape if our disappearance would be covered by the outbreak of fighting. People might then believe we were casualties of that action. Now there is no chance for my flight to go unnoticed. My family could be punished, as could Tomas and all the students who dared to be my friends. If I turn myself in, they might be safe. Unless Dr Barnes gives me the drug used in The Testing interview. Unlike during my Testing days, I have nothing to counteract its effects. My secrets will be in the open. My family still at risk. Right now the only war that is being waged is here. No matter what happens, there will be consequences to this night.

I race for the moonlit doorway. Hands grab me from behind and yank me back. Instinctively, I lash out with the knife. I feel the blade make contact with fabric and flesh, and Damone screams. His grip loosens and I run.

I am in the doorway when I hear the footsteps. I run faster, out of the shed, towards the bridge. I stumble over a small bush. That one moment is all it takes for Damone to catch me. His body hits mine, and we crash to the ground. I roll to the side and am stopped as hands close around my throat from behind and squeeze.

I can't breathe. Pressure builds in my chest. The world goes hazy around me. I claw with my free hand at the fingers digging into my flesh and then do the only thing I can do. I grip the knife and stab behind me with the last of my energy.

The knife punches into flesh. I hear a gasp as the hands release their hold on my throat. Blood runs over my hand. The knife plunges deeper. Air slides into my lungs. There is a loud thunk, and Damone's body slumps on top of me. Gasping for breath, I struggle out from under the weight and hear "Let me help you."

Not Tomas's voice. Raffe.

I look up. He is standing in front of me holding a large wooden bat in one hand. The other is held out in front of him. I close my hand around his and climb to my feet. Only then do I look down at the body sprawled on the ground.

"Is he dead?" It hurts to speak, and my voice sounds unfamiliar. Low. Harsh. Swollen.

"Not yet." Raffe puts the bat on the ground, grabs Damone's legs, and begins to drag him. Not towards the residence and the help that lies inside, but away.

"What are you doing?"

"We can't risk Damone telling Professor Holt about this."

"We can't prevent him from talking."

"Yes." Raffe looks up at me. "We can. No one will question a student disappearing from the University. Especially one who is barely making the grade, like Damone. Students know failure requires a price. Some are too cowardly to pay it."

"I don't understand," I whisper. But I do. Raffe is dragging Damone to the ravine. If Damone isn't dead now, he will be when he hits the bottom. "We can't kill him."

Raffe stops at the edge of the crevice. "If we don't, we'll both suffer the consequences. I'm willing to face Professor Holt if you are. Your choice." He puts his foot on Damone's back and waits.

My choice. Save Damone or myself. Kill or be killed.

I wish Tomas were here to help me make this choice. I know the one I should make. All my life I've been taught to respect each and every life. To do whatever is necessary to preserve it.

Moonlight glistens off the blood on my hands. I picture myself running inside. Calling for a doctor. Following the teachings my parents instilled in me.

But I don't. I tell myself Damone has lost too much blood to be helped. That no matter the choice I make, he will die. Both are true. But I know in my heart the real reason behind my choice. Choosing to attempt to save Damone's life means ending my own.

I look out into the darkness, willing Tomas to step from the shadows. When he doesn't, I take a deep breath, swallow the bile building in my throat, and nod.

That one movement is all it takes. Raffe puts his arms under Damone and rolls Damone onto his back. Someone lets out a low groan. Raffe from exertion? Damone from pain? Before I can find out, Raffe gives one final push, and Damone's body plunges over the edge.

I can't breathe. Bending over, I put my hands on my legs and force air in and out of my lungs. Without missing a beat, Raffe walks back across the grass, grabs the bat and drops it into the emptiness below. "Okay. Let's get going."

There is no guilt in his voice. No concern for the life he has just taken. None of the tears that make my body tremble and my eyes burn.

"Cia. We have to go." He grabs my arm and pulls me towards the shed. "We don't want to be out here if someone inside starts wondering what the shouting was that woke them up. If we don't want to get caught, we have to get out of here now."

I flinch at the icy tone of Raffe's voice. Nausea rocks my stomach. A knife slick with blood is clutched in my hand. A body lies broken at the bottom of the ravine. Raffe appears unfazed as he picks my bike off the shed floor and wheels it out to me. A moment later, he returns with one of his own.

"Where are we going?"

"You're not going anywhere with him."

Tomas.

I turn and see him step out of the darkness into a patch of moonlight. His face is filled with worry and rage as he looks from me to the knife in my hands to Raffe.

"I should have figured you'd turn up." Raffe takes a step towards Tomas. "Did you and Cia plan to meet tonight, or did the two of you figure out some kind of emergency contact method?" When neither of us answers, Raffe shrugs. "Doesn't matter. Cia didn't need you to come to her rescue. She saved herself from Damone. The two of us were just about to head out. Do you want to come with us?"

Tomas stiffens at the implication that Raffe and I planned to go somewhere together without informing him. I start to explain, but realise this isn't the time or place. The longer we stand here talking, the greater chance there is of someone hearing us. If someone finds us here, they will see the knife and the blood that stains my hands. They will know what I have done. All of us will pay the penalty for my crime. I will not allow that to happen.

Sliding the knife into my bag, I take a step towards Tomas. "Look." The word scrapes my swollen throat. "We have to get out of here now."

"I'm ready when you are." Raffe sets down his bike,

heads back to the outbuilding and returns with another. "This was Damone's. I don't think he'll mind if you use it, Tomas. Now, if both of you are ready, I think we should get moving."

I look towards the edge where Damone lost his life, feel the throb of my throat where his hands tried to end mine and climb onto my bicycle. Tomas does the same, but refuses to look at me as we begin to pedal.

Both Tomas and Raffe let me take the lead as we ride across campus. I push my legs as fast as they will go, desperate to leave the sorrow and fear of my actions behind. But there is no forgetting the feeling of my knife puncturing Damone's flesh or watching his body plunge into the ravine. I want to collapse to the ground and howl with frustration, guilt and sorrow. But I can't because there is more at work here than a boy who wanted my success for his own and was willing to do anything to get it. There will be time enough for guilt and recriminations later. Now I have to decide what to do about the boys riding behind me. One I would trust with my life. The other just saved my life, but I do not understand his motivations. I need to if Tomas and I are going to survive this night.

When we are several blocks away from the University's entrance, I stop and wait for Tomas and Raffe. When they arrive, I ignore the frustration on Tomas's face and turn to

Raffe. "This is as far as we are going to go until you answer some questions. I know why Damone came outside tonight. Why did you?"

"Because I was following you." Raffe pushes up the sleeve of his jacket. In the moonlight, I can see three angry-looking scars. "You helped me during the Induction, not because you were trying to get ahead but because it was the right thing to do. That made an impression." He shrugs and rolls down his sleeve. "A couple of days after the Induction ended, I heard Griffin and Damone say that if they couldn't beat you in class, they'd find another way to get rid of you. A few days later, Professor Holt asked Griffin to keep an eye on you. He said she was concerned about your suitability for leadership and wanted Griffin to report any unusual behaviour. Griffin asked Damone and me to help him follow you. I drew that duty last weekend."

My heart skips. "You saw me leave the residence."

"You were too fast for me to keep up." He gives a small smile. "This time I was ready. Apparently, so was Damone."

I shake my head. "I don't understand. Why not report me to Professor Holt?"

"Because I'm not like Griffin and Damone." Raffe glances in the direction we came from. "I grew up believing that going to the University and helping revitalise this country were the greatest things a person could do. Two years ago,

I started to realise that things weren't as perfect as my father and his friends claimed. Something happened—"

"What?" Tomas asks.

Raffe shakes his head. "There isn't time to get into that now. The two of you can either trust me or not, but if we're going to do whatever it is you planned, we'd better get moving or we'll never make it back by morning. Unless, of course, you guys don't plan to go back."

"Of course we're going back," I say, wondering if Raffe has somehow overheard Tomas and me discuss our plans to leave. If so, what else did he hear?

Though we have studied together, Raffe is not a friend. Not someone I understand. His actions tonight should elicit my trust, but part of me can't help wondering if that was the reason he helped me in the first place. Damone had more ambition than brains. It's not a surprise he would jump to betray a fellow student in order to better his standing. While I didn't like Damone, I think I understand what lay behind his actions. Raffe is a mystery. I do not want to believe someone would aid in someone's death just to gain the confidence of another. However, Will's actions in The Testing proved almost anything is possible if someone wants something badly enough. It's possible Raffe pushed Damone to his death in order to delve into my secrets. My father once told me to trust no one. I take Tomas's hand and hold tight. No matter what secrets we had in the past, I know I am right to trust Tomas. Unless I want to return to campus and ignore my chance to help end The Testing, I see no choice for now but to take Raffe with us.

"So are we going to stand here and talk all night, or do what you planned to do?" Raffe asks.

"Let's go," I answer.

"No." Tomas lets go of my hand. "Cia, you can't trust him."

Maybe not, but I see no other option. Asking Raffe to give us a moment, I lead Tomas down the street and explain about the air-field and the answers I hope to find there. "The president is going to propose the change in law and ask for a vote soon. We may not have another chance to look for the answers the rebels need. I don't know if I can live with myself if people die and I didn't do everything I could to prevent it. Can you?"

I look at the dried blood on my fingers. Maybe if I prevent more deaths, I can live with the one I am responsible for. Maybe Tomas will be able to live with Zandri's death, too.

Tomas studies Raffe across the darkened street. In the silence, I think of Will and his betrayal during The Testing. Tomas believed he could not be trusted. I insisted Tomas was wrong, and we almost died. I would not blame Tomas for walking away from me now. Instead he pulls me close and says, "No, I couldn't live with myself either. Let's go."

United, we walk back to where Raffe waits with our bicycles. I pull the Transit Communicator out of my bag, turn it on and tie it to the middle of my handlebars with shoelaces I took out of a pair of boots. Between the Communicator's compass and the map book, I should be able to get us there and back without getting lost or turned around.

The map showed a number of ways to get to the airfield. My choice is a route two miles longer than the others. A road just beyond the revitalised boundaries of the city. Speed is important, but speed will mean nothing if we are spotted. Three people riding down the city streets in the middle of the night would attract attention.

Raffe says nothing as we pedal to the east. Revitalised streets give way to those abandoned to time. The road is bumpy and buckled. Using the dim light of the moon, I steer clear of the most damaged areas and keep riding. Finally, we reach the road that heads to the south. Here the tarmac is smooth and in perfect repair. I feel my shoulders tense as I glide along the asphalt. The road's condition acts as a warning. A roadway is only this well tended if it is important to the United Commonwealth Government. Though I doubt officials would travel in the dead of night, we need to take care.

The glowing display of the Transit Communicator marks

our progress. I keep picturing Damone. His lanky body. Angular face. The calculation in his eyes except when he laughed. Laughter transformed him into someone young and carefree. From what he said during the Induction, laughter and fun were not priorities in his family. Success was. Perhaps if he had laughed more, he would not have made the choice to trade my life for his gain. He would not have been a tool for Professor Holt to use against me.

I think of all the lives lost in the Seven Stages of War. Of those who were sent by their leaders into battle and instructed to kill. Did those in charge understand the implications of their orders? Or were they, like Damone, thinking only of what they hoped to gain?

We are less than a mile from our destination when Raffe asks us to stop. "Do you think the two of you can tell me where we're headed? The only thing this way is the old air-force base."

"That's where we're going," Tomas says.

"Why? You wouldn't have seen the warning signs during Induction, but Cia did."

"Someone isn't paying attention to the signs," I say. "There are people living inside that fence, and I want to know who."

Raffe looks like he wants to push for an explanation, but I cut him off by putting my feet on the pedals and going forward. If he doesn't want to follow, he doesn't have to. But he does. As we pedal the last mile, I see Tomas and Raffe scanning the horizon, looking for signs of whoever might be living in this unrevitalised area. Off to the east, a howl echoes across the plains. A reminder to keep alert for more than human-made tracks.

I spot the fence a hundred yards south of a bend in the road. We hide our bicycles in a thicket of bushes and listen for sounds that we are not alone. Dried leaves crunch under our feet, and the wind rustles grass and tree branches. Other than that, everything is silent.

Taking a deep breath, I put my hands on the fence and climb. Our feet hit the other side at the same time. Raffe starts forward, but I turn back and scan the fence, looking for a landmark to tell us where we entered. The shadows of twisted trees and scraggly bushes spread across the landscape. Nothing unique marks this spot. Digging into my bag, I pull out the extra shirt I packed and tie it near the top of the chain link. There's a chance someone will see the fabric and wonder at it, but I would rather take the risk than waste time looking for our entry point later. Between the marker I've left and the Communicator's compass, we should be able to find our way out.

"How did you know to mark the fence like that?" Raffe whispers.

Tomas answers, "It's what we do in Five Lakes to make sure we can find our way back when we venture outside our colony's boundaries."

Raffe nods. "That makes sense. So now what?"

I pull out my penlight and shine it close to the ground. "Now we look for tracks and listen for sounds that will lead to whoever lives here."

I glance at the watch on my bag. We agree to search for an hour. It isn't much time, but it's all we can afford if we want to make it back to the residence before dawn.

I watch the compass and walk with my hand cupped around the penlight's beam – a trick Zeen taught me to limit the amount of light that can be seen at a distance – but juggling the two is awkward. Especially when the terrain becomes less level as grass and trees give way to broken pavement and collapsed buildings.

"You'll be able to look for tracks faster if you let me hold that." Raffe reaches for the Communicator, but Tomas's hand is there first.

"I think it's better if I take it." Tomas looks at the readout and points. "South is this way."

Raffe jerks at every rustle and snap. It makes it hard to focus as I study the ground. I am about to give up when my light passes over a section of dirt in between broken tarmac. The dirt is dry and hard, but recently must have been soft enough to capture the tread of someone's shoe. The print is faint. Too faint for Raffe to understand what he is seeing. But Tomas does. I spot another shoeprint fifteen feet from the first. Then another. The brown and yellow grasses growing through the tarmac are stamped down in a manner that suggests someone has recently travelled this way. But as encouraging as that is, a glance at the watch tells me we will need to start back soon. If so, I will have to accept that this trip and the death that came because of it have been for nothing.

That's when I see it.

A flickering glow in the distance. A fire.

My blood quickens as I turn off the flashlight and slide it into the pocket of my bag. I flinch when my fingers brush the handle of the laboratory knife and then close around it. My hand shakes as I pull it free. Never do I want to be forced to take another life, but I am not naïve. Whoever is by the fire may attack. If so, I will be ready.

Step by careful step, I move closer and crouch behind what must have once been some kind of vehicle. Tomas follows my movements and soundlessly joins me. Raffe arrives moments later. My heart pounds as I peer around the twisted metal and squint into the firelight.

People are lounging near the fire. Behind them is a one-storey structure that looks to be mostly intact. I hear the murmur of voices, but I'm too far away to understand what they say. Part of me wonders why they are awake at this time of night. Then a memory flashes. Tomas and I huddle together on another night. Not beyond pieces of twisted metal, but in a small building with no roof. In my memory, Tomas tells me to get some sleep. He'll wake me in a few hours so I can keep watch for other Testing candidates or animals that might mean us harm. These few must be the ones designated to safeguard their group's sleep. That means there are more people nearby.

Someone laughs and shouts, "Hey, new guy. Bring us some water."

"My name isn't new guy." The door to the structure opens. A man appears and walks towards the fire. "It's Cris. If you guys are such hotshots, you should have figured that out by now."

I hear Tomas suck in air as the firelight glints off a large silver gun strapped to the man's side. But it isn't the gun that makes Tomas catch his breath. It's the sound of the voice, the sight of the blonde hair and the face that is familiar to us both.

The man taking a seat by the fire isn't named Cris. It's my oldest brother, Zeen.

CHAPTER 18

There is more laughter. More conversation. Tomas's hand finds mine, but I barely feel his touch as I close my eyes and then open them again. Zeen is still here. Wearing the gun at his side as easily as he wears his smile. My heart soars at the sight of him, even as confusion swirls through me. After so long without a glimpse of my family, to see Zeen's grin and hear his laugh is like a balm for my soul. I want to race to where he sits, fling my arms around him and bury my head in his shoulder the way I did when I was little.

But I don't. Because Zeen is using a different name, which tells me he doesn't trust these people, whoever they are. No matter how much I want to, I cannot go to him. Not without more information.

I glance at the watch on my bag. The time I set aside for this expedition has elapsed. To return to the residence without being discovered, we have to leave now. We need to be in our beds when Damone is found missing. Otherwise, questions will be asked. Questions we do not want to answer.

Only, I can't leave without knowing what Zeen is doing here – I have to stay. Raffe and Tomas don't, though. I will not risk their futures at the University or their lives just because I'm risking my own.

Leaning towards them, I whisper, "It's getting late. If you go back to the University now, you'll make it before dawn. There's something I have to do first."

Tomas shakes his head. "I'm not leaving you here."

"I'm staying if he does," Raffe whispers.

"This has nothing to do with you." Tomas's voice is quiet but firm. "Besides, Cia and I can move faster and more quietly if you're not with us. The last thing we need is for your heavy footsteps to get us all shot."

When Raffe looks to me, I nod. "Tomas is right. Head back to the fence. Look for the marker. I promise we'll be right behind you."

"You'd better," he whispers. I watch him retreat into the darkness. Leaves rustle. A branch snaps. Then quiet. I feel a stab of guilt knowing Raffe has to navigate his way back on his own, but I am glad Tomas is with me. He cares about Zeen too.

Tomas and I circle to our left, careful to stay low. My blood races as one woman picks up a shotgun and rests it on her lap, but she doesn't turn in our direction. When we get closer, I tell Tomas to stay where he is. I am smaller and faster and will be safer on my own. Tomas looks unhappy, but he nods understanding. I dart behind a partially collapsed wall twenty feet away from where my brother sits, and listen.

The conversation drifts from subject to subject. The way game is being stolen from snares. The new housing they've been promised will be finished soon. Someone snores. A woman says she's glad their shift is almost over. One of the men snorts and says she's just happy to be sliding into bed with her new husband. There is laughter. A few jokes. The minutes pass. My heart jumps when I hear Zeen ask about some kind of schedule. Someone says it will be decided in the next couple of days. The conversation shifts to breakfast and whether they can convince the cooks to make pancakes. I hear Zeen say he'll mention it to them. He's going inside to work on boosting the radio signal. There's some good-natured teasing about him doing extra work to please Symon as all but one of the sentries follow Zeen into the building in search of food. Other than the one dozing by the fire, everything is quiet. But I've got the information I sought.

This is Symon's rebel camp.

That fact alone should make me feel safe. But if Zeen thinks it's important to keep his identity a secret, there's a good reason. Until I know what that reason is or why

Zeen has come here in the first place, I cannot hope to be reunited with my brother. Luckily for me, there is one person I am certain knows the answer to both of those questions.

I move quickly back to Tomas. Together, we hurry past the twisted vehicle and towards the warped trees I remember passing. When we are far enough away from the rebel campsite for it to be safe, I pull out my penlight. Our feet fly across the ground as the sky lightens. As we run, Tomas uses the Transit Communicator to guide our way.

Dawn is breaking as we reach the chain-link fence. Tomas spots the marker to our left, and we race towards it. I grab the shirt as I climb up and over and hit the ground running on the other side.

"Are you okay?" Tomas asks. "What is Zeen doing here with the rebels?"

"I don't know," I say as I reach for my bike. "But, I—" I stop cold as I realise all three bikes are still hidden in the bushes.

"What's wrong?"

I turn and scan the fence, looking for movement behind the chain link, and answer, "Raffe never made it back."

Wind blows the leaves on trees. A rabbit races through the underbrush. Otherwise, I see and hear nothing, but I know Raffe is out there. Where? Even without the Communicator to guide him, he should have found the fence and followed it to this location long ago. Something must have happened. Could one of the rebels keeping guard have caught him? Did Griffin or someone else from the University track us to this place?

Fear pricks the back of my neck. I turn towards the fence and Tomas grabs my arm. "What are you doing? We have to get to the University before people know we're missing."

"I can't leave Raffe." I can't be responsible for another death. "You're a fast rider. You can get back before breakfast if you go now."

"I'm not going without you."

"You have to," I insist. "If anyone wonders why I wasn't around this morning, I can tell them I was working at the president's offices. A Biological Engineering student doesn't have that kind of excuse. It's the only way you'll be safe."

"I don't care if I'm safe."

"But I do. I love you." Tears tighten my bruised throat. One falls down my cheek, but I keep the others back and say, "You have to go. If something happens to me, I need to know you'll get word to my father that Zeen is here and that you'll help get him out of harm's way. Please." I stand on tiptoe and press my lips against his. In the kiss I put all my love, hope and fears. Tomas pulls me close and deepens the kiss. I feel the heat of passion mixed with despair and know he will do as I ask.

Stepping back, I say, "I'll signal when I get back to campus."

With one last kiss, he places the Transit Communicator into my hands. "I'll be waiting."

"I know." I race towards the fence and once more begin to climb. As I jump to the ground, I catch sight of Tomas heading towards the road. Back to the University and the dangers that lie there. I hope he stays safe.

Alone, I retrace the path we took towards the rebel camp, looking for signs of Raffe. I can hear laughter far in the distance. The rest of the camp must be waking up. Without the cover of darkness, I don't dare venture closer. Instead, I turn and search to the east.

Thirty feet from the path we originally travelled, I see a freshly broken branch hanging from a bush. Several feet to the north, I spot patches of recently trampled grass. I follow the trail past a pile of rusted metal that must have once been part of a small airplane and stop dead in my tracks. Twenty feet ahead is a five-foot-wide fissure in the earth. The trail I've been following leads right to it.

For a moment, I can't breathe. With small, trembling steps, I cross the barren earth and look down into the gaping hole. I am prepared for the worst. Instead, I find two wide, very blue eyes looking up at me. Standing on a thin ledge about nine feet below is a dirt-streaked Raffe.

"What are you doing here?" Raffe asks. "Where's Tomas?"

Relief makes my knees go weak, and the bafflement in his voice makes me laugh. "What's it look like I'm doing? I'm rescuing you. I sent Tomas back to the University so no one would realise he or the bike he borrowed was missing." I realise helping Raffe out of the hole would be much easier had I let Tomas stay. Frowning, I add, "Give me a minute to decide how I'm going to get you out of there."

I take the bag off my shoulder and study the contents. Nothing I brought with me will help Raffe reach the surface. I shield my eyes from the early morning light and spot a weeping willow tree. The branches are both flexible and strong. When my brothers and I were younger, we used to weave them into ropes and swing from the trees in our backyard. They were helpful then. Maybe they will work just as well for me now.

Climbing the tree, I use the pocketknife my father gave me to cut a dozen long branches. The branches are less pliable than the ones back home. Still, after pulling on them to test their strength, I'm pretty sure they'll do the job.

I tell Raffe to hang on and begin weaving the branches together. In no time, I have a makeshift rope of twelve feet. I loop one end to a squat but sturdy-looking brown bush just above where Raffe waits. I tug on the rope several times to make sure the knots will hold and then throw the rope down.

Lying on my stomach, I peer over the edge. "Grab the rope and climb up."

"You want me to use that?"

"Do you have a better idea?" I ask.

Raffe's answering smile is grim. "If I did, I'd already be out of here." He grabs the rope, wraps it around his right hand, and tugs. "Okay. Here goes."

I glance back at the bush as Raffe lets the rope take his weight. The bush shudders. The knot shifts, but holds. For now. How long the little bush can withstand the force of Raffe's weight is questionable.

Determination colours Raffe's face as he pulls himself up inch by agonisingly slow inch. Below him, the dark, deep hole threatens. His feet search the hard dirt wall for leverage, but the dirt crumbles under his boots, making it almost impossible for him to gain a foothold.

Leaves rustle. Something snaps. A gasp rips from my throat as the rope shifts. The bush bends, and the roots begin to pull free of the ground. I grab the rope to alleviate some of the pressure, but the bush shifts again. Half the roots are showing. A glance over the edge tells me Raffe is still several inches from the surface.

"You might want to hurry," I say.

Raffe grunts and pulls himself up another inch. The edge is just above him. One more pull, maybe two, and he will be

Joelle Charbonneau

close enough to reach the top. If the rope holds.

Raffe's hand crests the edge. Instinctively, I scramble to my feet and grip his wrist with both of my hands and then lean back and pull. Raffe's head appears. I feel a surge of triumph that is quickly replaced by terror as my boots start to slide across the dry earth towards the ravine. Raffe outweighs me by at least sixty pounds. While years of physical activity back home have made me stronger than most of the University candidates, I cannot hope to support Raffe's weight much longer.

Sweat runs down my back. I fight to dig into the ground with the front of my boot. Raffe's shoulders appear. His left hand grabs hold of a seedling as the bush holding the rope gives way. He lurches downward a fraction of an inch, sending me pitching forward. I hit the ground inches from the edge and scramble back as Raffe heaves himself up and over.

Raffe and I lie on our backs, breathing hard. We are dirty, covered with sweat and safe.

Raffe speaks first. "You helped me again. Why?"

"Because it was the right thing to do." I dig through my bag, pull out a bottle of water and take a drink. Handing the bottle to Raffe, I say, "As soon as you feel up to it, we need to get going. There's someone I need to talk to."

"Tomas?" he asks.

"No. We're not going back to the University yet."

"Then where are we going?"

"President Collindar's office."

I wash Damone's blood off my hands and coat with some of the water and change my blood-streaked pants for the extra ones in my bag before setting off for Tosu City. There are fewer skimmers in evidence on the streets today, probably because the government is shut down on weekends in order to give officials time to spend with their families and to tackle personal revitalisation projects at home. Even the president isn't in residence, which is why there is only one guard at the entrance and no staff wandering around when I arrive.

The guard checks my identification bracelet and allows me to enter. Raffe is denied entrance. He has to wait outside. I tell him I'll be back in a minute and climb the stairs.

I spot Michal hunched over a small desk in the corner of his office, and feel a stab of betrayal. Since hearing the recording on the Transit Communicator, the only person I've felt I could trust was Michal. He confirmed that the recorder's stored memories were real. He helped me communicate with my family and directed my fear and anger into assisting the rebellion to remove Dr Barnes and bring an end to The Testing. I thought I could count on him for honesty. I was wrong. If Zeen is here with the rebels, Michal must know about it. Most likely, he facilitated an introduction and helped put the gun on my brother's hip, shoving him into the path of danger.

Michal looks up and smiles. "Hi. I wondered if you'd drop by. Do you need a desk to work at?"

In case someone is listening, I reach into my bag and pull out the short analysis of the communication system I wrote for the president. "I'm just dropping off my work. Where should I leave it? I don't want the president to think I neglected to do my assignment."

Michal glances at the papers in my hand and stands. "Follow me." He leads me back downstairs, through a couple of offices, to a small room I don't remember seeing on our tour. "You can put your report in this box."

Closing the door, he lowers his voice. "The president and her officials plan on announcing the debate about control of the University and The Testing on Monday morning. Per protocol, there will be three days of discussion. A vote will take place the day after the debate ends. If that measure is voted down, the other faction will be ready to begin their attack as soon as the vote of confidence is taken. If the president loses the vote, the members of the rebellion will be positioned throughout Tosu, ready to take out Dr Barnes and his team. People in unrevitalised areas are being armed with weapons and instructions."

I think about Zeen and feel panic bubble inside me.

"Why won't the president wait?" It would give the rebels more time to find a peaceful solution. And more time for me to convince my brother to get out of harm's way.

"Too many people know she plans on proposing a change of law. If she backs off now, she'll look weak. Dr Barnes has too many supporters ready to remove her if a vote of confidence is called. The other faction has convinced her that the only way to stay in power and end The Testing is to act now."

"Did you know this was a possibility when you brought my brother here?" I don't give him a chance to deny it. "I saw him, Michal. He's calling himself Cris. Why did you bring him here when you know there's a chance he'll die?"

Michal shakes his head. "Zeen overheard your father and the magistrate discussing options to keep students from being selected for this year's Testing. When he confronted them about their plans, he realised you might be in danger and insisted on coming to help you. Your father couldn't talk him out of it, so he contacted me and asked that I find a way to bring him here and keep him safe. I thought if he was with the rebels, he'd be less likely to track you down on his own. I was the one who suggested your brother change his name so no one would associate him with you or your family. Just in case..."

In case the rebellion isn't successful. So our family won't be punished if Zeen is captured or killed. The way it sounds, both are strong possibilities. Unless, in the next couple of days, someone can find and present the proof required to remove Dr Barnes and his officials from power with a point of law instead of a war.

"I have an idea." Before Michal can enquire about my plan, I ask him to wait for me to return, then I open the door and walk to the exit. For this to work, I have to put everything on the line. I have to once again go against my father's instructions; I have to trust. Tomas would tell me this is a mistake, but he is not here, and I can see no other way. Zeen's life and the lives of the other rebels are at stake, not to mention those of all future Testing candidates and the country itself. There is only one way I can think of to find the information the rebellion needs. If I am making the wrong choice, I will just have to live with the consequences.

I find Raffe waiting outside the entrance and say, "I need your help."

I take Raffe to the same building where Michal once spoke to me in secret. Perhaps I should have asked Michal to come, but he would have objected to taking this risk and exposing the rebellion. So I tell Raffe about The Testing, the candidates who disappear or die, and the need to put an end to the system once and for all. I tell him the end can only come if certain information is found. My throat is still swollen and sore from the abuse at Damone's hands. My words sometimes drop to a whisper, but I keep talking.

When I finish, the room goes silent. Seconds stretch to minutes as Raffe's eyes search my face. Is he looking for the truth? Is he trying to decide the best way to report this conversation to his father or to the University officials? I clench and unclench my hands and wait.

Finally, he asks, "Colony students who get wrong answers die during The Testing?"

"Not all of them, but yes. In The Testing, death is often the punishment for failure. And for some, causing those deaths is the path to success."

Raffe rakes a hand through his hair. "What about Tosu City students who don't pass their Early Studies exams? My father said my sister was assigned to a job in one of the colonies. Is that true, or is she..."

The unspoken word hangs between us as he waits for my answer. For the first time, I understand the motivation behind his aid – the event that happened two years ago and changed everything for him. He is looking for his sister. Now he assumes I might have an idea where she is.

"I don't know." The unhappiness on Raffe's face makes

me wish I did. "Maybe if we can get Dr Barnes removed, we can find out."

Raffe takes a deep breath and nods. "Then I guess I should get started."

Before I can ask what he plans to do, Raffe opens and closes the door, leaving me alone to wait and worry.

Time passes slowly. Though my throat is still sore, I eat an apple and swallow some water. I think of Tomas. Did he make it back to the University without anyone noticing he had been absent? Is he worried that I might not return? When I stand and stretch my muscles, my eyes stay glued to the ground below.

An hour passes. Two. Part of me wonders if Raffe was caught, while the other part wonders if he was telling the truth about his sister. Raffe's father is in charge of the Department of Education. Surely he would be able to protect his daughter from the punishments Dr Barnes might exact.

The clock taunts me as its hands move from one number to the next. Closing my eyes, I picture the people I love. My parents. Zeen. My other three brothers. Daileen, who so badly wishes to be chosen for The Testing and join me at the University. Tomas. Would they understand what I am doing now? I know my father would agree that putting a stop to The Testing with bloodshed is just as wrong as ending lives because of incorrect answers. Fighting death with more death was the choice that led to the Seven Stages of War. Our country barely weathered the consequences. We may not survive if the same choice is made again.

I hear footsteps outside and hold my breath. Is it Raffe, or has someone Raffe alerted come in his place? Was putting my faith in him correct, or will I now be punished for once again ignoring my father's advice to trust no one?

The footsteps pause.

The door swings inward.

Raffe stands alone in the doorway. In his hands are a bag and a gun.

CHAPTER 19

Raffe turns the gun around and offers me the handle. I look at him before wrapping my fingers around the hard wood grip, and he gives me a satisfied nod. "I grabbed this out of my dad's private office. Since you're trying to stop a war, I thought it might come in handy. This will too."

He reaches into the bag hanging from his shoulder and pulls out a palm-sized machine. A recorder.

"I'm pretty sure the recording in this machine and the others in the bag are what you're looking for. And you're right, Cia." His expression darkens. "What's on these recordings needs to end."

"It'll end as soon as Michal gets the recordings to Symon," I say.

But when I leave and return with Michal, Raffe refuses to hand the recordings over. "No offence," he tells Michal. "But I don't know you. If you want to deliver this to your people, you'll have to take me with you."

Michal stiffens. "I'm not taking the son of one of the

biggest advocates of Dr Barnes into rebel headquarters. Not only do I not trust you, but even if I did, Symon and the other members of the rebellion would see you as a threat. They'd eliminate you as soon as you walked into camp."

That Michal believes the members of the rebellion would kill so easily makes my blood run cold.

"Raffe is on our side. He's trying to find out what happened—"

"Look," Raffe says, cutting me off. "There's nothing I can say that will make you trust me. All I know is I have the recordings from The Testing. If you want them, you'll just have to make sure your friends don't see Cia and me. Otherwise, the two of us are walking out the door and taking the recordings with us."

I blink at Raffe's assumptions not only that I will side with him over Michal but that I plan on going back to the rebel camp. However, when I think about it, I know he's right. I have to go. While I do not doubt Michal's dedication to ending The Testing, President Collindar's first assignment taught me that the only way to know the truth is to see it for myself.

But while I know what I need to do, I hesitate. If Tomas safely returned to the University, he is now waiting for me to signal him. Hours have passed since the time he must have expected me. Does he think I have been killed or captured? Will he stay in his residence and trust that I will make it back, or is he already planning to leave in search of me? I should let him know I am okay. But without knowing if my absence has been noted by Professor Holt or my fellow students, I cannot take the risk. If I return to campus now, I may never have this chance again.

Straightening my shoulders, I walk over and stand next to Raffe to show we are united. We will all go to the rebel camp.

Michal sighs. "It won't work. The three of us together will attract too much attention on the Tosu streets."

Raffe smiles. "Cia and I already know the way to the air-field. Just tell us where to meet you, and we'll be there."

That Raffe knows the location of the rebel camp decides the issue for Michal. He tells us to meet him at the fence near a revitalised evergreen tree whose trunk is surrounded by a circle of stones. Once we arrive, he'll lead us to a place where we can watch Symon's headquarters unobserved.

"Wait ten minutes before leaving the building, and make sure you aren't followed." Turning to me, he says, "Those recordings better be exactly what we need, or I'm turning him over to Symon as a potential traitor." With this threat hanging in the air, Michal disappears out the door.

"That went well." Raffe looks at his watch and takes a seat. "I can see why you like him. He's a lot of fun."

Despite my concerns about Michal, I leap to his defence. "Michal lived through The Testing. He helped me survive it. The two of us will do anything it takes to bring it to an end."

"He might do anything, but you won't. You'd never kill someone for being a potential threat."

"How can you be sure? Look what I did to Damone." The blood has been cleaned from my fingers, but I can still smell the stench and feel the way it spilled across my hands.

"Damone attacked you. You had every right to defend yourself. If you hadn't, you'd be dead. If I didn't trust your judgement, I wouldn't have brought you the gun. The only question is whether you know how to use it."

I clutch the wooden handle, remembering the feel of pulling the trigger, the kick of the weapon, the way eyes widen when the bullet you shot punches into a body and ends its life. The scars on my arm tingle.

"Yes," I say, sliding the gun into the pocket of my bag. "I know how to shoot."

"Good." Raffe checks his watch and heads for the door. "After what I heard on those recordings, I think there's a good chance that even if everything goes according to your friend's plan, you're going to need it."

Raffe leads the way as we ride through the sunlit Tosu City streets. Though we are both tired, he sets a fast pace. Every couple of blocks, he points out a landmark as though giving me a tour. Occasionally, he waves to someone as they pass. I understand. He wants us to be seen and remembered as two University students enjoying a beautiful day. Because no one who sees us would believe we have caused death and are now working hard to bring part of the government down.

My muscles are taut. My pulse races but I smile and laugh. I tell myself that everything I have done will be worth it in the end. The recordings are the proof the rebels have been looking for. The president will play them on the Debate Chamber floor. Those who support Dr Barnes will have no choice but to vote with the president and remove him from office. The Testing will end without bloodshed. No one else will have to die.

We arrive at the fence and look for the tree Michal indicated. I spot it four hundred yards from where Tomas, Raffe and I entered before. We hide our bicycles in a thicket of weeds, scale the fence and wait for Michal. Fifteen minutes later, he appears on the horizon from the south.

"Ranetta and the other faction's leaders are scheduled to meet soon to finalise plans for their attack. As soon as that happens, they'll start deploying to positions around the city as well as co-ordinating with the rebel University students and Tosu citizens who are willing to fight for their cause. Symon plans to make one more plea for peace.

He's at headquarters now, trying to come up with a way to convince Ranetta and her faction to hold off on their attack. You can't go inside headquarters without being seen, but there is a broken shed in the middle of a copse of trees where you'll have a good view of the building. That's the best I can do." Michal holds out his hand. "Before I take you inside, I want to hear one of the recordings."

"Fair enough." Raffe digs into his bag, pulls out the recorder and hits Play.

"I guess I'll be walking the rest of the way." I jump at the sound of my own voice.

"Don't worry, Cia. You won't be alone. I'll walk with you." Tomas.

"You don't have to."

The words are familiar. I close my eyes and try to remember. I see a road. A bicycle broken into pieces.

"Yes. I do," Tomas says. *"I guess this is where we part company again. Cia and I wouldn't want to hold you back."*

"Funny, but I was just going to say the same thing." Will's voice. Then a gunshot.

Suddenly, I am back on the road. Tomas doubles over. His hands turn red as blood from the gunshot spills over them.

"What the hell are you doing, Will?"

I see Will smile at me from behind his gun. Feel the fear

as I relive the understanding that I have been betrayed by a friend.

"Isn't it obvious? I'm getting rid of my competition. I didn't come all this way just to be told I'm not good enough to make it into the University. I made that choice when Gill failed. My brother wanted to help this country ever since I can remember and he knew how much our colony could benefit from our selection. He made me study so we could do it together. They made a mistake not passing him through. If less than twenty candidates pass this test, they won't be able to make the same mistake with me. I tried to kill you earlier, but you got away. That upset me at first, but it turned out to be a good thing since travelling with you and Tomas helped me get so close to the end.

"Thankfully, a couple of the others were easier to kill before I ran out of quarrels. Both Gill and I are championship crossbow marksmen. He always takes first, but I give him a run for his money."

"And you think I'm just going to let you shoot me now? I've already proven I won't go down without a fight."

"You're smart, Cia, but you don't have the killer instinct. I could walk away right now and you wouldn't fire at me."

"You wanna bet? Go ahead and try me."

For a moment everything goes silent. I hear Tomas whisper my name. Then gunfire fills the air.

And I remember. My knees buckle, and I grab the trunk of a tree to keep from stumbling to the ground as whatever barrier Dr Barnes and his officials created to keep my memories at bay disappears.

Ryme offering me corncakes.

Will and Gill at the dinner table, laughing.

Holding Malachi's hand as life drains out of his body. His blood staining the tiles as officials carry him out of The Testing room.

Jumping across a bridge.

Being chased by mutated humans. Claws raking down my arm. Searing agony mixes with churning fear as I turn, fire and kill.

"Cia? Are you okay?" Michal's voice cuts through the flood of memories. I look up and see him and Raffe wearing similar expressions of concern. The recording is no longer playing.

I take a deep breath and pull my thoughts back to the present. There is time enough to sort through the past. To remember. Now is the time to make sure what is contained in those memories never happens again.

Straightening my shoulders, I say, "I'm fine."

Michal searches my face. Finally, he nods. "I have to get these to Symon. Once the president plays all these recordings on the Debate Chamber floor, officials will have no choice other than to vote against Dr Barnes. A few might argue that the acts on these recordings were not sanctioned by Testing officials, but they won't stand a chance against public outrage."

The idea of Will's betrayal, Tomas's near death and my attempt to kill being played aloud on the Debate Chamber floor makes me dizzy as I shift the bag on my shoulder and follow behind Michal and Raffe. People will know the choices I have made. They will hear the things we've all done and pass judgement. A small price to pay, I tell myself, for bringing The Testing to an end.

Twice we stop at the sound of nearby voices. Finally, we reach the broken outbuilding where Michal instructs us to wait. Two rotting grey walls are wedged in between a group of squat, twisted trees. Eroded sections in the front wall give us a good view of a long stretch of pavement four or five hundred yards away. On either side of the pavement are buildings. A handful of rebels hurry across the compound, long black guns slung over their shoulders. Zeen is not in sight, but he is here. Somewhere. And soon, because of these recordings, he will be safe. We all will.

Michal points to a building less than a hundred feet from where we are crouching. It's a small red-brick building set in the middle of a grove of trees.

"No one who comes by should question the two of you.

But if someone asks, pretend to be new recruits who are looking for time alone. You should be fine." Michal holds his hand out to Raffe, who passes over his bag. "Don't move from this spot. I'll be back soon."

We watch through rotting wood as Michal hurries through the trees and disappears inside the brick structure. After ten minutes, he walks out. I gasp when a man with grey hair appears behind him.

I know that man.

Closing my eyes, I sift through my memories. He stood on the other side of a fence during The Testing. He gave me food and a drug that helped me keep my family safe from secrets I would have been compelled to share during the interview. Michal once told me I'd met Symon during my Testing days. This must be him.

Symon claps Michal on the shoulder and walks with him in our direction. I hold my breath as they pass by our location, and I hear a familiar voice say, "I can't thank you enough for bringing these recordings directly to me."

"I would have brought them to the president myself, but I know you wanted me to bring anything I found to you, Symon," Michal says. "Once she plays these recordings on the Debate Chamber floor, the members will have to vote in favour of her motion. Dr Barnes will be removed. You can tell Ranetta when you meet with her today. She will be relieved to know there won't be a need for any more senseless death."

From a crack in the one side wall, I see Symon sigh. "I know it seems that these recordings should guarantee the president wins the vote. However, I have learned that when dealing with the brightest minds, you have to expect some will question and have different opinions. Just as you do."

My heart races. Those words. I've heard words like those spoken in just this way. By this same voice. In the early morning hours to Professor Holt.

I shift to get a better look at Symon. He shakes his head and takes a small pistol out of his pocket. "I'm an expert at dealing with those kinds of questions and the trouble they cause. That's why Jedidiah assigned me to this post."

Two shots split the air. Michal's eyes widen. His hands reach for his chest and he crumples to the ground. Terror claws my swollen throat, but the hand that clamps over my mouth prevents sound from escaping. I swallow the scream and hear Raffe whisper against my ear, "Keep still. You can't help him."

He's right. The bullets were fired directly into Michal's heart. He was dead before he hit the ground. Even knowing that, I must use every ounce of my willpower to sit motionless as the blood flows unchecked from Michal's body. To not cry out. To not strike back at the man who stole his life. I fight to breathe as Symon places the recorder on the ground next to Michal's lifeless body, points the gun at it and fires two more times. After picking up the shattered recorder and the bag containing the recordings, Symon walks back to the building without giving Michal a second glance.

A sob rips from my heart. Tears stream down my face as I take a halting step forward. I want to hold Michal's hand as I did for Malachi, but Raffe pulls me back. Silently he points to two men coming out of Symon's headquarters. They stride quickly to where Michal lies. One takes his feet. The other grabs his shoulders. Together they cart Michal's body away.

"Come on." Raffe grabs my hand and pulls. "We have to go."

I take one last look at the ground stained with Michal's blood. Tears burn my eyes and sear my throat as I dig through my bag. When my fingers close around the handle of Raffe's gun, I turn and run.

My feet fly over the ground. Tears blind me. I stumble over roots and debris, but I don't fall. Raffe's grip on my hand keeps me upright and moving. The scene I witnessed plays over and over in my head as I try to make sense of Michal's death. Symon, the leader of the rebellion designed to remove Dr Barnes peacefully and destroy The Testing, has just committed a murder to ensure the plan he created fails.

Why?

It isn't until my fingers grip the fence that I recall Symon's words and begin to understand. "*When dealing with the brightest minds, you have to expect some will question the direction we are taking.*"

The Testing was created to ferret out the best and the brightest young minds and mould them into leaders. But the best leaders form their own opinions. They want to go their own ways. How better to control those differing opinions than to allow them to think their views are being heard and even acted upon? If those who want change think they are part of a rebellion, there's no reason for them to start one of their own. By allowing them to think they are helping one or two students like me during The Testing, Symon has convinced them that they are having a real effect. Symon's argument for a peaceful solution wasn't to save lives; it was a delaying tactic to ensure that The Testing could continue to take them. To ensure that the rebellion would never take place. Year after year of caution. Year after year of Testing candidates' deaths.

Until now.

After so many years of inaction, the rebels to whom Symon has counselled patience are no longer willing to wait. They have planned an attack. An attack Symon and Dr Barnes know about. Possibly they've even encouraged it to eliminate those who have become too hard to control. To keep The Testing safe to select the next generation of leaders even if it means plunging a country into war.

If nothing happens to alter Symon's plans, my brother, the rebels and hundreds of selected Testing candidates will die. Dr Barnes and his team will win.

I refuse to let that happen.

But the only way to stop it is to create a new rebellion. A rebellion free of Dr Barnes's control.

For that, I will have to step up and be the leader the University is teaching me to be.

Deep in my heart, I hear Michal's voice whisper the words he said before I began the fourth phase of The Testing. *"You're smart, Cia. You're strong. There are people like me on your side who know you can make it. Please, prove I'm right."*

I'm not sure that I can, but I have to try.

Raffe and I ride to the University in silence as we absorb what we have witnessed. As our bicycles glide under the iron entrance, I put my hand in my pocket to signal to Tomas that I am back and realise my pocket is empty. The switch I created is gone. So is the special transmitter I created to prevent University officials from following my movements.

When did I lose them? Have Dr Barnes and his officials

been able to track our movements the entire time we were away from campus?

Raffe doesn't seem to notice my concern as he suggests we split up. He will go to the residence and see whether Damone's absence has raised an alarm. I will wait fifteen minutes and then follow. If it's safe, Raffe will be standing near the entrance.

But even if an alarm hasn't been raised, it still may not be safe. Not if Dr Barnes knows I was not on campus. That Raffe and Tomas were with me. Before I can warn Raffe about the tracking devices and what Dr Barnes might know, he rides off, promising to see me soon.

I notice the dirt streaked on my hand and head for the library.

My eyes dart around as I look for friends and enemies while I prop my bicycle next to the building. Taking measured breaths, I walk straight to the bathroom and scrub the dirt from my hands and the tears from my cheeks. I straighten my clothes and unfasten my hair, untangling it with my fingers. Then I step back and study myself in the reflector. Aside from the grass stain on my right knee, all evidence of my actions is gone. My appearance will give no one reason to question where I have been. I look normal. And yet I barely recognise the girl staring back at me. I wonder if, when this is over, I will know her at all.

As I walk back outside to my bicycle, I finger the bracelet on my wrist and see the faces of those who have died. Michal. Damone. Rawson. Zandri. Malachi. Ryme. A scruffy boy named Roman. A stunning redhead called Annalise.

Face after face. Some I cannot name. All are dead. Soon more will follow. Unless I am as smart as Michal believed me to be.

If Raffe can get more recordings, there is hope. If not, the president's vote will fail. By the end of the week, most of the rebels, including Zeen, could be killed. The city might be at war. I have almost no time to make a plan. To decide who I trust. Who will trust me.

Tomas. My heart wants to keep him from harm, but I cannot do this without him, and I know he will not let me. The only way to dispel the shadows that chase us both is to face them. I know he will agree and we will face them together. But no matter how much I might want to, Tomas and I will not be able to do this alone. More help will be needed. But who?

Raffe.

He says his sister sat for the University Early Studies exam and failed. His quest to find her makes him a natural ally, but I cannot help but wonder if he will be like Will and ultimately betray us.

Can I trust Stacia and Naomy? Nothing in my Testing

memories says that I can't. But I remember Stacia's cool smile. One she gave as she approved of choosing leaders who will do whatever is required to win.

As my residence comes into sight, I scroll through names and faces. Vic. Enzo. Brick. Kit. Will. They all are smart. Some have skills I know I will need. Others are willing to do the unthinkable to survive. I think of Ian and wonder what he will do. Will he take up arms with the rebel faction, or can I convince him to join with me? If I am to succeed, I will need to stop the rebels from attacking. To do that, I need someone on the inside who can give me information or convey my messages.

I stop on the far side of the bridge. Raffe waves to me in the distance to signal it is safe to return. But I hardly notice as I reach into my bag and close my fingers around the Transit Communicator. Zeen's device. The one that has pointed me in the right direction, hidden my secrets and kept me safe. A device designed to communicate with another that has been too far away to reach.

Could it be close enough now? Knowing that I have this half, could Zeen have brought the other one? Is he waiting for the right time to contact me? Or for me to reach him?

Raffe waves again, but I don't put my feet on the pedals. Instead, I hit the Call button and say, "Hello."

The seconds stretch to minutes as I wait for a response.

Finally, I tuck the Communicator into my bag and head across the bridge. As I stash my bicycle in the outbuilding, I look for signs of my confrontation with Damone. But all I see is grass deepening to a rich green. Trees stretching to the sunlight. Spring is ready to bloom, bringing with it another demonstration of how the conviction of a people to bring hope to the world can succeed.

I don't know if I am ready to be a leader or if I can stop the war that threatens all I love, but as I hurry up to my rooms and close the door behind me, I know I will do everything in my power to keep the hope of our country and those who struggled for it alive.

And that's when I hear it. The sound of static. A muted voice. It makes me want to cry with relief and fear.

"Cia. Are you there?"

Tears threaten as I lift the Communicator out of the bag and answer, "Yes, I'm here."

I just hope I am ready for what comes next.